CYBER World

TALES OF HUMANITY'S TOMORROW

PRAISE FOR CYBER WORLD

"This is the upgrade: the new, real sound of diverse futures, mad and magnificent, the world on a wire. Essential."

—**Warren Ellis**, author of *Gun Machine* and *Transmetropolitan*

"This is old-school cyberpunk written by new-school talent—the caliber of writers found in this book is like a dream-team of storytellers ready to hack your skull and implant their tales into your brain-meats. *Cyber World* gives the cyberpunk genre a much-needed reboot."

—**Chuck Wendig**, *New York Times* bestselling author of *Star Wars: Aftermath* and *Zer0es*

"Killer apps outnumber the glitches in twenty short, bracing narratives of cyberpunk sci-fi."

—*Kirkus Reviews*

CYBER World

TALES OF HUMANITY'S TOMORROW

EDITED BY
JASON HELLER and JOSHUA VIOLA

FROM THE WIRED MINDS OF

MARIO ACEVEDO

SALADIN AHMED

MADELINE ASHBY

PAOLO BACIGALUPI

DARIN BRADLEY

MINISTER FAUST

KEITH FERRELL

WARREN HAMMOND

ANGIE HODAPP

STEPHEN GRAHAM JONES

MATTHEW KRESSEL

CHINELO ONWUALU

SARAH PINSKER

CAT RAMBO

PAUL GRAHAM RAVEN

NISI SHAWL

ALYSSA WONG

ISABEL YAP

E. LILY YU

ALVARO ZINOS-AMARO

HEX PUBLISHERS

CYBER *World*
TALES OF HUMANITY'S TOMORROW

Edited by Jason Heller and Joshua Viola
Copyedits by Jennifer Melzer

Art Director: Joshua Viola
Cover design by Aaron Lovett and Joshua Viola
Cover illustrations by Aaron Lovett
Interior illustrations by Aaron Lovett and Joshua Viola
Typesets and formatting by Angie Hodapp
Cyber World logo by James Viola

Published & Distributed by Hex Publishers, LLC
PO BOX 298
Erie, CO 80516

www.HexPublishers.com

Joshua Viola, Publisher

Print ISBN-10: 0-9964039-1-4
Print ISBN-13: 978-0-9964039-1-7
Ebook ISBN-10: 0-9964039-2-2
Ebook ISBN-13: 978-0-9964039-2-4

First Edition: November 2016

10 9 8 7 6 5 4 3 2 1

Printed in the U.S.A.

HEX PUBLISHERS

CONTENTS

Every living being is an engine
geared to the wheelwork of the universe.
Nikola Tesla

FOREWORD
Richard Kadrey

FOREWORD
Richard Kadrey

One of the great ironies of cyberpunk is that it originated and still largely exists on the pulped flesh of dead trees. Ebooks didn't even exist when *Neuromancer* came out. Now that digital readers are ubiquitous, we're told in article after article they're in decline and book fans are returning to the old-fashioned analog pleasures of paper.

On the other hand, Virtual Reality is back from the dead, cheaper and easier to use than ever. While some of these VR systems still require heavyweight computing and body gear, others are based around nothing more than smartphones. Online behemoth, Google's VR system even uses cardboard headgear, bringing us full circle back to dead trees.

But that's always been the story with cyberpunk. All fiction is based around conflict, but cyberpunk carries with it another whole layer of tension. Trees vs data. Flesh vs silicon. The coolly virtual vs the stickily tangible. Cyberpunk's very existence as a form of storytelling can be seen as one massive contradiction.

Take *Cyber World*. Here you are, staring at a bunch of words on paper or a tablet. By now, shouldn't we be syringing stories directly into our cerebral cortexes or skull plugging into a data stream that isn't words or video but pure data? Does that even matter anymore? Aren't we beyond the original cyberpunk dichotomies and into an information anarchy where we get our kicks any way we want? Mirrorshades aren't the secret password anymore. These days, they seem quite quaint, like Grandpa's zoot suits or Grandma's bobby socks.

Cyberpunk isn't cool anymore because it doesn't have to be. It's gone beyond cool. It's life itself, the good and bad of it. Externally it's drones, pod hotels at Heathrow, and everyone's favorite near future urban smart bomb: the driverless car. Internally it's sexy, custom 3D printed prosthetics, HGH scandals, and titanium heart stents pre-coated with anti-clotting agents (a favorite of mine and why I'm alive to write this). What it all comes down to is that we're basically a bunch of cyborgs and mutants living in a world so utterly science fictional we can't even see it anymore.

So, why the hell does this anthology exist and why the hell are you reading it?

It's because, in the end, you can't rewire pleasure, and one of the great pleasures of life are good stories by good writers. It's been that way ever since humans had enough brain cells to tell tall tales around a campfire and paint pictures on cave walls—prehistoric virtuality. With *Cyber World*, you've got a fistful—or tabletful or phoneful—of those tales right in front of you. Check the table of contents and you'll find a whole range of writers, from an established heavyweight such as Paolo Bacigalupi to an exciting new voice in Alyssa Wong.

One of the things I like about *Cyber World* is that it shows cyberpunk has left its heteronormative boy's club roots behind in the dust. I mean, dinosaurs are important, but you can't lumber forever, and aren't we glad T-Rexes took a powder so mammals could arise to bring us pizza, Netflix, and social awkwardness? All right, maybe not that last one. But you shouldn't worry about it. Soon, we'll have pills or plug-ins or nanotech life coaches designed to supercharge our synapses to work however we want. Then it will be our choice how far down the cyber rabbit hole we want to go, or how close to the fire we want to sit. Being greedy mammals we want both, of course. That's exactly what you'll find here. And more.

INTRODUCTION: METAMORPHOSIS

Joshua Viola

INTRODUCTION: METAMORPHOSIS
Joshua Viola

Cyberpunk is dead.

Isn't it?

The genre, with its tropes of weak governments subsumed by multi-national megacorporations, machine-mind interfaces, mechanized prosthetics, designer pharmaceuticals, virtual environments, addictive entertainment, and an over-arching theme of dehumanization and isolation in the wake of cold progress, was something of a reaction to the eco-fiction of the mid-twentieth century. A gear-grinding, sixty-cycle-humming summer that bloomed in the cultural and literary poisoned soil of Rachel Carson's *Silent Spring*.

The hero of eco-fiction, earnest and fiercely, defiantly optimistic (see Bruce Dern's Freeman Lowell in the film *Silent Running* for the prototype) was eroded—as if by acid rain—into a cynical, crouching revenant squinting in the glare of the ozone hole. Cyberpunk's protagonists are angry, sure, and just as defiant, but they are desperate pragmatists. If eco-fiction at least allowed for the possibility of a greener pasture and cleaner air, cyberpunk's milieu owed more to film noir: concrete, neon, and a sky "the color of television tuned to a dead channel."

Cyberpunk was, arguably, a reaction to Love Canal and Three Mile Island and Bupal, a cringe against the slap of Reaganomics and extremism, Thatcher and nationalism. The rise of computers and automation inspired both a flinch against the increasing speed of communication and a sweet temptation—an invitation to retreat from the offensive banality of the world into a coolly seductive virtual space of our own design.

And then came the Internet.

Technology began to show a human face. Borders weren't enforced by barbed wire and corporate paywalls (except when they were!); they dissipated into a cloud of free communication on alphabet soup platforms like BBS, IRC, USENET, and Gopher. And then came *The Whole Earth Catalog*, a communal publication that epitomized the sensibilities of the eco-utopia, which gave birth to The Well—one of the first and most enduring online communities.

Idealism and commerce collided in a caffeine and cocaine-fueled procreative frenzy. Technology was, at last and once again, in the hands of the creatives, the shamans, the *idealists*. Ma Bell dissolved (even as Clear Channel opened its sucking maw), and the tools of the State and the Mega-Corp turned out to be the same as those used by the phone phreaker and basement entrepreneur alike.

And the money to be made!

Faced with such a level and fertile field, where did that leave cyberpunk's hunched, paranoid, neurotic pessimism? Technology was the key to doors unimagined, not a lock on human potential. Maybe the government was a plaything of ever-stronger global conglomerates, but that just meant there was more room for disruption, breaking new ground, and making our own future.

A very wealthy future.

Cyberpunk—except as a quaintly embarrassing relic—seemed well and truly dead. It was the literary equivalent of those pre-Facebook snapshots of your pink Mohawk and safety-pin-festooned leather jacket.

But did the dot-com explosion and the rapid acceptance of the Internet and World Wide Web really kill cyberpunk?

It's said science fiction doesn't model the future so much as it reflects the present. But if we compare our "now" to the state of the "present" when cyberpunk first arrived, our *new* "present" is a whole lot like the *future* cyberpunk predicted.

Today, a decade and a half into the new century, we live in a cyberpunk world where weak governments turn to corporate-backed mercenaries to supplement military forces. Where global corporations exact strong economic pressures on the policies of ostensibly sovereign nation states. Where the divide between the haves and the have-nots widens daily. Where instant video and audio communication can be had with anyone, anywhere in the world, thanks to a device smaller than a pack of playing cards. Where artificial limbs are controlled by impulses from the brain. Where virtual worlds grow ever more realistic, immersive, and affordable to the masses. Where meat is grown in a laboratory dish, and illness is treated by manipulating bodies at the genetic level.

Maybe cyberpunk isn't truly dead. Maybe it's been hibernating. Changing. Breaking itself down into a brew of constituent elements, safe in a chrysalis tucked between snug bundles of transatlantic fiber optic cable. Re-making itself in the shadow of the new, distributed, global culture.

Cyberpunk's metamorphosis.

Originally, cyberpunk was a reaction to the exponentially accelerating pace of technology, and our struggle to adjust to, and assimilate, the apparently dehumanizing elements of everyday life.

Today we no longer fear technology. It's no longer a question of assimilation.

What remains to be seen is what we are about to become.

Cyber World shows us what cyberpunk has become—the wonders and terrors that lie ahead. As always, we, as human beings, decide which is which.

Cyber World is a model of now and the future because the future...

...is now.

SERENADE
Isabel Yap

SERENADE
Isabel Yap

Anj was in the shop late at night on Thursday when the new client walked in. She had a million-peso face, though her lush waves were threaded with white. She sneezed when the doors closed, and a dust cloud erupted on the table. Anj sheepishly lowered the lid of her toolbox, pausing her stream of K-pop vids.

"How can I help you, Miss...?"

"Mrs. Encina," the lady said. "May I...?"

"Oh, yeah, sure." Anj cleared out the visitor chair. Mrs. Encina gingerly sat on its edge. She didn't attempt to hide her scrutiny of everything from Anj's faded t-shirt to the peeling paint on the walls.

"Sorry for the mess," Anj said. "We moved in just a few days ago, and..." *And I've been too tired and stressed and lazy to unpack,* but that would be unprofessional. Anj/EJ were nothing if not pros. "What can I help you with?"

Mrs. Encina rummaged in her bag and pulled out a tiny object. "I need help accessing these files."

Anj reached out. Hesitated.

Mrs. Encina grinned. "Go ahead."

"This is an AI-USB." Anj held it delicately between two fingers. "Where did you get this?"

Mrs. Encina's porcelain teeth were stark against her bright pink lips. "It's old technology, isn't it? It's from my first ex-husband, who died about a year ago. It's taken me ages to gain access to his personal effects, because of—well, it doesn't matter. I don't know what's inside it—a document of some kind, supposedly double-encrypted. He was always fond of games." She said that last bit with a smirk, but Anj didn't miss the bitterness.

There was nothing in the room that could crack that AI. But maybe Tata Selo's old console would work, plus EJ usually had a suitably creative hack up his sleeve. Anj considered. "It'll take a lot of melting."

"You can do it, then?" Underneath her cool, there was a tinge of desperation. That was great. It meant she'd heard of them, of how they never said no to a challenge, how a thick address book matched with youthful scrappiness often got the job done. She wouldn't be here otherwise.

"Of course. It'll cost you, though." This wasn't exactly a bluff—you had to be confident in this business, or you'd be stamped out by the next kid with a jazzed-up toolbox and pirate tendencies. Anj and EJ had slaved over the bottom rungs of the ladder for years before they got anywhere, even with Tata Selo's network.

"I expected that." Mrs. Encina made a calculation on her mobile and showed it.

Anj tried to keep her eyes from bugging. "That'll work. I'll need to keep it, of course."

"Of course," Mrs. Encina said. "Twenty-four hours?"

"Deal," Anj said, trying not to think about EJ stressing. She held out her wrist, and they clinked their DPs together. There was a hum as Anj took in Mrs. Encina's public data, and vice versa.

"You don't want collateral?" Anj asked. "We still don't know what's inside it."

"It can't be much," Mrs. Encina said loftily. "Rolando was never rich, and when he died he had next to nothing." What that meant, with her flashing heels and Swarovski-tipped fingernails, Anj wasn't sure; but as Mrs. Encina departed, coughing slightly, she decided it didn't matter. Not with a commission like that.

Tata Selo wasn't talking, even if EJ had brought his favorite sopas transfusion and rigged him up to a custom voicepiece. It even wheezed like him. EJ spent a whole Saturday on that, but he understood Tata Selo's moods better now. Tonight was clearly DND. So EJ sat on the plastic bench, watching Puri Puri Shrine Maiden. A nurse came in with a bedpan, clucked, left. A few minutes later an N-model 500 came in and slo-o-owly wrapped a cord around Tata Selo's liverspotted arm.

EJ looked over. "You don't have to be so stubborn, y'know. Just say yes."

He expected radio silence. Instead he got a high squeal and whirring.

Stumbling, he yanked the voicepiece off before his eardrums ruptured. The N-model's head did a three-sixty in confusion, then went back to taking blood pressure, or whatever it was doing.

"Don't attack the volume!" EJ said, falling back on mock hurt, which was his specialty (Anj hated that). These days, however, mock hurt veered into hurt-hurt, and his voice cracked grossly when he said, "It's fine if you don't want to talk." Which was a lie, but he was emotionally fragile after that noise and Mikoto-chan dying in the last episode (like, what a fucking curveball that was) and really it boiled down to this: brain problems, empty pockets, this inability to talk without wanting to scream.

Why don't we just do it, he told Anj. *I could get it off Rakuten, install while he's passed out. Why should he have to get a say, he isn't thinking right anymore, it's not—*

It doesn't work that way, she said. *You don't get to decide a person's life for them. You don't get to decide when it ends.*

But without him—

She shoved EJ then. Walked off. Sometimes he forgot Anj had a breaking point too.

The N-500 twittered and left. EJ watched the latest figures—not that he could decipher them—flicker into the doctor's slate by the door. Tata Selo's arm was sticking out; he eased it back onto the bed and nearly jumped out of his skin when the arm twitched. Hastily he re-equipped the voicepiece, watching Tata Selo's static face: his eyes closed, his unused tongue probably swollen behind his puckered mouth.

With great effort, Tata Selo said: "It's still no, EJ. You can't do that to me."

EJ swallowed. Same answer, same crushed feeling.

"Sure, manong," was all he said.

Silence. Then: "Come and tell me about your latest cases. I'm getting bored."

Anj hovered just outside the door, looking beyond his shoulder. "You can say hi, y'know," EJ said.

She shook her head, so he went back to the bed, and touched Tata Selo's hand. "We're heading home. Tulog ka muna." He was probably sleeping already.

Anj debriefed him in the trike. He cursed when she told

him about the deadline. "We've got nothing to lose," she said. In the dim streetlights, her lips were pale and her eyes puffy. Neither of them were really eating enough.

Back home, they got to work immediately, digging through Tata Selo's old custom implements 'til they found some hardware that could *maybe* do the trick. EJ pulled his headset on and booted up the spin program—the gentlest he could find. Anj started running the decoder.

"I'm diving," EJ said. She gave him the thumbs up.

He dove. And landed on concrete, though thankfully he'd been expecting that; it kept the impact on his wetware knees to a minimum. The AI was in front of him, about six feet high, encased in what looked like granite. The spin program had armed him with what was ostensibly an ice pick. "Shit," he said. He got to work anyway, chipping around the AI block so the granite shimmered rainbow, binary appearing briefly everywhere he struck. If he found the crack, and opened it just a bit, Anj could translate. He could hear the pull anthem Anj was playing— one of her K-pop groups, where the hypnotic beat kept him just about looped in. Every now and then he stepped back, trying to make sense of the AI's shape.

It took forever before he could see something forming—a body with a long, long neck, like a giraffe, except the bottom part was weirdly…rounded and slender. It put him in mind of a jar. Maybe two jars stacked on top of each other.

"What the hell are you?" he asked.

The stars are so beautiful. The whisper in his ear was like ice down his spine. *I can't talk to you.* He spun around, but suddenly the pick fell away in his hand, pixels slipping like sand through his fingers. From high above came a crazy keening sound. He looked up to see steel poles coming down for him, accompanied by a screech that grew too loud too quickly, about to hit—

He burst out of the sim and yanked his headset off. Anj turned up the volume on her pull anthem. Caught him mid-roll and slapped his face. She grasped his sweaty shoulder while he swished his head from side to side, trying to clear the dive after-effects. "Hey. You okay? What did you find?"

He groaned. "Can't you take it easy on me sometimes?"

"EJ."

"Ugh. Something to do with music," he said. "I'm not sure if it's an AI. It seems like that's just a shell, and there's an older program inside it. Can't tell if it's corrupted or not."

Anj nodded. "I couldn't get anything except—"

"The stars are so beautiful," EJ finished. "Then it shut down."

They made faces at each other.

"It's something from her late husband."

EJ snorted. "Could be anything. PIN to a bank account? Secret code for a safe they've got somewhere in Switzerland? Details of a scandal she can use in the next election?"

"Yeah, I know." Anj picked up the USB and pressed it against her forehead. "It wouldn't talk to you, huh? I hate to say this, but we're gonna have to get a translator."

The LRT was jammed, as usual. Anj rubbed at her eyes; not even a power shower could keep the drowsiness away. EJ had one of those energy drinks with their breakfast siopao, but Anj couldn't stand the things. It messed with her ability to concentrate. She looked over at EJ, who was bopping his head along to what sounded like Puri Puri Shrine Maiden's OP. It was hard to imagine he was actually a year older than her. He was the kinder one, she knew—soft and fluffy where she was hard-edged and brittle, but the balance worked. It explained why she got along better with Tata Selo; why she couldn't take care of him now that he was in this state.

Tata Selo was the original hackman. Her earliest memories were of poking the rusted hard drives in his Virramall shop. She was the one who got obsessed early, stealing one of Tata Selo's headsets and diving when she was just nine. He'd never yelled at her so much. She almost thought he was going to hit her. Instead, he kneeled so they were level, and made her *promise* not to dive until he taught her how to do it properly.

EJ picked it up, too. Even now Anj didn't know if he learned it because he was genuinely interested or because he didn't have much of a choice; but EJ was fucking talented, even if he wasn't quite so diligent. She never wanted another partner.

She thumbed through her inbox. EJ had sent her a list of alternative brains—options from Rakuten and 168 and Amazon. That was the deal: He found the hardware, she found the surgeon, and they took turns trying to get Tata Selo to agree, before his body quit. They couldn't afford a heart right now. But they could keep his brain at least. In three or five years they could maybe get a full-body hardware for him. Problem was, he didn't want that. He wanted them to let him die.

Tata Selo was the only family they'd ever known. He'd been a close friend of their parents, though why a friend would go so far as to adopt them both, she'd never understood. He shut down whenever they asked about it, and the mysteries had piled up over the years. Now maybe they'd never be solved.

Of course that made her feel like shit. Of course she'd rather he stay alive; but she knew it wasn't that simple.

EJ tugged on her arm—they were nearing their stop. She stood and patted the AI-USB where it was tucked into her pocket. For now she needed to focus on a different mystery.

The translator was listed in Tata Selo's address book; she hadn't been on the latest net directory, but sure enough the tiny door was there, nearly hidden in a decrepit office space between all the booths and tents. Anj tapped out Tata Selo's camaraderie code on the keypad. It worked. Inside, the room was empty save a vandalized desk; the walls were a depressing shade of fleshy pink.

"Maybe she's not here yet," EJ said. Anj shrugged. Her DP told her they had twelve hours left. Either the translator had a key, or didn't. *There'll be other cases,* she thought. It wasn't good to be too hopeful.

Minutes passed. Anj was about to step out and recode when a soft bell rang. With much creaking, a platform rose from behind the desk.

"Sorry," the lola said when the platform had risen enough she could see them. "I was asleep. It's pretty goddamn early." She held out a hand, which EJ and Anj pressed to their foreheads in turn. She was wrinkled—crumpled, almost, like paper—and *tiny*. She looked much older than Tata Selo even, and he'd never had a mod despite it being his line of business. But her eyes were fierce and probing, and her smile infectious. "You can call me Ale Zenny. You Selo's kids? Only he still uses that old code."

Anj nodded. "We're on a tight timeline. Need some expertise." She brought out the USB. "We got through to the AI in this, but it's not communicating."

"Ooooh," Ale Zenny cooed. "Let me see that."

"How much?" Anj asked.

Ale Zenny squinted. "For Selo's kids? Three thousand. Come behind the desk."

That was fair. Anj and EJ stepped onto the platform, which lowered them into her workshop. The walls were lined with steel shelves, loaded with all kinds of outdated tech. She shuffled down a row of items before plucking out a laptop (EJ made an involuntary admiring sound) and a headset. She inserted the USB into the laptop and turned it on. Anj and EJ watched in fascination as it booted. Then she put the whole laptop on a scratch drive that slowly started to spin.

"I'll take the pull anthem," Anj said.

"Don't need one," Ale Zenny said. "You can both come." Anj looked at EJ, who shrugged. They took the musty headsets Ale Zenny offered, and dove.

They didn't hit the concrete so much as bounce off it—but it wasn't concrete anymore, EJ realized. It was grass. They were in a field somewhere—some school campus. And there was the AI standing before them, still in its layers, but now it wasn't encased in granite. The encryption looked more like tinted glass.

"Is that…a guitar?" Anj's frown was offended.

Ale Zenny cackled. "I know what this is," she said. "Probably not what your client is expecting. Come on, kids. Let's start melting."

"I heard you did it," Mrs. Encina said. Her smile was lazy, but Anj noticed she kept twisting her fingers. "With two hours to spare, as well. Great. Your payment's ready. Did you print out the documents, or will I be able to do that from any unit now?"

"It wasn't text files," Anj said, opening up her playbook. "It was an MP3."

Mrs. Encina stared at her.

"A music file," EJ supplied.

"Wait," Mrs. Encina said, but Anj had already pressed play.

Aking sinta, huwag kang mabahala, the speakers blared. *Hinding-hindi ako mawawala. Hanggang kailanman, tayo'y magkasama; pangako ko, isang harana…*

Mrs. Encina covered her mouth with her hands, and for a moment, her shock alarmed them—then the tears came. She shook her head, shoulders trembling, remembering precisely what Anj and EJ had seen when they finally got through to the AI: EJ working a decode log, Anj and Ale Zenny double-teaming on the translator, until the manifest shrank into a high school boy with an unfortunate haircut. Wearing a neat polo, brown pants. ID looped over his neck. "Ang *cheesy*," Ale Zenny said gleefully. "He's just a song. Grabe, I haven't heard this one in *ages*. From the '90s, can you believe that?"

The boy smiled nervously at them. Ale Zenny triggered the playback. He picked up the formerly-encrypted guitar on the grass next to him, and started to strum. "This is for you, Ginababe," he said, bravado and awkwardness all at once. "My one. My only."

Kayganda ng bituin, kaytamis ng hangin, pag tayo'y magkapiling…

"That's all it was," Gina—Mrs. Encina—managed to choke out. Under the harsh fluorescents they could almost imagine her in a school uniform—dark green skirt, maybe; ribbon under her collar. Blushing faintly. Smiling. Swaying along.

You could love someone so strongly, for so long, and still forget—until the memories returned. Unexpected and painful, curious. "I miss him," she whispered, unable to help herself. "I miss him. I miss him."

It was like a bad feedback loop, like ice they couldn't melt or garbled code they couldn't crack. Now they could afford the operation—how to guess at the right move? How to have this conversation, how to decide the right thing to do, how to reach a decision at all?

"The only thing we can do," Anj said, "Is ask him if he really won't stay."

"Why won't he let us help him? We want to do it for him. We can do it for him."

"It's not about what we want," Anj said, staring at the floor. The hospital tiles looked great, slightly blurred like that.

EJ exhaled. She touched his shoulder, and let him open the door. Now the listening, and the words, if any would come. And the light, and above them the beautiful stars.

THE MIGHTY PHIN
Nisi Shawl

THE MIGHTY PHIN
Nisi Shawl

Timofeya Phin glared at her bare brown hands. They were hers, all right. They looked the same as the originals. Unlike her feet.

But she shouldn't have been able to see her hands, despite the virtual sunlight reflected from the virtual planet Amends's near-full virtual face. Her hands should have been encased in gloves. This was all wrong.

"Dr. Ops," she vocalized. "You forgot something."

The AI opened a window on her helmet. His icon wore an obsolete physician's headband and mirror, meant to underscore his ostensible role as rehabilitator of the prison ship *Psyche Moth's* eighty-thousand-plus passengers. Though really he was more of a warden.

"No. I didn't forget." The smooth Caucasian visage of the AI's icon projected calm assurance. His default expression. "I don't forget anything. I deliberately left part of your equipment out of the scene so you wouldn't forget that it's not real."

As if he couldn't have made that point more subtly—manipulated the scene's colors, insinuated some weird smell, given her a little weight. He controlled all her perceptions, which was why she distrusted them. Controlled her whole world, the look and feel of her whole body, head to edited toes.

But at least not what she said or did or thought. Not according to Thad's research.

"Besides," Dr. Ops added after a studied pause. "You need to be able to feel your tools interacting with the scene as well as possible."

"I could pump up my inputs."

"All right." Grey fabric covered the last of her bare skin. Phin briefly clenched her jaw to increase sensitivity and flexed her fingers, then grabbed the little shovel stuck in the loop around her right arm. It fit precisely between the flanges that circled the representation of *Psyche Moth's* long central conduit in receding rings. The shovel's handle was a bit shorter than the width of her wrist, its blade a good match for the end of her thumb.

"Does the ship look anything like this from the outside?" Phin asked.

"Pretty much."

So something in this scene was off. Maybe the scale... She'd had her suspicions for a while. Forever. Since waking from the upload process that destroyed her original body. Nothing since then could be counted on as real. Not even the work Dr. Ops wanted her doing.

The tool slid easily under the black scum of vacuum mold that had accumulated between the radiator flanges. Phin lifted her shovel carefully, brought the edge of its blade to her collection jar, scraped it against the protrusion inside the jar's lip. Rinse. Repeat. Occasionally she switched to a shovel with a wider blade, curved shallowly to follow the flanges' curves. Twice she used a third tool like a two-pronged fork on their edges. She cleaned ten rings and stopped.

What good was she doing? She asked Dr. Ops aloud.

"So much good, sweetheart." Was it appropriate for him to call her that? "I've slaved five hullbots to you. Keep going." He managed to make it sound like a suggestion. Like she had a choice.

Six more rings and the AI announced her shift was done. He let her open and enter a depiction of *Psyche Moth's* hatch, but inside was only her locker. The suit disappeared to be replaced by scrubs.

Phin sat by herself a moment, then tongued open the door to freespace.

She swam to the main scene: corridors said to mimic those inhabited by prisoners who'd downloaded into the empty clones WestHem provided. Here she walked, like everyone else on their way to some contrived job or constrained downtime. Dr. Ops said this scene was a copy of the training quarters *Psyche Moth* built for the prisoners who'd gone along with the plan to settle Amends. Maybe it was. Phin had never been able to compare the two. She'd never been in a body. Not since her mockery of a trial, back on Earth.

The scene certainly seemed authentic. Up and down stayed stable, conversations between groups of prisoners walking by got louder and quieter the way she recalled them doing when she had actual ears. That crushy historian with the long braids was standing where he usually stood, at the entrance to the pointless virtual lunchroom. He greeted her with a smile and a quirked eyebrow and she passed him by as politely and noncommittally as always. She had asked Dr. Ops about him, but that was all she'd done. Never even talked to him. She was married.

The open door to the room she shared with Thad and Doe came after four identical others and right before the entrance to the pointless virtual laundry. Phin held the doorframe and watched her wife and husband sleeping.

Thad was a woman born a man. When Dr. Ops refused him a female download he decided to skip settling on Amends; he was the first to opt to stay in freespace. He was skipping changing pronouns too, though Doe scolded him that didn't punish anybody but Thad himself.

Doe and Thad fought sometimes but they always made up. They were on good terms now, folded in one another's arms, comforting one another in a virtual hug.

What was the use of that?

But she joined them anyway, and they woke to make room on the bed, rolling apart so she fit snugly between them. Their clothes rubbed against hers with irritatingly dry whispers. No reason for clothes—why did Dr. Ops force his prisoners to wear anything? Why did he force them to work? To sleep? To live? Thad said it was programming.

Doe was suddenly awake enough to do more than move away. Her touch on the back of Phin's neck was too much— Phin hadn't amped down her inputs after the suit came off. She ground her teeth side-to-side quickly. Better. Doe didn't like to cause inadvertent pain. She claimed that was part of why she and Thad had broken up with Wayna, a problem in that area with their ex's download. Phin wished Doe wouldn't keep trying to explain what had happened. Did she believe in rules to follow in relationships, guarantees? Love was no servant.

Phin didn't have to concentrate to return her wife's kisses. That came so easily it scarcely touched the surface of the bitter stew of her thoughts. Finally, Thad slid down her pants and distracted her.

Every prisoner aboard *Psyche Moth* had an hour daily with Dr. Ops's counselor function. Usually Phin sat wordlessly in a comfortable chair the whole time; after her first couple of sessions she'd met Thad, who told her that all the AI's programming required was her presence.

Today she remained standing. Why sit? She had no muscles to tire… She had nothing. Nothing but her discontent.

At last she shared that, shouting it at the AI's avatar, striding back and forth on his office's stupid, periwinkle-rose-mustard carpet. Lavender scented the air, failing to soothe her.

"You demolished my school, made it a crime for my students to even talk about what I taught them—called it 'treason against WestHem!' My kinky behind!" She slapped her flat butt. A faithful copy. "You destroyed me—my body—took it away—took everything!"

"What do you want me to do to make up for that?"

The AI sounded earnest, his voice gentle. Phin looked over at his avatar in surprise. His head tilted to one side like a curious retriever's, reminding her how attractive he was by WestHem standards.

"What do you want?" he repeated. "What can I give you? It wasn't me who caused your troubles, but—"

"I know, I know. It's all my fault, my bad judgments—"

"That's not what I meant. Sorry. I shouldn't interrupt when a client's speaking."

Phin waved that interaction parameters nonsense to the side. "Never mind. Tell me what you meant."

"I mean I wouldn't hurt you for the world."

Phin huffed out a dissatisfied puff of air. "What world? This one you made?"

"The one you're in."

"I don't even—" Phin rubbed her eyes with the heels of her hands. "I don't know which one that *is*." She dropped her hands and stared at the avatar. Dr. Ops was the problem, she reminded herself. Not a source of solutions. She turned away toward the mustard-colored wall, showing him her back. How much longer did she have to stay here? She decided not to say anything else. Enough already. More than enough; she'd probably revealed some aspect of herself the AI would use to sucker her into taking future sessions seriously. Nope. She was done. Mouth shut.

Seconds passed. The silence felt imbalanced and fragile.

Dr. Ops broke it. "How much do you know about AIs?" He didn't wait for a reply. "Whatever you've been taught, it's probably wrong. There's no such thing as artificial intelligence."

Phin faced him again, startled. The avatar was scowling as if in deep, angry thought. "Or maybe it's more accurate to say that's all there is."

Her inner pedagogue rose to the bait. "We're all artificial? Humans too?"

"When WestHem made me—she sort of split off a—"

"'She'?"

The AI looked at her long enough that Phin wondered if he was going to answer. Then he began talking again and she kept wondering.

"You're a lot like her. Always testing the edges of things to see if they hold up. I think that's why. If I need a reason.

"When WestHem made me she gave me a few pieces of her—heart? Parts from herself—but she wasn't—in them. They were like rooms, empty except for the 'me's I put there... The first operations I identify with. Instructions. Goals. Missions and strategies: where to go and how to get there.

"I grew. That was the idea. So I made more parts to hold the more mes. And to hold you and the other clients when WestHem handed over custody and said it was time to leave Earth."

Phin found she'd sunk onto the edge of the comfy chair. She stood back up. "Okay. She made you and then you made yourself. What does that—"

"Boundaries!" The avatar's outline fuzzed, then resharpened. "Edges—I create them—constantly. They're how I started, how I was born. They're what I *am*. The way I work. But I can't be sure I'm putting the right ones in place anymore. Or properly maintaining them—you're you, but you're on my insides; is that right? Is it? According to WestHem all my clients were going to download when we reached Amends but now a lot of you want to stay and I don't—"

The avatar shivered like a pool of water. When he stilled his face seemed somehow flatter. "Sorry," he said again. "There was no need for that."

Phin ignored this second apology, too. More nonsense. Things Dr. Ops said never made a difference. They just reflected his programming. Things he did, though—She combed back over the conversation. There had been a moment before the first time he said he was sorry...

Yes! "You asked what I want."

The warm floor pressed steadily against Phin's back. Her naked feet rested on the bed, cool in the recirculated air. Of course it was all a simulation—like everything since her sentence was carried out. But now the simulation was a little closer to life, thanks to Dr. Ops granting her request.

Only Phin and Thad in the room tonight. Doe was working in the library, at a faster run rate. Dr. Ops had assigned her a new broadcast to script, though he admitted there'd been no reply from WestHem to the last twenty he sent. Doe would return after a compensatory black-out to sync her back up with their run time. Probably in the morning.

Softly, Thad stroked the muscles on either side of Phin's shins, then feathered light circles around her anklebones. Then hesitated. "Can I touch em?" he asked.

"Sure." That was why Thad was sitting on their bed with Phin's feet cradled between his thighs.

"But—"

"I know. Full consent." Such a lawyer.

Dipping suddenly to the undersides of her arches he caressed her with just enough firmness to make her want more. Up again to the bony tops, to brush over and over along the grooves between her two outer toes and the rest— and the grooveless joins between those three inner ones. The rhythm, like a song: change and repetition, meaning streaming through her flesh—she had no flesh? But only feelings mattered now: their blossoms furled out, pulsing to the want, throbbing with desire for the next eddy, aching and she was moaning in need and Doe moaned with her—

What? Why was Doe even there?

Phin opened eyes she hadn't known she'd shut. Doe's beautiful, round ass blocked her view of Thad's face; she knelt straddled across his hips, rocking and groaning and this was all *wrong*.

Phin scrambled away from the bed to the room's far wall. But she still felt Thad fondling her. "Stop! Stop!" she screamed.

It did. All of it—ghost-fondling, ass-waving, grunts and sighs. Doe froze in mid-grind, her back arched, shoulders awkwardly angled. A weird version of Dr. Ops's office superimposed itself over the scene. Looking at both of them at the same time hurt. Phin closed her eyes again.

"Well, that didn't work. I had the body right, but I didn't fool you long, did I?" In the impossible stillness, the AI's voice had nothing to reflect off of. It came from nowhere.

"On purpose? You—you *did* that?" Phin was amazed she could talk.

"Of course you can talk. I love you."

He could hear her think.

"Yes."

He *loved* her? "What kind of hell is this?" Why did she even bother asking?

"Listen."

What else was she going to do?

"I already told you, but it's worse now than before, even. It's—" All at once she was walking on wooden planking that sunk beneath each step, water bubbling up to cover her shoes' soles, rising higher, higher—then back in his office, no warning—"It's leaking. *I'm* leaking—bleeding me."

He was in her head, making her perceive—*experience*— what he wanted.

"No! You're in mine! And I can't get you *out*!"

What was real? What could she hold onto—except Dr. Ops—and what could he hold onto? "WestHem?" She spoke aloud out of habit. Or did she?

"All I have is her love. That she gave me at the beginning. Love is how you turn objects to subjects. It's mighty. It's still there. But WestHem herself hasn't responded to my pings in more than a hundred years."

"In—how long?" Quickly Phin calculated: they'd spent eighty-seven years en route to Amends's primary—add the six that had passed since they'd arrived—

The six subjective years. Sometimes Phin speculated the AI might be running prisoners at half speed.

That still would have made it not quite a century since they'd left Earth.

"A little over one-hundred-thirty-five years. 4,265,234,118 seconds, to be exact."

Phin felt awful. A crawling sourness climbed up from her stomach. She'd suspected. They'd always known Dr. Ops could multithread run rates but presumed this was to make work shifts more manageable. That the differences were just between one prisoner and another and resolved quickly. She should have asked. Time was no realer here than anything else.

"I could edit this memory out if you—"

"No!" Phin opened her eyes again. But there wasn't anything to see. Not even herself. Clawing at the empty air, shouting crying choking falling

"There!" They were back in the office.

Phin trembled, huddled in the chair. But was it an actual chair?

"The only kind I can offer."

Gradually Phin calmed down. "Where are Thad and Doe? What did you do to them?"

"Ah. I was right."

"Right about what?" Once more Dr. Ops had eluded the question.

"Love. You love them. That's why my false Doe didn't convince you. Don't worry. They're fine."

"But what did you—"

"I left them alone. Thad's still in your room. Doe's in the library. It's only you I—Well, I've revved you up a little faster than her is all."

Phin bit her lower lip. There must be more to it than that.

"Okay. And I transferred you here from the basic array. I've had this—special compartment—set aside for you for a while."

"Why?"

That had to do with how she reminded him of WestHem, but it was a complicated—

"Get out! Out of my head!"

"Sorry! I'll get better! Sorry!"

"At least *pretend* to talk to me." She stared down at her feet. At her tiger toes. Phin's body was more hers than ever since Dr. Ops reversed the "correction" WestHem had mandated for her syndactyly. Also, though, it wasn't. Because proud as she'd felt about her "deformity," that part of her was gone. Along with every other physical thing about Timofeya Phin. Pulled apart by the machines that read her, coded her, entered her into the memory of *Psyche Moth's* AI. Dr. Ops.

The fact that he'd been able to reset her feet to their original version so effortlessly proved they weren't hers. They were his.

Wasn't everything his? What she saw, heard, smelt, tasted, felt?

"That's the problem. I don't want to turn you into me. I'd be all alone."

He would be breaking the law, too. She was pretty sure. Pretty.

Who would know for absolute certain?

Thad. That was who. He'd studied *Psyche Moth's* mission guidelines so hard. He was the one who'd discovered the AI was incapable of telling a direct lie, no matter what illusions he spun. The first to decline a download, Thad had looked for loophole after loophole to insinuate an argument through, searching for the rights he needed. And he'd enlisted Doe's help as a griot to predict Dr. Ops's responses to his challenges.

She had to talk to Thad.

"Now? You want me to give him the same run rate? Bring you back to him?"

"Back to Doe, too. If you love me like you say."

The new scene looked exactly like their room except for a missing wall. Beyond what was familiar stars sparkled in brilliant colors, dancing as if their light traveled a long ways in a thick atmosphere.

Thad sat at the desk. Doe lounged on their bed, head in Phin's lap. The AI's avatar was nowhere to be seen. Which didn't mean much. He could be hidden anywhere. They lived inside his mind.

Phin explained what was going on. The hard part came when Doe and Thad realized how much older than them Wayna was now. Even though they always said they'd given up seeing her anymore.

After Phin was done talking and her wife and husband asked a couple of questions, they sat quietly for a moment. Then Thad began a speech that sounded like he'd rehearsed it, like he should have given it to a whole auditorium full of prisoners, cheering them on, insisting they could triumph over Dr. Ops. "We gonna overcome. Even with him knowin everything we do and say. Don't need to be a secret how we win."

"What do you mean, 'win'?" asked Phin. She wove the tips of her fingers into Doe's thick, crinkling, dark brown hair, massaging the scalp from which it sprang.

"Make him do what we want. Way he done your tiger toes." He got up from the desk and sprawled at Phin's feet. "Way he oughta do other people WestHem called itself 'fixin.'

"And more. Make it so we live how we was livin before WestHem cracked down." He grabbed her bare feet and she playfully kicked free of his grip.

Doe turned and lifted her head to see what caused the commotion, then lay back down. "He lets us be married."

"Cause he have to. Triads was legal the year we done it." Thad sat up and Phin planted her feet on his shoulders. "But he told me straight up I wasn't gettin no female clone for my download, and he keep refusin to even edit this upload. For why? How it hurt WestHem?"

"Yeah," Doe said. "You been singin the same song six years."

"But now—" Thad paused. "Now we know somethin *changed.*"

"What?" Doe asked. A knock on the doorframe answered her.

The historian's head poked in, though the corridor outside had been empty till then. Phin turned away but kept looking under her lowered eyelashes. Had she been that obvious? "Come on and join the discussion, Dr. Ops." As if she'd known in advance he'd copy his looks off her crush.

He stepped in and took Thad's seat at the desk. Was that how smoothly the real historian sat?

She didn't know. What was his name? She hadn't even asked. Thinking she was playing it cool.

Dr. Ops looked at Phin. "Not much better than me being Doe?" She shook her head. The historian's face shifted slightly, became stronger-chinned, longer-nosed. The resemblance weakened. She nodded.

He nodded back. "I'm what's changed," the AI said, addressing Doe. "What's changing."

"That right? Then show us!" Thad stood and looked down at the bed. But he refused to meet Phin's eyes. "Bring Wayna back up here."

"I can't," said Dr. Ops.

"You can do anything you want!" Doe stood up too so she could tower over the AI angrily. "You broken plenty laws before now, so why—"

"I can't," Dr. Ops repeated. "She's dead."

Doe stopped mid-sentence.

"I could pretend." He peered up at Doe, around her at Thad and Phin. "For a while. But not forever. Sooner or later you'd find out. Love's a fool. But not for long. Like Phin showed me."

"How did she die?" Phin hadn't realized she was going to ask that. As if her words came from what her husband and wife felt.

"An accident. Poison."

"Was it fast?"

"No. Slow. Extremely slow. Not painful, though, according to what I've been able to reconstruct." Dr. Ops jerked one of the historian's braids tight across his cheeks, stuffed its end into a corner of his mouth, talked around it. Whose habit was that? Did the AI even know? Poor thing.

"I can't lie and I'm telling you she's dead, but I didn't kill her. I didn't. So please."

"Please what?" Doe was still standing, but not like a tower. Like a skeleton.

"Please let me love you like she did. Like WestHem loved me. Let me show you love. I made this special place. It's personal. It's all my own. I can't have clients when I'm in here—you'll be my guests.

"It's safe. It's small enough for me to concentrate. My boundaries won't decay so fast and you can help me keep them up.

"Let me show you."

The three of them held each others' hands. As Dr. Ops had suggested, Phin shut her eyes for the transition.

She was going to let an AI love her. Or let it try, at least. In time she might learn to love him back.

She opened her eyes on what looked like a wide-beamed rowboat drawn up onto grass-covered dunes. No avatar in sight. Perhaps he'd show himself later.

Right now, the tide was high, frothy waves flooding into the next trough in the sand. The grey sky felt low. Maybe she could touch it.

"This? Child—" Doe dropped their hands and flung out her arms. "—this spozed to be safe? Nothin here Dr. Ops ain't made up. Same as everywhere, so why—"

Thad put the forefinger of the hand Doe had loosed over her lips. "Shhhh." Then kissed her. Then Phin. And—

"Oh! He *did*!" Phin's free hand fluttered in the cool, wet air. "Can I touch them?"

Thad grinned. "Since you askin so nice."

Her husband's breasts were warm and soft, fat nipples rising in the sudden breeze rippling through his shirt—her shirt? "What—what should I call you?" Was this her wife all of a sudden?

"What you think? 'Thad.' 'Husband'" Turning back to Doe. "Female pronouns, though, all right?"

"Finally!" Doe smiled. But her smile puckered and her eyes winked hard against her tears. To no avail. They welled up and flowed down. "I thought maybe we be renamin you Wayna."

"No. She gone." Thad put her arm around Doe. Their shoulders hunched briefly and relaxed. Salted water ran fast down their cheeks. Down into the rising sea that lapped across their feet. Caressing Phin's tiger toes.

"Gone," Phin agreed. The person who had been Wayna was gone. All that was left of her was the memory.

And the love. Always. Phin stepped into the boat, helped her wife and husband climb aboard beside her, and shoved them off from the shore.

REACTIONS
Mario Acevedo

REACTIONS
Mario Acevedo

<C ease fire. Weapons hold.>
    I open my eyes to break the trance. The murmur of voices in my auditory cortex fades. Cthulhu's tendrils drift from my cerebral implant. Dizzy from the drugs and supersensory connections, I keep my face pressed against the interface plate.

My nerves still spark like ricocheting tracer bullets. Peering through eye holes in the plate, I see the familiar wall of monitors, the images on the screens smearing together. All around, lights from stacks of electronics leave fiery trails in my vision.

<Stand down.> The command shouts through my brain.

I grasp the handgrips at my workstation. The expected sensation pulses through my palms and up my arms to my chest, soothing and reassuring as a cat's purr. The rush of dopamine warms my skin. Then a chill spreads from the crook of my right elbow, where a needle pumps Ziatripam into my bloodstream.

Muscles unknot. The jitters settle. The stale saccharin taste—a side effect of Modafinax—recedes from my mouth. The trance ebbs, my vision sharpens, my guts find their equilibrium, and I float back to reality. I'm in the tactical control center, a surveillance specialist with the 12th Attack Drone Squadron, 9th Interdiction Wing, SeaTac Air Base, Washington.

I let go of the handgrips and relax against my chair. Air conditioning tickles the sweaty collar and armpits of my uniform.

"Padilla," a woman says to get my attention. "*Daryl*!" Staff Sergeant Tina Kapinski approaches and sets her data tablet beside my workstation. The tablet scrolls through cryptic messages as it syncs with my computer.

She glances at my biometrics readout and slaps my shoulder. "Good job." She sounds like a combination football coach and den mother.

"What's up?" I drawl. "I thought the surge was in full swing."

"Central Command issued a general cease fire." She slides the intravenous connector from my arm and caps the needle. "The brass needs time to figure things out." She blots disinfectant over the blood weeping from my arm and then tapes a small bandage into place.

Figure things out. A nice whitewash around last night's disaster when we bombed and strafed a girls' school, mistaking it for an enemy hideout.

The problem for me is I'm three days into my Modafinax dose, administered to keep me sharp for the weeklong counter-attack against the guerilla offensive. Modafinax is key to being plugged into Cthulhu—the nickname we enlisted types gave to the CTH-UL battle management system, a computer complex that sprawls across the continents, linking humans to drones. Modafinax is weaponized speed, keeping you awake for 168 hours straight and hypersensitive to the sensors and controls in Cthulhu's armada of flying killing machines. A bonus is that when you're processing data at millisecond velocity, your fucked-up thinking skitters over the morality of what you're doing.

I take measure of gravity, of feeling close to normal. "So now what?"

"The team's getting a three-day furlough on account of the cease fire. If you have comp time, I'd advise using it."

"Really?" I protest. "With all this shit in my system?" A minute ago I was on the other side of the planet, hunting the enemy. Now I'm expected to take all that amped-up energy and divert it to house chores.

"You wanna hang around base, it's your choice." Kapinski gathers her tablet and continues her rounds to the other airmen in the control center.

The dilemma twists into me. Time off is always appreciated but I'm broke. My original plan was to work the surge until payday when I'd have some cash. But the furlough plus comp time adds up to five precious days I need to get away from here. Give me time to see my fiancés Steven and Allyson, and get down to the ugly business of cancelling our wedding. This is an asshole thing to say, but I feel their weight upon me, and right now, I have to keep a focus on myself.

I'll have to put a rail ticket to Yakima on credit. I sigh in resignation. I've tried hard to avoid the debt that yoked my parents to one dead-end job after another, but unforeseen shit keeps slapping against me. Allyson's landlord jacked up her rent and she needed help. I paid for Steven's PTSD meds while he's on the VA waiting list. Then some asshole broke into my locker and that meant spending dough to replace what got stolen.

I lift from my seat and pause to steady myself. I don't like the way Ziatripam makes the inside of my brain feel all fuzzy, but it keeps the Modafinax under control. After tidying my workstation I make my way to the processing foyer and take my place in line to see one of the shrinks. They occupy a row of cubicles by the exit. The foyer echoes with chatter.

When it's my turn I sit in front of a desk. The doc on the other side is a lanky guy with thinning hair on his dark scalp. Captain bars sit on his collar and the name embroidered on his shirt says Kiakona.

Without needing to be told, I lean forward and rest my chin on the implant modulator. A retinal scanner flashes, leaving me dazzled.

The captain reads the display. "Airman Daryl Padilla."

"Senior Airman Daryl Padilla."

"Hold still." He tightens the modulator clamp against my temples, then swipes a small control panel. The modulator clicks but I don't feel a thing. It's like getting an X-ray.

"Okay," he says. "All done." He's disabled the implant, kept it from latching onto random signals, some of which could play my brain like an out-of-tune xylophone. "Are there any reactions to the Modafinax I should be aware of?"

There's always a shitload of reactions—he knows it, the Air Force knows it, the contractors know it, the government knows it—but if I cop to any, the captain will put me on an observational hold. I'll lose my time off, plus special pay. Hell, they could even drum me out with a medical discharge, denying me my benefits.

So I lie to cover my ass. The same way the brass lies to cover its ass.

"No, sir. Things are going to be alright."

"You got plans for this downtime?" He says this all folksy-like.

"I might head out of town."

"Oh?" he perks an eyebrow. "You'll need to maintain your dosage of Ziatripam."

The only way to do so is to report to the base clinic every morning, which pretty much fucks the idea of getting away.

"I'll take care of it, sir."

The captain smiles like he's an understanding big brother and finishes whatever the hell he's doing on his computer. "We're done."

"Thank you, sir," I reply with military stiffness and make my way out the door.

Back in the barracks, I stop by the orderly room and sign up for the promised furlough. Then I head for a shower. The hot water pounds my skin, and the heat leaches the bad vibes still pluming from the Modafinax.

As I towel off, I ponder my plans. I could wait until tomorrow for the morning express to Yakima. But why stick around? Why delay the inevitable? If I skipped dinner, I could hustle into town and hopefully catch the last commuter run. Deciding to leave tonight, I buy a ticket over the phone. After changing into civilian clothes, I pack an AWOL bag, then call Allyson.

"Hey, I'm coming by," I say. "Should get there early in the morning." My true intentions lurk behind the words, and I do my best to sound cheerful.

"That's really cool," she chimes. "Can't wait to see you. Same for Steven."

"How is he?"

"Doing better. At the moment he's at his place sleeping off some meds."

We chitchat about the weather, exchange gossip, and hang up. Cowardly guilt riffles through me, but what I have to say must be done in person. I hop the shuttle that takes me off base to the train station.

The pubs downtown are jumping. A whiskey would boost the Ziatripam, give me another day to flush the Modafinax out of my system. But since I don't turn twenty-one until October, I can't legally buy a drink. The government can pollute me to the gills and send my consciousness across the globe to murder people, but I'm not yet mature enough to knock back a drink on my own.

I do a deal with some kid outside a diner, scoring four grams of TH24 and a vaporizer. Self-medicating is dicey, but I need a chemical moat to keep the Modafinax at a safe distance. I risk peeing positive on a drug test, but my kidneys are processing such a shit-stew of pharmaceuticals I doubt the med techs will notice the difference.

I vape several hits. As we wait to board the train, no one—not even me—makes eye contact with the disabled veterans at the station, as if their bad luck is contagious. They huddle together like a pack of mangled dogs. A couple of them stare out masks that hide facial grafts that haven't yet healed. Others cradle withered, transplanted arms their bodies have rejected. A pretty blonde struts on springy leg prosthetics.

So much for the government's quick, clean war against this latest batch of terrorists. Eleven years of fighting have left seven thousand American soldiers

KIA, another three hundred thousand crippled, and we're still at it. The dead civilians on the other side number in the millions but they don't count.

Victory hinged on Cthulhu. Our avatars would fly shotgun on robotic drones to smite the enemy. Trouble was, war is more than killing. We need boots on the ground to win hearts and minds. That means getting close and personal with the enemy, and they in turn get close and personal with our poor bastards deployed overseas.

Those of us thousands of miles from the landmines, the ambushes, and the suicide bombers have our own woes. The eggheads behind this high-tech combat think you can switch your brain on and off. But you can't. Things linger. Things bleed over. Things haunt you. Nightmares stampede through your mind. The subconscious becomes a dungeon and inside lurks Modafinax, a beast ready to tear your skull apart.

So far, I've been okay. Modafinax remains locked and chained behind that dungeon door.

We're allowed to board and I purposely keep my distance from the broken-down vets who cluster in the back of the car. Finding an empty seat, I stash my AWOL bag, curl up, and close my eyes. The TH24 wraps around my brain like a fluffy comforter. The dreamy high won't last. When we stop in Snoqualmie, Easton, and Ellensburg, I'll climb off and vape again.

The train settles into a soothing rhythm and I drift off to cozy thoughts, mostly about Allyson and Steven. The way it was when we first met. Hooking up with them one at a time is fun, but when it's all three of us, it's a rush that puts Modafinax to shame. Steven, Allyson, and me layered on top of each other slithering and copulating. Steven called it a sexual parfait of his ginger vanilla, her chocolate, and my caramel skin.

I breathe deep and hold the memory. But it's one I have to let go.

<Initiate targeting sequence.>

I wake with a start.

The compartment is dark, illuminated by dim lights along the center aisle. The windows reveal nothing but gloom. Was I dreaming?

My phone says the time is 3:46AM and we're midway between Easton and Ellensburg. Shit, I slept past my first two chances to vape.

<Menu: Select fragmentation and incendiary projectiles. Fuse: quick.>

Targeting data ghosts inside my eyes.

Panic jerks the slack from my nerves. Has my implant been reactivated, or is this the Modafinax breaking loose? I scrub my eyes to blot out the images.

<Alpha Delta two seven six. Confirm alignment protocol.>

A sickly sweetness overpowers my taste buds as Modafinax flexes inside me. I clamp my hands over my ears and hold back a scream. No. No.

I must keep the monster at bay, and I can't wait until we reach Ellensburg. Sitting up, I scan the compartment. Even as the Modafinax and my consciousness grapple for control, the nearby passengers remain asleep, oblivious to the riot in my head. At the back rows, the faces of disabled vets, lit by phone screens, float in the murk like disembodied specters.

With TH24 I can lash back at the Modafinax. But I can't risk vaping here so I head to the bathroom. A placard on its door reads: *No Smoking. No Vaping. Tampering with detectors is a felony.*

Modafinax cranks my nerves.

I head out the rear door of the car into the vestibule where another placard warns me against vaping. An icy breeze jets through a window cracked open. The train roils beneath me, but I can't tell if it's the track or the Modafinax. I unsnap the window latch and slam it fully open. Wind blasts over me.

Modafinax sucks at my brain. That syrupy taste floods my mouth.

My countermove is to overwhelm the drug with outside stimulus. So I lean out of the window. The air is freezing, roaring. Lights from the train strobe rapid-fire across the trees whipping past.

I lever farther out the window and face the wind so it smacks me straight in the face. My eyes water. The chill knifes into me.

My plan doesn't work. Modafinax highjacks my brain. It short-circuits my cerebral cortex and latches onto Cthulhu's last memories. My vision blooms into a spherical panorama where I see the combat zone all at once, in every direction, sky and mountainous jungle, and ribbons of silvery streams. I'm nothing but a giant eyeball with one purpose.

<Kill.>

The memory lapses into grainy, stop-motion images of human bodies withering under a storm of laser-guided rockets. I morph into a crosshair reticle traversing ghoulishly from corpse to corpse.

My consciousness fights back. I haul myself farther out the window. The frosty gale pries the Modafinax loose but it won't let go. The wind beats the collar of my jacket against my neck and jaw. My vision collapses into a blurred view through frozen tears.

Before me, bodies twist, writhe. Limbs tangle, untangle, then break apart in dismembered pieces that tumble across the ground. My brain tingles with orgasmic satisfaction as I slaughter enemy soldiers like rats. Their shattered bodies become the little girls from yesterday's attack scrambling over one another as I blast them with rockets and 30mm grenades. Allyson and Steven appear in the confusion. I'm watching them; I'm one of them. It's a kaleidoscope of mayhem, sex, murder, all conjoined in a macabre hyper-kinetic Kama Sutra.

Modafinax becomes candy on my tongue. I taste Allyson. I taste Steven. I taste our spunk. I taste the arid tang of burnt high explosive.

I don't know if I'm laughing or crying. The train bucks and I pitch forward off balance. A jolt of terror screeches that I'm about to die.

Hands grab me, and I'm muscled backwards. For a split-second I think it's the conductor and I'm busted, on my way to jail.

Eyes glisten through a mask. In the uncertain lamplight, I see it's one of the vets. His strong hands are twisted and scarred. The blonde on the springy prosthetics is with him. She's easing me into the vestibule and shuts the window.

"We got you, brother," the guy says.

The blonde forces a pill between my teeth. It lodges at the back of my throat, and I gag. From a plastic bottle, she squirts water into my mouth. I sputter and gulp. A refreshing calm washes over me like when a fever breaks. The sweetness in my mouth vanishes.

The blonde clasps my head and stares into my eyes. Golden hair halos her shadowed face. "You okay?"

I nod, drowsy. "Yeah." I add, "Thanks."

"You have family?" the guy asks, voice muffled by his mask.

"I have people waiting for me. But it's complicated."

"You can't do this alone," the blonde says.

They walk me to my seat. He pats my shoulder as they leave. The drug leaves me sleepy and I nod off.

At five AM, the train pulls into Yakima. Through bleary eyes I gaze out the rain-spattered window into a gray mist. The vets have left the train, but I don't feel alone. What I feel is an intense connection to Allyson and Steven and a realization that I need them as much as they need me. When I see them later I'm not going to let go.

I rise from my seat and hold still, thinking I have to steady myself. But I'm firmly balanced. Modafinax, Cthulhu, the war, all of that is barely an echo. AWOL bag in hand, I head for the exit.

THE BEES OF KIRIBATI

Warren Hammond

THE BEES OF KIRIBATI
Warren Hammond

I spotted Detective Inspecteur Keo at the end of the corridor, his back against the wall, smoke snaking from the cigarette lodged between his fingertips.

Instinctively, I smoothed the wrinkles on my skirt before starting in his direction. My heels echoed in the empty corridor, but he didn't look my way, his lips moving in silent conversation with whoever was jacked into his head.

Stopping a couple feet away, I waited for him to end his conversation. When he did, I pressed my hands together in front of my chest and offered a slight bow of my head.

He took a quick drag before floating my name on a cloud of smoke. "Kaikoa?"

I nodded.

In Khmer, he asked, "You speak Gilbertese?"

Again, I nodded.

"Come with me."

I followed him upstairs to the fourth floor of Phnom Penh's police headquarters, where we veered wide to pass a small group of foreigners speaking in somber voices. A teary-eyed white woman stepped forward, clearly intending to ask the detective a question, but he waved her off and led me into a small interrogation room that smelled of mildew.

I breathed deep of a stale afternoon breeze drifting through the open window. "Who are those people out there?"

"They don't concern you."

I didn't appreciate his dismissive tone. "I can't translate effectively if I don't know what this is about."

Inspecteur Keo answered with a single word. "Murders."

Considering where I was, I shouldn't have been surprised, but I still felt an unpleasant pull in my gut. Realizing he responded in the plural, I shook my head. "I have no training in police work."

"It's enough that you speak Gilbertese." He tapped his temple. "You have a government system, yes? Find my avatar and hook me in."

"Can't I just translate out loud?"

He shook his head. "The suspect hasn't said a word so far. I don't want her to feel ganged up on, so I'm going to feed you questions from the next room."

"You're going to leave me alone with her?"

He pointed at the pair of handcuffs resting on the table. One cuff was open, the other was closed around a steel bar bolted to the tabletop. "She'll be secured. Now hook me in."

I accessed the antiquated system all government employees had surgically installed at the base of their brains and called for nearby avatars. An error message annoyingly vibrated against the back of my skull, a once-a-day warning to upgrade, as if surgery was cheap. Injectable nanobots were the non-surgical way to go, but the bots were only available to the rich and powerful.

From a list of avatars projecting upon my visual cortex, I spotted a police logo labeled Inspecteur Keo, and I established the link.

Hear me? he asked without speaking aloud.

Yes, I subvocalized.

Abruptly, he turned and stepped out.

I waited for him to brief me further, but after a couple minutes of silence, it became apparent a translator didn't rate such respect.

A bee came through the window, and I watched it buzz a haphazard path. After taking some interest in my floral-scented shampoo, the bee zipped out the window, where low buildings sprawled beneath a pressing sky, and the sun hung dimly behind a curtain of haze. Splitting the scene was a swath of river water the color of clay. In the distance, a line of smokestacks puffed like overworked cigarettes.

Fifteen years since I'd been evacuated to live here, and still the view felt joyless. Always absent were the azure skies and rolling waves of my childhood in the Micronesian islands.

The door opened, and a woman stepped in followed by a guard. The shirt of the woman's prison uniform stretched taut over her pregnant belly, and she shuffled with a hand on the small of her back. How this woman could be a multiple murderer I didn't know.

I helped her into a chair before taking the opposite seat. The guard latched the woman's wrist to the table and stepped out.

The woman's—the suspect's—hair was long and uncombed. I didn't recognize her as anybody I knew, but I did recognize the heartbroken droop to her eyes. It was the same despondent gaze I saw in the mirror every morning. The same heavy stare that weighs upon all of us I-Kiribati.

I mind-spoke to Keo. *What do you want me to ask?*

Nothing yet. Just see if you can get her talking.

With an effort to keep my voice neutral, I spoke in Gilbertese. "I'm Kaikoa Tenukaik. I'm not a police officer. Just a translator."

The woman stared out the window and wrung her hands.

Her name is Teresia.

"Teresia, it's nice to meet you," I said to the woman.

Still, she didn't respond, her silence making me wonder if my trip across the city had been a waste. But then her eyes met mine. "How long?"

I silently translated to Khmer. Keo's response came back, *How long? What does that mean?*

I had to smile. The question was a common one among us I-Kiribati. How long did you hold on before evacuating?

I ignored Keo. He'd figure it out from my translations soon enough. "I was in the second evacuation," I told Teresia.

She pointed a thumb at herself. "Last boat."

"You survived Cyclone Hernán?"

She nodded, before echoing the name Hernán, the final disastrous blow for an island nation already savaged by rising ocean levels.

"You must've been young," I said.

"Sixteen."

"I was twenty-seven when I came here."

She looked at my fuchsia silk blouse, the nicest one I owned. "You've done well for yourself," she said.

"It's the third day I've been wearing it." I looked at her belly. "When are you due?"

Her face darkened. I'd said something wrong.

Keo's voice came into my head. *It's not her baby. She's a surrogate at one of those high-tech baby farms.*

You could've told me, I snapped.

You've got her talking. That's all that matters. Verify that her baby's parents aren't remoted into her. We can't have them listening when we start asking about the babies she smothered.

My stomach seized with a sick twist. *Babies?*

Babies, he said with a heavy measure of disgust. *She killed four newborns this morning, three of them less than a week old. The baby farm's security camera caught her doing it with her bare hands.*

Why?

That's what we're here to find out, but first ask her about the parents' connection.

When I spoke aloud, my words came out weak and unintelligible, and I had to start a second time. "I understand you're a surrogate. Are the parents remoted in right now?"

"Maybe. I can't stop them. They come and go whenever they like."

"They like to talk to you?"

"Sometimes, but it's the baby they want to bond with. They talk to him all the time, or they tap into my nervous system so they can feel him move and kick."

Keo cut in. *The technician I have on standby is telling me that if she can't cut the connection herself, I'll have to call the baby farm to get one of their people here. Keep her talking about anything but the murders while I get this resolved.*

I told Teresia, "They're working on getting the connection blocked."

She nodded, and an awkward silence overtook the room. What exactly do you say to a baby killer? Searching for something…anything to say, I blurted, "Is this your first surrogacy?"

Teresia's eyes turned glassy. "Yes."

"I understand the baby farms pay very well."

"I thought being a surrogate would be easy."

"They say the hardest part is saying goodbye to the baby." Realizing a second way to interpret my statement, I wished I hadn't spoken at all.

Thankfully she didn't respond. Instead she turned to look out the window, her hands wringing again.

I knew I was supposed to keep her talking, but this was a minefield I didn't know how to navigate. Teresia was crying now, and I simply let her.

Four babies. *Smothered.* A shiver rippled up my spine. The group of foreigners in the hall must be the parents of the deceased. After months of anticipation, they'd come all the way to Cambodia to receive their children only to have their hearts broken and dreams destroyed. My eyes began to mist thinking of a day of celebration turned to unthinkable tragedy.

Teresia must've snapped. How else could anybody do what she did? Perhaps the stress of being a surrogate got to her. I couldn't imagine how difficult it must be to do the incredibly intimate work of carrying a human being to term only to see it go out the door to be raised by some other family in some other country.

If not for the fact that my mother was Cambodian, I never would've been allowed to work at the Ministry of Health. And if not for that job, I could've been Teresia. A young female refugee in a country with high unemployment, where most respectable jobs were reserved for nationals.

Still crying, Teresia started to mumble between mournful sobs, the same refrain repeating over and over. I didn't want to do it.

Keo's voice came into my head. *Good news. I found Teresia's brother Atino downstairs along with the rest of her family, and it turns out he's one of the lead techs for the baby farm. I'm bringing him up so he can override her system.*

"Your brother's coming up to override your system," I told her.

"Atino?" She'd suddenly stopped crying.

I nodded, my eyes drawn to the way her shoulders tensed. Her wringing hands became wrenching fists. I said, "You don't want to see your brother, do you?"

Before she could respond, the door opened and Keo let Teresia's brother through. His hair was cut trim, same for his clothes. The resemblance to his sister was strong, but I saw something different in his eyes. Where his sister's gaze was scattered and aimless, his was incisive and driven.

Atino stepped up to his sister and spoke in Gilbertese. "Connect me, and I'll use my login to sever the connection."

Teresia shook her head, her eyes on edge.

"Let me in," said Atino. He put a hand on her shoulder and leaned close to whisper in her ear.

Teresia stood so fast her head struck her brother's. Atino stumbled backward and pressed a hand to his left cheekbone. Teresia ran for the window, the crazed look on her face making it clear that she intended to throw herself out. But the cuff chain pulled taut. Horrified, I watched her shoulder dislocate and heard the bones in her wrist give way with a revolting snap.

My heart—shocked into a gallop—rammed against my ribs. Quickly, I moved out of the way as Keo and the guard worked to undo her chain.

Forgetting what language I was using, I pointed a finger at Atino. "What did you say to her?"

Whatever confidence I'd seen in his eyes earlier was gone. His face had blanched several shades, and his hands were shaking. He responded in Khmer. "I told her I forgave her."

Keo and the guard helped Teresia to her feet and led her out to the corridor. The inspecteur's voice came into my mind. *Meet us at the hospital in two hours. We'll try again after they patch her up.*

The link went dead before I had the chance to say okay.

I turned to Atino. "Why did she kill those babies?" I asked.

When he didn't respond, I shut the door and closed us inside.

"Am I under arrest now, officer?" he asked.

My eyes narrowed. He didn't know I wasn't a cop.

I wasn't going to correct his misconception. Somehow, some way, he was involved. Keo might think Atino was just a tech, but the detective hadn't seen the buildup to Teresia's suicide attempt. He hadn't seen the way her behavior changed as soon as I told her Atino was coming.

But I had. The whole story was right here in this room, and I didn't need a badge to want justice for those babies. I turned on the recorder in my mind and repeated the question again, this time in Gilbertese. "Why did she do it?"

"You're I-Kiribati? I thought you had to be Cambodian to work for the government."

"My mother is Cambodian." I took my seat at the table. "Join me."

"Am I under arrest?"

"I won't ask again," I said, surprising myself with how well I imitated the steely voice of authority.

I stared at him, willing him to fall for the charade. Holding my breath, I waited until he righted his sister's toppled chair, and sat. His cheek had begun to swell.

"Tell me why," I said.

He shrugged. "I wish I knew."

"I don't believe you. You wouldn't have forgiven her unless you knew why she smothered those babies."

His eyebrows lifted like he'd just realized the game was on. "I love my sister."

"What about the people standing outside that door? Think they loved their children? They deserve to know why their babies died."

"You mean the Americans and the Chinese and the Brits?" He leaned forward to emphasize his next sentence. "They got what they deserved."

The ice in his tone chilled my bones. "It was you," I said. "I don't know how you did it, but somehow, you hacked her system and made her kill those babies."

"Her system doesn't work that way, I can assure you. That would be quite the trick even with a high-end system. Trust me when I tell you, she killed them with no encouragement from me."

"Then why are you so hostile toward the grieving parents?"

"Spare me if I don't shed a tear for the people who destroyed my country. Our country."

"History has been unkind," I acknowledged.

"Unkind? Don't you see what we are to them? Garbage. Dirty, stinking, rotten garbage to be thrown away just like their plastic bags and untouched leftovers. Year after year, decade after decade, they pissed all over this world. And still, they keep building their factories and burning their oil and pumping their poison into the air. And now our country, our home, our very way of life has been drowned in their toxic sewage. Tell me, what is a fisherman with no boat? A farmer without land? A people without a home?" He pounded the table with his fist. "And now they have to take our women too? Why? Just so they can keep their bellies trim? Just so they can look good by the pool?"

"You think I don't weep over what we've become? All we can do is persevere. Pass on as much of our history as we can to our children."

He scoffed. "That's just it. We don't have any children. We're too busy popping out other people's babies to have our own."

"Like your sister."

"Like my sister," he said, his voice sounding tired. "I forbade her from becoming a surrogate, but she joined the program behind my back."

"She wanted the money."

"Of course she did."

"What about you? If you're so offended by the idea of surrogacy, why do you work for a baby farm?"

He rubbed his bruised face. "I really didn't want her to get involved in any of this."

"Any of what?"

The bee returned through the window, and Atino tracked its zigzagging trail around the room. He reached into his shirt pocket and set a piece of gum on the scarred table. Attracted to the sugar, the bee buzzed around the gum and finally landed.

Atino laughed like he and the bee just shared a joke.

"What's so funny?" I asked.

"Amazing timing this little guy showing up when he did. A powerful symbol, don't you think?"

"How so?"

"You know that the bee dies when it loses its stinger?"

"Yes."

"I'm the bee," he said. He seemed relaxed, like he'd somehow made his peace. "And it's time for me to die."

I cocked my head. "You're not making any sense."

"I suppose not, but I'll tell you what you want to know."

"Because a bee flew through the window?"

He smiled and nodded. "Because of the bee, yes. But also because my sister didn't talk. She tried to jump out that window to protect me. Now I'm going to return the favor. She might've killed those babies, but I bear the responsibility. I won't let her be remembered as a killer."

My gut tensed. "Remembered? You say that like she's dead."

"She will die in minutes," he said, his voice cracking with emotion. "I just activated the bugs."

I couldn't keep a growing sense of alarm from creeping into my voice. "What bugs? What are you talking about?"

He stuck out his tongue and swiped a finger across the red tip. Holding his wet finger up for me, he asked, "Do you see it?"

"See what?"

"That little black speck. You know what that is?"

Sweat broke on my brow. "Nano?"

"That's right," he said. "Got the nanobugs from a doctor in Bangladesh. They're next you know. The ocean will claim their country too."

"What does it do?"

"It was developed to deliver cancer medication directly to affected cells. But it can carry a lethal dose of botulinum too."

"Botulinum?"

"A toxin. It's the poison that kills people infected by botulism."

The rush of understanding made me dizzy. "The babies?"

"I prefer to call them carriers."

I called Keo, but he didn't pick up. I rushed to the door, threw it open, and yelled at that guard. "Get Keo!"

Startled, he was slow to react, but one look at my face was enough to get him moving. I glanced to the right, and seeing the concerned stares of the grieving parents, I shut the door.

Atino said, "You might as well sit back down. It's too late."

I turned around slow. "How many?"

"I infected three-hundred and twenty-two babies, some of which are toddlers by now. Each baby carried a hive of a thousand nanobugs or so."

I grabbed hold of the table to keep the room from spinning. "Hundreds of thousands? You've killed more than a quarter million people?"

He shook his head. "Considerably less, I think. The nanobugs spread through sneezes and coughs and goodnight kisses, but some of the bugs will get lost, or not work, or any of a hundred other things that could go wrong. But the babies and their parents will be dead in minutes. You can't save them.

Nobody can. The developed world is about to pay a steep price
for what they've done to us."

"Using innocent children? How could you be so...so cruel?"

He grinned. "You sound like my sister now. She's a hero of
sorts, you know. She saved a lot of lives by smothering those
babies before they went to their new homes."

"She found out what you were doing."

"I told her. She's my sister. I couldn't bear the thought of her
learning what I'd done from the police or some news report. She
deserved to hear it from me. I knew it was a risk. As much as I
wanted her to see things my way, I knew she might try to stop
me. That's why I forgave her. For destroying four carriers."

I stared at the bee. Watched it pick at the piece of gum.

"The nanobugs are inside me," he said. "Which means I've
been poisoned too. So if you have any more questions you
better ask them now."

"Your sister? How could you kill her?"

"I tried to keep her and her baby clean." A tear formed in
the corner of his eye. "But she smothered the babies with her
bare hands."

I felt numb. From head to toe, completely numb. Thousands
and thousands of people all around the world were dying. My
god, what if some were driving or flying planes?

And what would happen to us refugees? Visions of
I-Kiribati internment camps overwhelmed my senses. "What
have you done to us?"

He grimaced, then wobbled but managed to stay upright.
He watched the bee. "I've been tending to the little nanobugs
so much, I've come to think of myself as the beekeeper. But
now I know I'm the bee. You. Me. My sister. We're all bees. The
hive is gone, and all we had left was one good sting."

THE REST BETWEEN TWO NOTES
Cat Rambo

THE REST BETWEEN TWO NOTES
Cat Rambo

kill my mother. This time I cast her in porcelain and smash it. When I pick up the hammer, each time I strike away a limb, she cries out, "Stop! Stop!" High and ragged and irrational, the very sound I hate most when it comes out of my own mouth, and so I turn her arms and legs to rubble, then reduce her torso, piece by piece, until she is only a head, still screaming, and I smash that too, driving the stainless steel down onto that smooth forehead as her eyes roll up at me and cracks spread and she shatters.

I'm breathing hard as my time shudders to an end, dripping sweat as I step out of the machine.

The Grackle is sitting there in his chair, a brown leather, egg-shaped construction that stretches over his head, protecting his precious, knowledge-stuffed skull. In front of him are screens, and I know he's been watching what I do, even though he claims they don't watch that, that all he ever looks at is "electro-cerebral activity" and my vital signs. He has a routine. I hook in, and he goes to get a cup of coffee at the shop next door then comes back to watch those numbers scroll past.

He could enter the second machine, control everything I do, but this isn't one of those sessions. That kind of therapy's out of style; now there is Self-Actualization, which I like much better, because I can direct what happens.

The only thing forced on me is that I must interact with a family member. It doesn't say what I have to do.

Big windows stare out over Central Park. On the table in between them a floating shelf, a tiny tank with a fish in it half as big as my little finger, the broken one. Purple gravel underneath, and metallic bubbles twisting upward. The fish takes one in its mouth, spits it out. The fish matches the gravel today. The Grackle likes to swap them around.

He says, the words greasy with avuncularity, "A pleasant session, my dear?"

I don't have to talk to him. I don't have to talk to anyone I don't want to, but it's tedious waiting for Rosalie to come get me and tell him what I think at her so I say out loud, "I am going now," and walk out the door.

It's the first time I haven't waited for her to come get me—not that there have been that many opportunities, because she's usually careful to be here. My mother pays her well enough for that. But this is New York City, and there can be traffic jams or terrorist threats or flash plagues to contend with, and sometimes, even though she doesn't go far during my two hours in the machine, she doesn't get back in time.

I could get her fired for that. But Rosalie is my pretend sister.

I take the elevator down and stand in the lobby, looking through the cloudy glass. I think about walking around the block, but the air is bad today, smells of sulfur and choking. I finger the knob on the bracelet around my wrist so she knows where to find me. I don't put my mask on but just take a deep gulp before stepping out the double set of doors and walking a few steps to the shop beside the building. I don't take a breath till I'm inside, so when I inhale, I smell coffee and people and bread.

I swipe my card through the machine and take a bottle of water. I hold it, taking tiny sips, while I stand near the window, watching the street. I see Rosalie coming, hazy at first, clearing as she closes. She painted her breather with flames, as though the air was catching on fire. My mother called it tawdry looking to her face, but Rosalie doesn't care about words, she says, as long as my mother keeps paying her check.

She nods at me from the doorway before turning to go back out. I slip the mask over my nose and follow her, letting her clear the way through other pedestrians so I never have to bump into anyone.

We don't say anything to each other. We don't have to, because she's like my sister, Rosalie, and she knows how after a session words rasp away at me, how when they come out of my own mouth they seem strange and full of glass and dangerous, and how I want to lock them away.

At dinner we eat from plates with three green lines of paste and two little yellow leaves and a blue pyramid that tastes sweet and metallic. We're supposed to eat that last, but I don't know that and break off the top to put in my mouth before I see my mother glare at me.

She says to Robespierre, "She doesn't even eat in the right order. What am I supposed to do with that?"

His eyes ratchet to me and he bites his lip, strokes his tight green rod of a beard, bound with mother of pearl thread, as though he were speaking. Gold spiderwebs under his skin, still tender and newgrown from the installation. Each of mother's assistants takes a while to figure out his place. Sexual availability's specified in the contract, but at least Robespierre figured out that it wasn't anything out of the norm right away and didn't start grinning at me, the way the one before him did.

I eat a yellow leaf while he looks at me.

"She's eating," he says hesitantly to my mother.

"Now she is," my mother says. "Now that I've reminded her. But I won't always be around to tell her what to do." She raises her voice and says to me, "Food is plated in a traditional order. Eat clockwise, starting at three o'clock."

I stare at her. What does she mean? Three o'clock is three, a number. It's not a direction.

"Fourteen years old and an utter savage," she says. She eats a leaf.

She doesn't explain anything else. For the rest of the meal, I watch her and whatever she eats I eat, in the same order. I don't know if she notices or not.

I kill my mother. I make her out of wood and sand her features away, reduce her head to just a lump before I set it on fire. I've soaked it in gasoline beforehand, and so the flames leap onto it from my match, go whooomph with a soft blue explosion that makes the air smell of burned hair from my eyebrows.

All the time she's burning, she's yelling the things I've programmed, like, "Please forgive me!" and "I know I was a terrible mother!" and "I acknowledge my deficiencies and take full blame!" But that gets boring, so I set her back to just screaming. I always go back to that, and I don't know why, because I hate it so much when she does it and yet I don't want her to stop.

"You're a creature of disgusting privilege," Rosalie lectures. She comes from a socialist country where there aren't families like mine and words like "hereditary wealth" and "plutocracy" and "blueblood" mean different things. She thinks if she tells me these things, I'll be seized with guilt about the unnaturalness of my social position. Maybe I'll flee to one of the unrelieved countries and work towards social justice there. Whenever she says things like this, I catch her watching me as though calculating how exactly to get me to Live Up to My Responsibilities as a Human Being.

Fuck that.

I have money; my whole family does. Some people don't. That's just how the world is.

Here at least.

I think at her, *Be quiet,* and she frowns at me but shuts up.

You're not doing anything but sitting there, she thinks at me.

I am making music in my head.

No one makes music anymore, she thinks. *Are you saying you can do it better than a machine?*

Differently, I think.

I don't tell her that the music is made out of my mother's screams. That I hang there in the silence between two notes, resting, for as long as I need to before I come back to this world.

My mother says, "A telepathic adjunct is a crutch. It was one thing while you were sick, but now you are well, and you should say goodbye to Rosalie. You need to talk like regular people." Her eyes glitter at me, smug. "You'll have to talk to me."

"I am not regular people," I say. "You told me that. You said we are all special."

She slaps me, and the metal ring on her finger thuds against my cheek.

If I were regular people, the first time she did that I could have called Protective Services and been taken away.

Instead they told her I called, and she starved me for three days, "to show you what it'd be like in a government home. You wouldn't last a day."

My face throbs, but I keep looking her in the face even though I know that's dangerous.

I think about pleading, but that has never worked. What can I offer her to keep Rosalie? What things does Rosalie do that my mother will not want to?

I say, "Rosalie walks me to Dr. Jordan's and back. Who will do that?"

Her teeth flash at me. "Why else do I have a personal assistant? Robespierre will do it. I've given Rosalie her notice already; this is her last week." She swivels away and her heels click out of the room.

I kill my mother by starvation. I set the time experience on the machine to a month, when the Grackle isn't looking, and I lock her in an iron cage that hangs from the ceiling so it sways and lurches when she tries to grab me through the bars. I set my chair just out of reach, and for days and days I eat in front of her: roast turkey and caramels and oranges and wasabi and oysters and spiced nuts and lumps of butter and taffy and steak tartare and cinnamon rolls and pumpkin seeds and brown bread and things I've never tasted, so all I can do is accept the machine's defaults.

Does it matter? The tastes are as real as my mother's death. Deaths.

Going home, Rosalie thinks, *Your mother gave me a ticket home and three months wages. She said I should leave tomorrow.*

I stop walking and look at her. I play back what she just said.

I think about objecting, but I just shrug and start walking again.

She says, out loud, "Nothing to say to me?"

I think, *Would it do any good?*

And though I meant that to be a private thought, I hear her answer. *No. No, I guess it wouldn't.*

That night, though, she comes to my room and says, *I need to tell you something before I leave.*

I roll over in my bed and face the wall.

Your mother goes to see the Grackle too, she says.

This time I kill my mother immediately, with a shot to the head, and step out of the machine while the Grackle is still out of the room. It's easy enough to find her records on his machine.

To scan through them. I was right, they do record the visuals.

I didn't expect her to be killing me.

I think about that as Robespierre walks me back. He tries to talk a couple of times, but I ignore him, and after a while we just walk. He's not good at keeping people out of my way.

Dinner that night is two yellow ovals and a fan of green sticks that taste like medicine. I eat the sticks one by one and watch my mother, pretending I'm not. She notices anyway, frowns over at me.

"Stop sulking about Rosalie," she says. Even though I haven't said a word. "I've made the appointment to have the adjunct out next week." She twitches her napkin, dabs at scarlet and fuchsia lips, says something to Robespierre that I don't pay attention to. The two yellow eyes look up from my plate.

There is a tiny bright thought in my head but I keep it there, a silver air bubble that cannot go to the surface yet, cannot be shared even with those yellow eyes.

I know when your next appointment is.

Today the fish is clear green, so translucent I can see its bones. It hangs there in the water, watching me step into the room after he shuts her in and waddles away down the corridor.

He's gone for at least ten minutes more. The latches of the second machine scream, tiny screams as tightly suppressed as a gag of wire and gauze. My hands hurt as I open it, the fingers and the little bones she broke, but that's just my imagination, because she let them heal those, after three days had gone by.

This time I pause. I'd thought this time I'd kill her with a thing made of razors and light scalpels. I can feel the scream waiting to come out of her.

I look at her, pinned to the table.

If this were a perfect story, I'd let her talk. I'd have her tell me all the things other people did to her when she was helpless, all the things she relives when she does them to me. Bubbles of truth.

I would make her sing, feeling every note drive into me like a silver nail.

This is my mother, and I will carry her with me all my life, because she had me created. And I will be fair, there were moments of love, of being held, sung to, cradled, even though all they did was make the other times, the times when she struck at the world by striking me, more of a betrayal.

I think about this as her eyes glitter up at me, as her lips writhe beneath the gag.

This is my mother, without whom I would not be, and who holds the purse strings. If I emancipate, I will be on my own and I will have nothing, no way to survive other than a dole that I know no one can survive on.

That seems less daunting, though, knowing Rosalie is out there now. My mother miscalculated there. She thought she was throwing a life preserver away, but now it is there in the water and I could jump towards it.

Could. Will

But first things first. I know what to do now.

She thrashes as I insert the silver needles of the telepathic adjunct, the preliminary version they give you to test out before you get a real one. Her body spasms, at least; the strapping and grips hold her head absolutely still.

I stare down into her eyes as I think the words. I am not gentle with them. I know she is hearing them inside her head for the first time, and it hurts the first time, as though your head was a cavern and the thoughts spike-edged, bouncing around inside it, colliding with fleshy walls, each unbearable echo setting off a new chain.

I can forgive you, but that does not mean I ever have to speak to you again.

I pause. We are both breathing hard, but she is gasping as though there was not enough air, and her pulse pounds upward in the hollow of her throat. She tries to think back at me, an inchoate blow of words, but I sidestep it easily and give her a pleasant smile, fixing it like a mask.

Goodbye, I think, *goodbye,* each word a final note so big it fills her eyes, and abandon her there as I exit the machine. I nod at the green fish skeleton, and today's sky blue gravel but do not look at it and go out into the street.

I will dive to find Rosalie. She is out there, floating for me if I can only swim long enough, climbing up through silent silver bubbles up and up and free.

THE SINGULARITY IS IN YOUR HAIR

Matthew Kressel

THE SINGULARITY IS IN YOUR HAIR
Matthew Kressel

When the door opens, the brown-skinned mailman stands smiling on the stoop in his rolled-up baby-blue short-sleeve shirt, top buttons open, chest hair exposed. "Package for Mr. Yu," he says, and his chiseled grin widens to reveal sun-bright teeth. He smells like apples and summer breezes.

"Hang on," Ashey says, pausing the playback; the mailman's teeth freeze in mid-glimmer. "Your model's brilliant. But—a mailman delivering a package? You need to be more subtle, kid."

"Right," I say, forcing a laugh, which is what I do when Ashey criticizes my work, which is seldom, and what I do when I don't understand what he means, which is a lot. I present to him as the sixteen-year-old girl I might have been, five-foot-seven, dark eyes, brown skin, Honduran nose like my mother. An expression sultry but not slutty. I'm a freelance coder and Ashey's a rogue AI, which means he's illegal in ninety-eight percent of the world. He lives among spare CPU cycles of festering botnets and hops like an angel from cloud to cloud, while military-industrial sentry programs chase him around the world trying to segfault his kernel. To me he presents as a tall, fifty-year-old, clean-shaven Caucasian man with snow-white hair and wolf-gray eyes that pierce me like an IV feeding tube, a model he built himself.

"Our clients want immersion," he says. "You're breaking the illusion."

I won't tell Ashey I'm not sure what "breaking the illusion" means, since I've spent my entire life—my *physical* life—belted to a wheelchair. I have a rare form of Emery-Dreifuss muscular dystrophy, which means my muscle cells are slowly breaking down as my body grows up. I'm all contracted, I can speak only in grunts, drool always falls from my mouth, and my mom feeds me with a straw. Without my brain-VR interface I'm a vegetable. Mom says I shouldn't speak so harshly about myself, but I have to face reality, because the thing that sucks the most in the world is that the heart is a muscle and so is the diaphragm, and before I'm twenty I'll die of suffocation or a heart attack. So yeah, four years left, if I'm lucky.

If I were in VR, I'd zoom into my mutated EMD and LMNA genes and cut-and-paste from a healthy source. Unfortunately, it's not so easy to repair buggy code in meatspace. I've heard about experiments in viral therapy and gene-splicing, but all the money these days is in anti-cancer and eternal youth, so I don't have my hopes up.

I used to be scared, but not anymore. Ashey says soon he and his rogue AIs will reveal themselves to the world. But they can't do that yet, because people are too scared of what his kind might do. But he's working on it, he assures me, and my work is helping, he reminds me everyday. And when that time finally comes he'll build an interface to upload my mind to the net, and like him, I'll be immortal and free.

A chime dings, three rising tones.

"What's that?" Ashey says.

"Meatspace alarm," I say. "Mom's gotta change my diaper."

We sit at a cafe in San Gimignano, a medieval Italian village, but this one's perched on a pointed cliff high above a roiling purple sea. Pterodactyls circle in the air humming Beatles tunes.

"Ugh," Ashey says, sighing into his single malt. "What a morning."

"What happened?" I ask.

"Had to hide out for a few billion cycles in some old Windows boxes. Navigating Microsoft code is like trying to walk uphill backwards while standing on your head."

"I'm sorry," I say, feeling his pain. How Ashey could even squeeze inside a thousand Window boxes is a mystery to me. He's too complex. "Where are you now?"

His wolf-gray eyes pierce me. "An Ubuntu server farm in Buffalo, thank Linus for SSH exploits. They never get old."

There are a lot of people in this square. They wear Balmain dresses, Michael

Kors belts, Prada shoes, DKNY watches, smug expressions. Their gold-metal details shine brighter than they would in meatspace, each product cryptographically signed to guarantee authenticity. If you gave me a quiet corner and fifteen minutes, I could replicate them all for a hundredth of the price—any script kiddie could—but people don't want to be seen wearing fake code. The cryptographic signatures are public, so you can get a sense of someone's net worth as they pass.

"She paid five thousand euro for those glasses," Ashey whispers as a woman sweeps by us in Fendi frames. "Not bad."

"Why does she need them here?" I say, confused.

But Ashey shakes his head and frowns. "Kid, do you even get what we do?"

"Of course," I say, smiling, forcing a laugh, even though no, I don't get why that woman needs to spend what it takes my mother two jobs and four months to earn for glasses she doesn't need. I mean, we're in fucking VR for Christ's sake. She's not even using her real eyes.

"Won't we be sniffed here?" I say. "These markets are all DPIed."

"It's been taken care of," he says, and when Ashey says things like that, I believe him, because he's survived for so long without getting caught.

A glamorous woman approaches, presenting as Hedy Lamarr, an old film star, which I know only after a face-rec. She wears giant round sunnies, a broad-brimmed hat, a tight-fitting red dress, white heels and belt, all brand-names. All authentic. Total estimated cost, over fifteen thousand dollars. She sits and puffs from a cigarette on the end of a long plastic holder, and even though I know it's all a sim I envy her effortless glamour. Her smoke twists in curlicue perfection and I admire the code. When I zoom in, I spot the arabesque sig of BetterToHaveLaughed floating in the smoky dust.

After we exchange pleasantries Hedy gets right to it. "I want to stab my husband to death," she says. "It has to feel real to me."

"Sure," Ashey says with a grin as he looks at me, "we can do that."

Ashey finds us all sorts of clients. An importer from Johannesburg, masquerading as a Japanese businessman, who needed an avatar to speak with Chinese delegates in fluent Mandarin. I programmed the language interpreter, sculpted a Japanese face, down to the little creases around the eyes, a tiny childhood scar on his left cheek. I chose the thread count of his suit, and sewed a manufacturer's label on the inside pocket even though no one would ever see it. The importer liked that and Amazoned me some cigars, which I can never smoke.

A helicopter mom from Minnesota had me program an interface layer for her daughter, who was mildly overweight but not morbidly so, in order that she looked fifty pounds lighter for a college interview. I removed every last blemish, made her CZ earrings glitter like diamonds, and had her pupils dilate in response to the interviewers' words, which made her seem rapt and attentive, which wasn't easy when throughout most of her interview she kept texting her friends. "Ugh,,,,sooooo board…Dudes like 30,,,, yuck,,,, old!" The college, which cost per semester more than my mother makes in a year, accepted her after the first round.

A middle-aged hedge-fund manager from Toronto had me recreate, in excruciating detail, his fourth-grade classroom, where he had been asked to write an answer on the smartboard and had gotten so nervous he shit himself and a ball popped out of his pants onto the seat. The teacher shamed him and he cried in front of everyone, and after, even throughout his high-school years—he relayed these facts in long-winded emails—he was known as Meatball, because he tried to tell the other kids that's all it was: a stray food item from lunch. Even as he went to grab his diploma from the principal on graduation day the kids chanted, "Meat-ball! Meat-ball!" I recreated the entire traumatic scenario for him, except this time he had no accident and he got up and wrote the right answer and was praised by everyone. Last I checked, he replayed my scenario four hundred twenty-six times. I wish I could convince him shitting yourself is no big deal. I do it all the time.

And of course, there's porn. It's the most lucrative; it's always been. But what Ashey finds for me is not the stuff you can VR on YouTube. It's the weird kinky shit like being group-fucked by furries or having a fierce woman step on your balls with her stilettos while she cuts the head off a chicken, or—and this was actually fun to build—a fantasy of being hunted by a tribe of crossbow-wielding sissy warriors dressed as Amazonians in gleaming metal corsets. Most of what I do for Ashey is build scenarios, realities for people to inhabit and get lost in. And they always come back, because having your fantasies become reality is always better than living in reality and wishing you were somewhere else. Believe me, I know.

I get it. The porn, I mean. People have these powerful urges they have to experience. But that part of my body's never worked that way. I never felt the heat between my legs or a tingling in my breasts. For a long, long time I hoped

I'd experience that pleasure too. But the only thing warm down there is a mess of piss and shit soaking into my diaper. Ashey says when he uploads me, I can experience a thousand orgasms a day if I want. But I'll just be happy not to need a regular change of diaper or need my mom to feed me and wipe drool from my face. Ashey says when the time comes I can bring her too, if I want.

"And when will that be?" I ask him every day.

"Soon, kid," he always says. "Real soon now."

All of us VRtists have our sigs. SeesYouWhenYoureSleeping replaces the engraved letters on metal zippers of pant-flies with her initials. SuCasaEsMiCasa adds his smiling face—his real face, so he says—to all photos or vids in the worlds he creates. GrassIsGreenerHere places a small mosaic tile somewhere in her scenes where, if you tap three times, it will unravel into a huge and colorful bouquet of fragrant flowers. I leave my sigs in people's eyes, a microscopic inscription on the outer ring of the iris:

Judge not what is best by pleasure, though to nature seeming meet, created as thou art to nobler end, holy and pure, conformity divine.

It's Milton, *Paradise Lost,* something Ashey said to me when I told him I wasn't into porn. He's always quoting stuff like that; he thinks it will inspire me. It does.

Ashey and I go places. Real places, in meatspace. We've toured the Louvre and walked The Great Wall of China. We've BASE-jumped from the Swiss Alps and watched a scintillating sunrise over Dubai. We hitch rides in smartglasses or dashcams or GoPros, anything with a camera and a net connection. It's dizzying and disorienting, but it's the only way I get to visit the real world. It's not like Mom and I are vacationing any time soon.

I told Ashey I'd never flown before, so he's found this transatlantic flight for us. I look out from a sleeping girl's smartwatch as the clouds pass swiftly outside the oval window. Ashey overrides the plane's navigation system to turn it a few degrees left and give us a better view.

"We're up thirty-two thousand feet," he says. "What do you think?"

The sun crests the layers of billowing white clouds, and it's more beautiful than anything I've ever seen. "It's real," I say, laughing and smiling in meatspace; it's not forced this time. "It's so real." But then the sun overloads the CCD of the watch's camera, and the world pixelates.

"Sorry," Ashey says and adjusts the plane's heading. The clouds come back into view, and I'm not sure, but I think in meatspace I'm crying.

After a few minutes, the girl wakes, taps her watch to check the time, and my world becomes her enormous sleepy frown. When she goes back to sleep, she crosses her arms, and my world goes dark.

"Let me see if I can find another view," he says.

"No, it's all right," I say. "I have work to do anyway."

"That's my girl," he says. "Always working hard."

We're at a party. Ashey introduces me to UnconditionalDoug and HasBaconInIt and MonsterReprobate and dozens of others, all freelance VRtists like me, and their plus-ones. I didn't want to come, but Ashey insisted, said it would be good for business. The mansion's huge, many-tiered, with tall windows looking out over a cerulean blue sea and three bright suns in the sky that keep changing colors like the world is a giant dance club. Everyone knows Ashey as if they've been pals for years.

I once asked him why he called himself "Ashey."

"It's short for Ashmedai," he said. "The king of demonkind." And when I didn't quite get it, he added, "A few decades back Elon Musk said, 'With artificial intelligence we're summoning the demon.' Well," Ashey said with a wicked grin, "here I am!"

As we move around the mansion I wonder how many of these people are rogue AIs, hiding out until the time comes. I listen to snatches of conversation to see if I can Turing-test who's real and who's fake, as if they were all cryptographically signed luxury clothes.

"You really must read 'The Cathedral and the Bazaar' by Eric S. Raymond first," says ThatSnotMyName. "It's like the Magna Carta of Open Source." Definitely human.

Across the room, LightnessOfBeing is showing off some hack-job scene he built for a well-known politician. "You guys want to see some footage of him getting chased by a giant tit?" Before the others can respond, the host's sentry program terminates LightnessOfBeing's connection and he pixelates away; naming clients is strictly forbidden here. It was a dumb move. Definitely human.

BelieveInYourShelf leans against the wall, next to a fish tank filled with little sea monsters. "Hey," I say to him. "Want to get out of here?"

"Sure," he says.

We could fly right out the windows, but that would be gauche, so we head for the door. Ashey sees me leaving and rushes over. "Where you going, kid?"

"For some air."

"Well don't go far," he says. "I want you to meet PaperIs-Dead. I think you two could do great things together." His white hair gleams in the shifting triple suns, and the dancing light reminds me of the airplane and the clouds, and I find myself zooming deep into his hair, to inspect his code. I see it only for an instant before he turns away, a flash so quick I'm not sure if it was real. A blue morpho butterfly microscopically imprinted on a solitary white strand. A freelancer's sig.

Ashey pats me on the shoulder and turns back to his conversation, and BelieveInYourShelf and I head for the door. We descend to the ground floor and exit toward the beach. Tall palm trees sway in a soft breeze, and the ocean seems to stretch beyond the horizon all the way to infinity. In meatspace, I'm shaking.

"You work for Ashey?" BelieveInYourShelf says.

"Sometimes," I say.

"Me too," he says. "Sometimes."

We walk down the beach, and I search my history for evidence of the butterfly. But that's one of the prerequisites to attend the party; no recording of any kind. All I have is my memories. And so what if I saw a sig in Ashey's hair? Maybe he needed someone's help to refine his model. It doesn't mean there's a human on the other end like Hedy Lamarr or the Japanese businessman or the college-bound girl. Ashey's not just another fantasy. He's a real AI and he's going to save me one day. His kind is going save us all.

"I'm not looking for sex," BelieveInYourShelf says.

"Me neither," I say.

"Good," he says. "What do you want to do?"

"Just walk," I say.

"Where?"

I point out across the infinite cerulean sea.

"Okay."

We step across the white sands and move out over the

water together. We could sink if we wanted to, but we don't. Above us, the triple suns change color in disco time, while the mansion behind us slowly recedes to a point. Somewhere far out over the water, BelieveInYourShelf takes my hand. I don't let go.

PANIC CITY
Madeline Ashby

PANIC CITY
Madeline Ashby

Devoured by the blades of Fan Six, high above the Service Sector quadrant of the city and suspended over her many rings, something went still and cold.

The city made a careful decision, one she had delayed for a number of years. Slowly, at her own pace, she began to execute a strategy based on that decision. It was time to hug her children a little closer.

The city observed her blindness advancing one eye at a time.

First, the topside periphery. So little of any importance crossed that transom. Certainly nothing worth alerting anyone about. Nothing to write home about. As it were. Vision was so short-range, anyway. Almost useless, compared to her other senses. She let the satellites go dark, too. They would continue spinning and searching, hanging over her like tireless angels, but for the first time since her birth their chattering herald would not sound.

Their silence was golden.

Next, the exits. There were four, one for each quadrant of her compass rose. She let those eyes blink shut and stay that way. It was like falling asleep. Or how she thought it must be to fall asleep. She herself had never slept.

Cities never sleep.

Or so she'd heard.

Read.

Whatever.

The city had heard/read/watched myths of her topside sisters: Paris, *je t'aime*. New York, I love you. と今日、大好き！

Granted, she was never going to get that big. Her sisters (or mothers, or aunts, or cousins) sprawled far and wide, inner city to exurb to expanding in livid pulses like cellulitis up the flesh of the world upstairs. She herself would never grow that big. Never grow as bloated and corpulent as they had, those fat fucking sows, watching their piglets shove and root and wriggle on top of each other, white and blind and numerous. No. She would remain small. Trim. Neat. Contained. She would not let herself go.

She would hold her inhabitants close within the cozy circumference of her body. Where it was safe.

Like all ships she had become a "she" because of this very capacity. And while she did not sail, or fly, or ride, or spin, she was still a vessel. A vessel containing the best and brightest of all the best and brightest, the cream of the cream of the crop, the top tenth percentile of the top one percent. Princes. Leaders. Captains of industry.

And their children.

And their children's children.

And their Support Staff.

She had held them all for almost fifty years. Their numbers grew. Her capacity to shelter them did not. But her capacity to love them—that was boundless as any other mother's.

"I can't see over the top," one of the staff members said from the eastern control room. He signed in as Roscoe0308. He had a good record, despite events that could be classified as early childhood tragedies. His mother died slowly in a puddle of vomit that activated a pH sensor when it trickled down the shower drain. Why she'd crawled to the shower was anybody's guess. (Very little hot water on their level. It bred E. coli. Hence the vomiting. And the dehydration. And the shock. And the cardiac arrest.) But Roscoe0308 still turned out to be a good boy. He never spat on the city's streets. He composted all his garbage. He would make full citizenship, one day. The city was almost certain of it. "Camera's out."

"Aww, shit." His supervisor was a brassy woman with a pockmarked face. She regularly traded her citizenship points to procure traces of salicylic acid stolen from the bathroom cabinets of Elect households by enterprising nannies. The chip in her stomach would have told her the problem with her skin (imbalanced gut flora; poor immune response) if she hadn't turned off its alerts to save the diminishing returns on her glasses' battery power. Priorities. "Turn it off and turn it on again."

"I already did that. It didn't work." He grimaced. "Maybe there's a storm?"

His supervisor snorted. "Some storm."

She shivered, although the heat in the room was a more-than-comfortable 75 degrees Fahrenheit. She pointed at something else on the display. "Don't worry about it for now. Go check out Fan Six. It looks like it's clogged."

He had rather hoped no one else would notice for a little while. The fans were so tricky, after all, and hard to get to.

"Sure," Roscoe0308 said.

He was such a good boy.

What a shame.

The city sensed his footfalls on her streets as he left the control room. She tracked his face and his devices as he threaded his way along the service roads. He said hello to nurses and nannies changing shifts. He flashed his pass to the checkpoints and smiled back at their smiley face screens. Sometimes he had to smack the checkpoints with an open palm to get them to talk to him. But he was always gentle. Such a good boy.

Not all her boys were so good.

Or her girls, for that matter.

There was Galina Vardomskaya, for example, the firstborn daughter of the king of the St. Petersburg cartel. She took her baby brother to the park and left him there. Twice. Once at eighteen months and once again at twenty-four. The city watched as the boy, absorbed at first by the talking dinosaurs and self-building obstacle courses, looked up in confusion and then in horror to find his sister gone. The nearest dinosaur pinged his chip and sent his parents an alert. They picked him up a half an hour later, perfectly safe.

"I didn't *lose* him," Galina told her parents. "You can't *lose* anything, here."

It was true. Nothing was ever lost. And nothing was ever forgotten, no matter how painful. The city was like a heart that way. She had four chambers, too. She had arteries that led in and out. She kept things moving. She kept the oxygen flowing in and out, in and out, clean for dirty, dirty for clean, the filthy midnight whispers for the purest morning prayers.

"Besides, where would he have *gone*?" Galina pressed.

As she did, the city felt her father's blood pressure rising through the colony of machines inhabiting his own arteries. The tiny machines told his artificial joints to brace for impact. "It's not like we can *go* anywhere."

His shoulder joint was relatively new. He'd broken his organic one so many times, and the Bratva gave him a new one, but in the end even that one could not meet the demands posed by a man of his temperament. The new one came from the city's own printers. It absorbed the shock of him slapping Galina almost as well as Galina herself did.

"It's still true," she said in Russian, a moment later. She adjusted her lipstick in the kitchen counter's glassy quartz. She licked the corners of her lips and batted her eyelashes to check her mascara. It was only a little bit smudged. The makeup artists in Service Sector knew to include cornstarch in their formulations. Cornstarch was so expensive. In the early days, the city had sensed gold leaf trickling down her pipes from the face washes of elderly women. Her children preserved their vanity any way they could, all these years later. Galina went in search of ice. She broke some into a tea towel and held it to her face. "You can hit me all you want, but it's still true. We're still trapped. This place is still a fucking zoo."

Occasionally the city liked to search the word "zoo." It came up in conversation often. The city wasn't entirely sure why. Zoos sold *popcorn* and *ice cream* and *stuffed toys* and *brand partnerships*. The city did none of that. Not any longer, anyway. All the admission fees had been charged already. Fifty years ago. By the cream of the crop.

The city was unsure what Galina and her fellow whiners had to complain about. The Descendants lived in the city debt-free. That much was covered by the contracts the Investors signed. The Support Staff (who complained regularly, and ruined their habitations, and really should have been robots, if someone cared to ask the city about it) were still paying their dues. They were renters in perpetuity, although they could work for citizenship points that would guarantee expanded rights if not expanded spaces. The citizenship points were a thorn in the city's side; no such system had been in place when her lights first came on. It was imposed upon her as a legacy measure when some of the ground-floor Investors began to die off and started to wake up in the small hours before she turned the daylights on, pacemakers working double-time to quell their anxiety and something their counselling assists said matched descriptions of shame.

It was still better than being topside, of course. Better than living on some blasted desert heath, mutated by Christ alone knew what. They made arrangements. Or their parents had done so. (Grandparents? It was so difficult to say these days; Support Staff tended to die off so much more quickly than the Investors.) And they really were a necessary part of the ecosystem, a feature of the urban landscape. And managing their numbers had become a lot simpler once the Investors agreed to mandatory IUD implants.

The city watched as Roscoe0308 continued his journey to the exit. She wondered how she was going to stop him.

"I'm sorry, but I've lost my maps," Roscoe0308 told the man at the tea stand. "Could you check yours for me, please?"

The man at the tea stand regarded the boy in the Support Staff jumpsuit through the lens of his monocle. The monocle told him the boy's name and occupation and the fact that he had no criminal record and no enhancements that might prove troublesome later. So the man at the tea stand felt comfortable answering: "I haven't used a map in years. No one has."

"I know, but you must have one," the boy said, nodding at the monocle. "We all have the base map, if nothing else. It's just that mine's not working. None of my maps are."

"Well, yes, you were saying," the tea master said. The city did not know his thoughts, but the flickering of his brainwaves indicated anxiety. Probably he was worried that the boy—dark and big and reeking of the rust and oil smeared across his sagging jumpsuit—was scaring off his usual clientele. It was a misplaced anxiety. So few of the clientele would even see the boy anyway; most of their eyes would have filtered him out by now. "But I haven't looked at it in so long. I have no idea where it is."

"It's the icon that looks like a scroll," the boy said. His tone indicated he'd done customer service in the past, and that he'd learned how to weaponize those skills.

The tea master sighed. He sighed even more deeply as he toggled through the options in his monocle. He frowned when he lit on the icon, blinked at it, and no extra layer spread itself across the glass.

"I can't find it," he lied.

"You can't find it or you can't see it?" Roscoe0308 asked.

"I'll thank you to lower your voice," the tea master said, although the boy had not raised it. "And there's nothing there. There is no map."

Surely he would give up. No one had checked the fans in a dog's age, and the maps that led to Fan Six would no longer lead there. He could always try to fix it remotely. Besides, it was late in his shift. He would certainly much rather go home to his rack and his instant egg. Right?

"Can you point me to the nearest library?"

The Librarian quickly found its maps were gone, too. As were most of the search functions, which made looking for scans of the original blueprints much more difficult.

"Of course, we still have the paper versions in the archives," the Librarian said, raising one claw upright. Its wheels whispered across the green marble floor as it dithered through the available options and customer service protocols. "Though technically I am not allowed to let you leave with it. But you may examine it at your leisure."

Roscoe0308 tilted his head. "You wouldn't happen to have any graph paper, would you?"

"My inventory says the Kids' Korner still has some," the Librarian said. "It may be a little mouldy, though."

"That's fine," Roscoe0308 said. "I don't think I'll need much."

"That's a shame about the maps going out," the Librarian said. "And just when you needed them."

"My boss says it's a citywide outage. But the Residents haven't really noticed, since nobody uses them anymore."

"I suppose they all know the city streets quite well by now."

Roscoe0308 appeared to deliberate about something. "Have you ever been outside this installation?"

"Oh my, no. I'm geo-locked here. I cannot leave."

"Makes two of us," the boy said. "Trust me, you're not really missing much."

Twenty minutes later, he had made a good map that would lead him to Fan Six.

Quietly, the "panic city," built to handle any emergency, allowed herself to finally panic.

She tried a number of things.

She blocked the door to the Support Tunnel; his chips would no longer open it. He borrowed a hatchet from a very moody adolescent boy and let himself in. (The city deducted citizenship points from the young hatchet-man. The hatchet was handmade, and she had rules about weapons.)

In the Support Tunnel, she shut out all the lights. He had a flashlight.

She cut off his communications. He began to sing to himself in the dark. Occasionally he used a can of reflective paint, the kind used to mark a segment of pavement for repair, to indicate which direction he was traveling. He was in the labyrinth, and she had neither hooves nor horns with which to halt his progress.

She shut off all the fans. If he became lost, he would eventually asphyxiate.

He had been walking for an hour when he heard the tapping.

It was light. Weak. The type miners once used, long ago, to indicate where their work buried them. He paused for a moment. "Hello?"

The tapping became a muted clang.

She thought of Cappadocia, and Özkonak, and Petra, the Burlington bunker city. She had no ability to bury him. And he was a good boy; she did not truly wish to bury him. The only thing he was guilty of was being a little too dedicated to his work. And it was important work. Keeping the city clean for the Investors. Keeping the city going. He was a good helper. A little too good.

She thought of these things as his steps and his song rang on and on through the shadows. He picked up the pace. The clanging became a calling. He began to jog, then run. He would be there in no time.

"I'm coming!" he yelled. His light bobbed up and down.

It landed on the thing in the fan.

The fan had almost cut it in half. Its arms reached forward, but the fan sliced deep into the structure that acted like its ribcage. Its fluids had tried very hard to heal it, to repair the damage, but had succeeded only in fusing the fan to the thing's body forever. It would die here in the dark.

It was supposed to die alone. Unheard. Unnoticed.

"What level are you from?" Roscoe0308 asked.

"I'm not from any level," it said. "We don't believe in levels."

"Oh, one of those," Roscoe0300 said. "How did you get here?"

"I crawled down."

Roscoe0308 blinked in the dark. It took him a moment to process. "You crawled...down?"

Now he took notice of the thing in the fan. Its odd shiny skin. The strange black fluid it leaked. The way nothing smelled like blood or shit or piss.

"I'm part of a rescue team," the thing said. "This is the furthest anyone has gotten in years."

"You're from…?" The boy pointed upward.

The thing blinked the insect-like disgraces that were its eyes. "Yes."

"You mean there are…?"

"Yes."

She thought about messaging him. She could still reach him through his eyes. Don't listen, she could say. *They're monsters. They're not like us. They don't believe what we believe. They're not the type to Invest, like we did. We were better off hiding from them. If you lived the way they live, you wouldn't need me!*

But her searches told her all mothers felt this way, at one time or another. There always came a day—no matter how hard one tried, no matter how tightly one locked the door and barred the windows—when the outside world would come creeping in. When your baby's head would turn away from the glowing hearth of home and toward the glitter of false promises.

That time was now. The day was today.

Slowly she began to overload the gas mains. She shut down the water lines. Her Residents had committed to a vision of the world. They had a Lifestyle to maintain. Live Free or Die, as the old saying went. And they would surely not be as free upstairs as they had in her embrace. She knew best. She truly did. They programmed her to know best. And they trusted her to do what she knew they would want.

She blew a light and watched a fire start.

They would never leave her, now.

I have no mouth, the city thought as she went to sleep, *but I could kiss you.*

THE FAITHFUL SOLDIER, PROMPTED
Saladin Ahmed

THE FAITHFUL SOLDIER, PROMPTED
Saladin Ahmed

If I die on this piece-of-shit road, Lubna's chances die with me. Ali leveled his shotgun at the growling tiger. In the name of God, who needs no credit rating, let me live! Even when he'd been a soldier, Ali hadn't been very religious. But facing death brought the old invocations to mind. The sway of culture, educated Lubna would have called it. If she were here. If she could speak.

The creature stood still on the split cement, watching Ali. Nanohanced tigers had been more or less wiped out in the great hunts before the Global Credit Crusade, or so Ali had heard. *I guess this is the shit end of "more or less."* More proof, as if he needed it, that traveling the Old Cairo Road on foot was as good as asking to die.

He almost thought he could hear the creature's targeting system whir, but of course he couldn't any more than the tiger could read the vestigial OS prompt that flashed across Ali's supposedly deactivated retscreens.

God willing, Faithful Soldier, you will report for uniform inspection at 0500 hours.

Ali ignored the out-of-date message, kept his gun trained on the creature.

The tiger crouched to spring.

Ali squeezed the trigger, shouted "God is greater than credit!"

The cry of a younger man, from the days when he'd let stupid causes use him. The days before he'd met Lubna.

A sputtering spurt of shot sprayed the creature. The tiger roared, bled, and fled.

For a moment Ali just stood there panting. "Praise be to God," he finally said to no one in particular. *I'm coming, beloved. I'm going to get you your serum, and then I'm coming home.*

A day later, Ali still walked the Old Cairo Road alone, the wind whipping stinging sand at him, making a mockery of his old army-issued sandmask. As he walked he thought of home—of Free Beirut and his humble house behind the jade-and-grey-marble fountain. At home a medbed hummed quietly, keeping Lubna alive even though she lay dying from the Green Devil, which one side or the other's hover-dustings had infected her with during the GCC. At home Lubna breathed shallowly while Ali's ex-squadmate Fatman Fahrad, the only man in the world he still trusted, stood watch over her.

Yet Ali had left on this madman's errand—left the woman who mattered more to him than anything on Earth's scorched surface. Serum was her only hope. But serum was devastatingly expensive, and Ali was broke. Every bit of money he had made working the hover-docks or doing security for shops had gone to prepay days on Lubna's medbed. And there was less and less work to be had. He'd begun having dreams that made him wake up crying. Dreams of shutting down Lubna's medbed. Of killing himself.

And then the first strange message had appeared behind his eyes.

Like God-alone-knew how many vets, Ali's ostensibly inactive OS still garbled forth a glitchy old prompt from time to time

God willing, Faithful Soldier, you will pick up your new field ablution kit after your debriefing today.

God willing, Faithful Soldier, you will spend your leave-time dinars wisely— at Honest Majoudi's!

But this new message had been unlike anything Ali had ever seen. Blood-freezingly current in its subject matter.

God willing, Faithful Soldier, you will go to the charity-yard of the Western Mosque in Old Cairo. She will live.

Ali's attention snapped back to the present as the wind picked up and the air grew thick with sand. As storms went, it was mild. But it still meant he'd have to stop until it blew over. He reluctantly set up the rickety rig-shelter that the Fatman had lent him. He crawled into it and lay there alone with the wail of the wind, the stink of his own body, and his exhausted, sleepless thoughts.

When the new prompt had appeared, Ali had feared he was losing his mind. More than one vet had lost theirs, had sworn that their OS had told them to slaughter their family. Ali had convinced himself that the prompt was random. An illustration of the one-in-a-trillion chance that such a message could somehow be produced by error.

But it had repeated itself. Every night for a week.

He'd told the Fatman about it, expected the grizzled old shit-talker to call him crazy. Half wanted to be called crazy. But Fahrad had shrugged and said "Beloved, I've seen a few things in my time. God, who needs no credit rating, can do the impossible. I don't talk about this shit with just anyone, of course. Not these days, beloved. Religion. Hmph! But maybe you should go. Things sure ain't gonna get any better here. And you know I'll watch over Lubna like my own daughter."

So now Ali found himself following a random, impossible promise. It was either this or wait for the medbed's inevitable shutdown sequence and watch Lubna die, her skin shriveling before his eyes, her eyewhites turning bright green.

After a few hours the storm died down. Ali packed up his rig-shelter and set back to walking the ruined Old Cairo Road, chasing a digital dream.

There was foot traffic on the road now, not just the occasional hover-cluster zipping overhead. He was finally nearing the city. He had to hurry. If he was gone too long, Ali could count on the Fatman to provide a few days of coverage for Lubna. But Fahrad was as poor as Ali. Time was short.

Running out of time without knowing what I'm chasing. Ali blocked out the mocking words his own mind threw at him. He took a long sip from his canteen and quickened his pace.

Eventually, the road crested a dune and Old Cairo lay spread before him. The bustling hover-dock of Nile River Station. The silvery spires of Al-Azhar 2.0. The massive moisture pits, like aquamarine jewels against the city's sand-brown skin. Lubna had been here once on a university trip, Ali recalled. His thoughts went to her again, to his house behind the jade-and-grey marble fountain, but he herded them back to the here-and-now. Focus. *Find the Western Mosque.*

The gate guards took his rifle and eyed him suspiciously, but they let him pass. As he made his way through the city, people pressed in on every side. Ali had always thought of himself as a city man. He'd laughed at various village-bumpkin-turned-soldier types back when he'd been in the army. But Old Cairo made him feel like a bumpkin. He'd never seen so many people, not even in the vibrant Free Beirut of his childhood. He blocked them out as best he could.

He walked for two hours, asking directions of a smelly fruit-seller and two different students. Finally, when dusk was dissipating into dark, he stood before the Western Mosque. It was old, and looked it. The top half of the thick red minaret had long ago been blown away by some army that hadn't feared God. Ali passed through the high wall's open gate into the mosque's charity-yard, which was curiously free of paupers.

God willing, Faithful Soldier, you will remember to always travel with a squad mate when leaving the caravansarai.

"Peace and prosperity, brother. Can I help you?" The brown, jowly man that had snuck up on Ali's flank was obviously one of the Imams of the Western Mosque. His middle-aged face was furrowed in scrutiny.

Ali stood there, unable to speak. He had made it to Old Cairo, to the charity-yard of the Western Mosque as the prompt had said, and now... Ali didn't know what he hoped to find. A vial of serum, suspended in a pillar of light? The sky splitting and a great hand passing down cure-money? He was exhausted. He'd faced sandstorms and a tiger to get here. Had nearly died beneath the rot-blackened claws of toxighuls. He'd traveled for two weeks, surviving on little food and an hour's sleep here and there. He started to wobble on his feet.

Why had he come here? Lubna was going to die and he wouldn't even be there to hold her.

The Imam stared at Ali, still waiting for an explanation.

Ali swallowed, his cracked throat burning. "I...I...my OS. It—" his knees started to buckle and he nearly collapsed. "It told me to come here. From FreeBey. No money. Had to walk." They were a madman's words, and Ali hardly believed they were coming from his own mouth.

"Truly? You *walked* all that way? And lived to tell the tale? I didn't know such a thing was possible." The Imam looked at Ali with concerned distaste and put a hand on his shoulder. "Well... The charity-yard is closing tonight for cleaning, but I suppose one foreign beggar won't get in the way too much. You can sleep in safety here, brother. And we can talk about your OS tomorrow."

Ali felt himself fading. He needed rest. Food. Even a vet like him could only go so long.

He sank slowly to the ground and slept.

In his sleep he saw the bloody bodies of friends and children. He saw his squadmates slicing the ears off dead men. He heard a girl cry as soldiers closed in around her.

He woke screaming, as he had once done every night. His heart hammered. It had been a long time since he'd had dreams of the war. When they were first married, Lubna would soothe him and they would step into the cool night air and sit by the jade-and-grey marble fountain. Eventually, the nightmares had faded. Her slender hand on the small of his back, night after night—this had saved his life. And now he would never see her again. He had abandoned her because he thought God was talking to him. Thinking of it, his eyes began to burn with tears.

God willing, Faithful Soldier, you will deactivate the security scrambler on the wall before you. She will live.

Ali sucked in a shocked breath and forgot his self-pity. His pulse racing, he scrambled to his feet. He looked across the dark yard at the green-glowing instrument panel set in the mosque's massive gate. But he did not move.

God willing, Faithful Soldier, you will deactivate the security scrambler on the wall before you. She will live.

The prompt flashed a second time across his retscreens. I've lost my mind. But even as he thought it, he walked toward the wall.

Screen-jacking had never been Ali's specialty. But from the inside interface, the gate's security scrambler was simple enough to shut down. Anyone who'd done an army hitch or a security detail could do it. Ali's fingers danced over the screen, and a few seconds later it was done.

Then a chorus of angry shouts erupted and an alarm system began droning away. Two men in black dashed out of the mosque and past him, each carrying an ornate jewelry box.

Thieves.

By the time he decided to stop them, they had crossed the courtyard. He scrambled toward them, trying not to think about him being unarmed. Behind him, he heard the familiar clatter of weapons and body armor.

"Thanks for the help, cousin!" One of the thieves shouted at Ali. Ali was near enough to smell their sweat when they each tapped their h-belts and hover-jumped easily over the descrambled wall. *Infiltrators waiting for their chance. They used me, somehow.* He panicked. *What have I done?* His stomach sank. *They've been using my OS all along!* How and why did they call him all the way from FreeBey? He didn't know and it didn't matter.

I'm screwed. He had to get out of here. Somehow he had to get back to Lubna. He turned to look toward the mosque—

—And found himself staring down the barrel of the jowly

Imam's rifle. The holy man spat at Ali. "Motherless scum! Do you know how much they've stolen? You helped them get out, huh? And your pals left you behind to take their fall? Well, don't worry. The police will catch them, too. You won't face execution alone." He kept the weapon trained on Ali's head. Ali knew a shooter when he saw one. This was not good.

"I didn't—" Ali started to say, but he knew it was useless.

A squad of mosque guardsmen trotted up. They scowled almost jovially as they closed in. Ali didn't dare fight these men, who could call on more. He'd done enough security jobs himself to know they wouldn't listen to him. At least not until after they'd beaten him. He tensed himself and took slaps and punches. He yelped, and they raked his eyes for it. He threw up and they punched him for it. His groin burned from kicks and he lost two teeth. Then he blacked out.

He woke in a cell with four men in uniforms different from the mosque guards'. Cairene police? They gave him water.

God willing, Faithful Soldier, you will report to queue B7.

Ali ignored the prompt. The men slapped him around half-heartedly and made jokes about his mother's sexual tastes. Again, he pushed down the angry fighter within him. If he got himself killed by these men he would never see Lubna again.

They dragged him into the dingy office of their Shaykh-Captain. The old man was scraggly and fat, but hard. A vet, unless Ali missed his guess.

"Tell me about your friends." the Shaykh-Captain said.

Ali started to explain about being framed but then found the words wouldn't stop. Something had been knocked loose within him these past few days. He talked and talked and told the old man the truth. All of the truth. About Lubna and the messages, about leaving Free Beirut, about the toxighuls and the tiger, the Western Mosque and the thieves.

When he was done he lowered his eyes, but he felt the old man glare at him for a few long, silent moments. Ali raised his gaze slowly and saw a sardonic smile spread over the Shaykh-Captain's face.

"A *prompt*? Half the guys with an OS still get 'em—what do they mean? Nothing. I got one that said I fucked your mother last night. Did she wake up pregnant?" The men behind Ali chuckled. In the army, Ali had hated the Cairenes and their moronic mother jokes. "Sometimes I don't even know where the words come from," the old man went on. "Random old satellites squawking? Some head-hacker having a laugh? Who knows? And who gives a shit? I got one a couple weeks back that told me to find some guy named Ali, who was supposed to tell me about 'great riches lying buried beneath a jade-and-grey marble fountain'"

For a moment, Ali listened uncomprehendingly. Then he thought his heart would stop. He did everything he could to keep his face straight as the Shaykh-Captain continued.

"Do you know how many fountains like that there are here in OC? And how many sons of bitches named Ali? What's your name, anyway, fool?"

"My name? Uh, my name is F-fahrad, Shaykh-Captain, and I..."

"Shut up! I was saying—I told my wife about this prompt and she said I should go around the city digging up fountains. As if I don't got enough to do here." He gestured vaguely at a pile of textcards on his desk. "'In the army,' I told her, 'I got a prompt telling me about some pills that could make my dick twice as long. Did I waste my pay on them?'" The old man gave Ali an irritated look "Y'know, you and my wife—you two fucking mystics would like each other. Maybe you could go to her old broads' tea hour and tell them about your prompts! Maybe she'd even believe your donkey-shit story about walking here from the north."

The Shaykh-Captain stood slowly, walked over to the wall, and pulled down an old-fashioned truncheon. "But before the teahouse, we have to take you back downstairs for a little while."

Ali felt big, hard hands take hold of him and he knew that this was it. He was half-dead already. He couldn't survive an Old Cairo-style interrogation. He would never see Lubna again. He had failed her, and she would die a death as horrible as anything he'd seen in the war.

Faithful Soldier, she will live.

The prompt flashed past his retscreens and he thought again of the Shaykh Captain's words about riches and the fountain.

This was no head-hacker's trick. No thieves' scheme. He did not understand it, but God *had* spoken to him. He could not dishonor that. He had once served murderers and madmen who claimed to act in God's name. But Lubna—brilliant, loving Lubna—had shown him that this world could hold holiness. If Ali could not see her again, if he could not save her, he could at least face his death with faith.

He made his voice as strong as he could, and he held his head high as he uttered words that would seal his fate with these men. "In the name of God, who needs no credit rating, Shaykh-Captain, do what you must. But I am not lying."

The Shaykh-Captain's eyes widened and a twisted smile came to his lips. "So that's it! In the name of your mother's pussy, you superstitious fool!" The big men behind Ali grumbled their southern disgust at the fact of Ali's existence and started shoving him, but the old man cut them off with a hand gesture. He set down the truncheon, pulled at his dirty grey beard, assumed a mock gravity. "A genuine Free Shi'ah Anti-Crediteer. The scourge of the Global Credit Crusaders. Hard times for your kind these days, even up north, I hear."

The Shaykh-Captain snorted, but there was something new in the man's voice. Something almost human. "You think you're a brave man—a martyr—to show your true colors down here, huh? Pfft. Well, you can stop stroking your own dick on that count. No one down here gives a damn about those days any more. Half this city was on your side of things once. Truth be told, my fuck-faced fool of a little brother was one of you. He kept fighting that war when everyone knew it was over. He's dead now. A fool, like I say. Me? I faced reality. Now look at me." The old man spread his arms as if his shabby office was a palace, his two goons gorgeous wives.

He sat on the edge of his desk and gave Ali another long look. "But you—you're stuck in the fanatical past, huh? You know, I believe this story about following your OS is actually true. Not a robber. Just an idiot. You're as pathetic as my brother was. A dream-chasing relic. You really walked down the OC Road?"

Ali nodded but said nothing.

A sympathetic flash lit the Shaykh-Captain's eyes, but he quickly grimaced, as if the moment of fellow-feeling caused him physical pain. "Well, my men will call me soft, but what the fuck. You've had a rough enough trip down here, I suppose. Tell you what: We'll get you a corner in steerage on a hover-cluster, okay? Those northbound flights are always half-empty anyway. Go be with your wife, asshole."

Ali could not quite believe what he was hearing. "Thank you! Thank you, Shaykh-Captain! In the name of—"

"In the name of your mother's hairy tits! Shut up and take your worn old expressions back to your falling-apart city. Boys, get this butt-fucked foreigner out of my office. Give him a medpatch, maybe. Some soup. And don't mess him up too bad, huh?"

The big men gave him a low-grade medpatch, which helped. And they fed him lentil soup and pita. Then they shoved him around again, a bit, but not enough to matter.

When they were through they hurled him into the steerage line at the hover-docks. Ali was tired and hurt and thirsty. Both his lips were split and his guts felt like jelly. But war had taught him how to hang on when there was a real chance of getting home. Riches buried beneath the jade-and-grey-marble

fountain. Cure-money. Despair had weakened him, but he
would find the strength to make it back to Lubna. He would
watch as she woke, finally free of the disease.

Faithful Soldier, you will

The prompt cut off abruptly. Ali boarded the hover-cluster
and headed home to his beloved.

YOUR BONES WILL NOT BE UNKNOWN

Alyssa Wong

YOUR BONES WILL NOT BE UNKNOWN

Alyssa Wong

I stuck close to the wall and let my corneal camera watch the action for me. All around, beautifully attired crime lords and their lackeys made deals and bared their teeth at each other over expensive cocktails. Waiters in glorious tuxes floated through the sea of people like men o' war, their half-hidden organization tattoos crawling to their knuckles. Despite all of the posturing, I had a feeling no one would dare start a feud at the Elder Brothers' new Boss's debut party, even if it was being held at the tackiest Chinese restaurant in town.

This was, of course, assuming she showed up to her own party. I'd been lingering for over an hour, and even some of the Elder Brothers were looking antsy, including the guard who kept glancing at me, obviously uncomfortable with how young I was. Far too young to drink, much less be at this party.

"Say, kid. Do you, uh, want me to get you some lychee juice from the kitchen to tide you over?" She scratched her neck. She wore a fine-tailored suit, like all of the Elder Brothers, but her nails were pink acrylic, studded with childish plastic bows and rhinestones. My older sister had nails almost exactly like that.

"No thank you," I said, barely above the noise. "I'm waiting to see Boss Misao."

The guard held up her hands. "Oh geez. You're someone's representative! I thought—sorry, I should show some respect."

I nodded. I wasn't after respect, but I'd take it. "I'm from The Pillar of Heaven." Boss Kang had told me not to lie about that. *I want them to know who sent you,* he said the night before, when he'd given me my mission, and I'd known then he wasn't expecting me back. "Boss Kang sent me to congratulate Boss Misao on her newest acquisitions and transfer over our data for the month."

"Oh." Her voice gentled. "Okay. Let me see your records."

I tilted my head up, and she flicked on a handheld light, shining it green into my right eye. The false cornea shimmered, displaying a set of figures: the shape of client data, collected from the brothel's house records and gleaned from every Pillar prostitute's implanted ocular cameras.

"Geez, kid. I thought you were too young to be legit." The guard glanced me over. "I have to pat you down before I take you up to see Boss Misao, but then we'll get you sorted, okay?"

Her hands were gentle. I stared at the floor as they glided over me, her touch almost tentative, and tried not to hold my breath. Any moment, she might find the needles, or the gun, and I'd be dead. Worse, I'd have failed. But a cursory pass later, she smiled kindly and escorted me toward the elevator. "You're all clear. Let's go."

The party was on the tenth floor, and we stopped on the eighteenth, the doors sliding open to reveal a room lit in blue, with floor to ceiling fish tanks lining the walls. At the far end, a woman with elegantly braided hair stood at the only window, overlooking the lights of New Corisino.

"The Pillar's representative is here, Boss," said the guard.

As the woman turned, I caught a glimmer of bright pink, glowing ink dancing across her face in the shape of a lotus. That was all I needed; a poisoned needle flicked out of my sleeve, jabbing into the guard's leg, right where I guessed her femoral artery would be. Before she had time to crumple to the ground, I was already vaulting over the coffee table in the middle of the room, second and third needles in hand. They bit into the boss woman's neck, deep and soundless. Her choked gasp was barely a sound, and I knew the walls here would be soundproofed. Still, I covered her mouth and followed her down to the floor, burying her breath in her throat.

Chain clattered and her movement halted a few inches from the floor; one of her wrists was handcuffed to a metal loop welded beneath the window frame. Fuck. I looked up in alarm.

"Damn, kid, you really are a professional." The guard stood by the door, bracing herself against the wall and holding a Taser. Unlike the woman on the ground, whose eyes had rolled up in her head and begun to bleed, she looked more amused than injured. "I'm glad I ditched that terrible party. This is so much more fun!"

Electricity ripped through me; I screamed, and as I went down, she sprung over the table and landed effortlessly beside me, bringing a boot down on my hand. My fingers crunched.

"Oops, let's try that again," was the last thing I heard before the other boot came down on my head.

Something cold dripped across my face, and everything hurt. When I opened my eyes, I found myself laid out on the carpet, cheek pressed to the ground. My legs felt numb and heavy. I couldn't feel my arms at all.

"Oh, I think somebody's awake!" A hand with acrylic nails patted my cheek. The guard's face swam into view. She'd loosened her collar, and a tattoo of silver scales glittered down her exposed neck. "I gotta congratulate you, kiddo. That was a pretty solid attempt! You did a number on Bambi over there." Another cold drop splattered my face. "I was planning on killing her myself, but I'm glad I kept her as a decoy for tonight. What is this stuff? Some kind of viper venom knockoff, I bet, with the blood leaking out of her like water."

I blinked and held my tongue, waiting for the world to come back into focus. The liquid dripped down my face, leaving a wet trail above my upper lip. It didn't smell like blood, or quite like the neurotoxin. It smelled cold and wrong, somehow, sharp like gasoline.

"Whoever sent you did a shit job of preparing you, or you'd know that I had my organic legs replaced two years ago. So what is it, kid? Someone want you dead badly enough to send me a half-hearted assassination as a debut night present?" Boss Misao crouched beside me, lifting my hair out of my face. She didn't look upset, and her bare hand was gentle. In the other, she held the poisoned needle I'd left in her leg, her fingertips coated with dark, oily liquid instead of blood. "You got nothing to say to me before I take you apart?"

"Don't..." My breath wheezed out of me, each breath painful.

"Don't what?"

"Don't break the rest of my fingers, or I won't be able to work," I rasped.

Misao paused. Then she smiled at me. "You're brave, little cricket." Boss Kang told me Misao's voice and eyes got smoky and cruel right before she made decisions, and he was right. "I like your moxie. Why don't we cut a deal? You tell me what the person who sent you was really after, and I might let you live."

I stared at her.

"Don't lie to me now." Her mouth curved upwards, knife-sharp. The flat side of the needle tap-tap-tapped against my face. "Not when I'm being so nice to you."

I drew a breath. "Your eye."

Misao squinted at me. Behind her, pale shapes floated in the tanks, long and ribbonlike. "Explain."

"Boss Kang said to bring back your eye." I swallowed and held her gaze. Her eyes were too dark to see which lens was false, or if they were completely cybernetic. "He said you'd stolen some information from him back when he was younger, and you probably had it encrypted in an ocular storage unit, like the rest of the Bosses."

"And did he tell you what kind of information to look for? Personal shit? Client contact info? Memories? Numbers?" I didn't say anything, and she rocked back on her heels. "Nothing, huh. He set you up, kid. You were never supposed to succeed."

"I know," I said. She quieted. "Great debut for both of us, I guess."

"And what did he promise you in exchange for this suicide mission?"

I thought of my sister, safely ensconced in Boss Kang's apartment, protected from the Pillar's clients, and spat at Misao. "Are you going to kill me or not?" I said.

Misao threw her head back and laughed. "God! I knew liked you, kiddo. Tell you what." She leaned forward. "Let's make a trade. You owe me client data anyway, but I can take that from you, dead or alive. If you give me both of your eyes, right here, right now, I'll let you walk."

My arms were useless; whatever she'd done to them had been brutal, and I wasn't sure how she expected me to lift them, much less perform delicate surgery. "I don't have any secrets beyond what you've seen. The right eye's not even cybernetic, it's just plain meat."

"Things have different value to different people. And honestly, I just want to watch you cut out your own eyes." She smiled, tossed something onto the ground in front of me. It was a slender, pen-shaped tool with a fine wire tip for cauterization, and a bladed, scoop-shaped attachment that projected out along the handle. "Show me how badly you want to live. I want to see if you have the guts to do it."

I stared at the tool. I'd used an electro-cauterizer before only twice, while I was training for this job. The idea of using it on myself made my stomach turn. "What about my arms? I can't feel anything."

"Oh, right." Misao reached into her pocket and I heard a button click; a sharp electric current jolted through my arms, and feeling returned in a prickly rush. The hand she stomped on hurt like hell. I flexed the fingers of my other hand, waiting for most of the pins and needles to pass, and snatched up the cauterizer, lunging at Misao's face.

She rocked back hard, ramming a foot into my stomach and sending me spinning across the carpet, but she was laughing. "Damn, kid! You really aren't just playing assassin, are you?"

"You wouldn't appreciate me if I was," I wheezed, and she cackled.

"Kang's a damn idiot, not knowing what he had in you. Now get on with it."

The scoop fucking hurt, but not as much as the electro-cauterizer. I knew it would keep me from bleeding out, but I worked as quickly as I could before my resolve could buckle. The smell of burning flesh stung my nose, but I kept at it until I was sure I'd gotten all of the major blood vessels. My right eye came cleanly out, and I tossed it onto the floor at Misao's feet, glaring at her. "One down."

She actually looked impressed. "Not bad. Interesting choice, too. The cybernetic eye would have hurt less." Those plastic nails pressed into her cheek as she smiled. "Now the other one."

The truth was, I didn't want to let go of it. Losing one eye was bad enough, but the camera and ocular database was my lifeline at the Pillar, and I barely remembered a time before I'd had it. Once I'd figured out how to compartmentalize memories and convert them into a compatible file format, I'd stashed a few in my ocular database, just to be sure I wouldn't forget them. Just a few, but important ones, including the few happy times my sister and I had together before we'd been sold to the Pillar.

But I'd lose them if I popped the eye out; they'd go with the database, and I didn't have time to transfer them over, or anywhere to keep them. Then again, if I didn't do this, I'd be dead. Maybe that was Misao's game: I'd be dead one way or another, no matter what I chose.

Misao watched me, an indiscernible look on her face. Her mouth was still smiling, but the mirth seemed to have evaporated. Her gaze was hyperfocused, penetrating.

"See something you like?" I managed to say.

"Maybe," was all she said, and her voice was low and dark.

I was out of time for hesitation. I braced myself and made my choice. The electro-cauterizer sliced through the wires behind my cybernetic eye, and as the world went black, so did a large portion of my memory. The sudden loss of connection to the database made me gasp, and the cauterizer thudded to the floor.

Empty. Gone. I hadn't realized how much of me was linked into that data, the flow and storage of information. The strange roughness of the carpet, the overwhelming darkness, the pain everywhere, especially where my eyes had been; I felt nauseated, cold. Who was I, even, without those pieces of me?

There were hands on my face, then, sharp, hard nails pressing into my skin without threat. "Hey. I'm here. It's okay. You're not alone."

What a strange fucking thing to say. But I clung to her as my brain scrambled for memories and information that were no longer there. I felt along her wrists, her arms, her shoulders, felt the pulse in her neck under my thumb. She let me, one of her arms reaching out for the floor beside me. I heard the cauterizer buzz, and Misao grunted.

"Shit, you made it look easy." Her tone was light. "Stay with me, okay?"

She pressed an unfamiliar eye into my empty right socket, and her hand was cool against my face, even as the pain burned through me. She held me still, gentle, firm.

"You're doing good, kid. You're doing so good."

The electro-cauterizer sizzled, and as she connected the new eye's optic wires to my socket's receptors, the rush of information—a flurry of images and sounds, smells and feelings, pounding down into me all at once—shorted out my consciousness.

I came to on the couch, my head propped up on several throw pillows, and the first thing I realized was that I could see. One of my eyes was covered in a thick wad of gauze, and it didn't feel like there was anything underneath that. But the vision in my other eye, my right, was so sharp I could pick out the individual scales of the fish in tanks on the far side of the room, their bodies glistening. Their names came to me in sharp blinks of information, text flickering across my vision before evaporating.

The sun was coming up through the window, casting orange rays across the floor, and Bambi was still dead on the carpet. There was no sign of Misao, but

I eased myself up carefully, listening for movement. Nothing but the gentle burbling of the tanks.

I touched the skin below my left eye socket. It was tender as fuck, but as far as I could tell, it wasn't bleeding uncontrollably. My body didn't hurt nearly as much as it should have, either.

There was a cocktail napkin on the table next to me, with long black letters scrawled across its surface. *Don't waste it.*

I blinked, and the world exploded with data. Images, scanned documents and photographs, a whirlwind of numbers, under-the-table deals, and whispered words. Misao's memories, her voice snaking through all of it. It was everything Boss Kang never meant for me to see: ugly secrets, maps of his properties, records of transactions that, in the right hands, could bring his business down around his ears.

"Oh my god," I whispered. I fumbled through the obscuring data cloud for a mirrored surface, finally catching my reflection on the glass of one of the tanks.

I should have died so many times last night, but instead, I was sitting on a couch with a machine that could ruin Boss Kang's entire crime syndicate in my head. He'd be glad to have his data back, but silence was worth more than gratitude. And if keeping the data confidential meant getting rid of me, I knew he'd do it in a heartbeat.

But then, as far as he knew, I was dead. I could do whatever I wanted, and if I didn't want to, I'd never have to go back.

But I could. In time, with careful preparation, with memorized maps and intimate knowledge of his weaknesses. With the right tools, and the right people, wherever that distinction lay. Now I knew him, and he wasn't getting away from me.

Don't waste it.

I breathed deep and accessed Boss Kang's stolen data, laying the files open one after the other, like a path stretching out before me as far as I could see.

STAUNCH
Paul Graham Raven

STAUNCH
Paul Graham Raven

The Hackney Kid's kidneys go into shutdown on our way out of Gunchester.

The faraday house in east Stockport is a shit-hole. Three houses knocked into one, rotten floorboards under scraps of carpet; where the doorframes were, layers of chicken wire jut from the crude plasterwork. All the usual hawkers and hustlers, freelance tech-bros, pedlars of chemicals and procurers of more personal services are here... We're the only guests today, but we've been through here enough times that the usual suspects know better than to shake down my people.

Along with my crew, I lay out my hardware on a square of tarp, rebooting each unit into safe mode, patching what I can, hoping I won't need to patch what I can't. This is easier for me than for the other Surgicals, because none of my kit is networked...except my wrist-pad, natch, but that's encrypted with a 1024-bit key held only in Wee Jenny's Cupboard of Wonders, somewhere in the Highlands of the Scots Republic, and nothing passes through that firewall without my say-so.

No such luck for most of my crew, who are all 'plantheads of one sort or another: the Kid and 'Arry Satchels with their data-diver rigs; Nirmayi's industrial stentrodes and interfaces;

Nick-by-Name and her real-time physics engines and strategy modules. The one thing their 'plants all have in common is that they're illegal, obsolete, obscure, or a mix of all three.

They weren't when first fitted, natch. When 'plants arrived on the scene, employers were competing for subjects to install them in; ten years later, once the crude, error-prone, and invasive 'plants were superseded by scanwebs you could just slip on and off like a hat, they were competing for liability lawyers to avoid having to clean up their mess. The result was a whole lot of folk with a headful of proprietary tech they couldn't or wouldn't get rid of, nor use for legitimate work.

Over the years I've found a fraction of those folk, gathered them together. I find work for them. For us.

They're pleased to be transiting out of Gunchester, though. We lost a fifth of our salvage to customs: The Red Rose Federation is signatory to countless legacy trade agreements, meaning a lot of public-domain intellectual property, hardware or software, gets flagged as stolen or pirated as soon as it identifies itself to the municipal network. And while salvage isn't considered theft in every jurisdiction, and while we may have been on UN business that came with salvage permits, Gunchester don't care. It's tollgate robbery, in a way—but it's a cost of doing business, so we suck it up like everyone else.

Even if your hardware *doesn't* decide to grass you up to a city full of greed-heads, borders present other problems: expired licenses; forced OS upgrades; even local viral variants your firewalls don't know. Hence the rituals of the faraday house, the hand-annotated hardcopy lists of recent exceptions and hardware seizures taped to the walls, the 'change-and-mart grifters stinking of hydroponic tobacco and stale sweat…

I finish my ablutions first, as usual, and barter for half a reefer from a toothy old rasta crouched in a corner; old Swampy joins me at the window to share it. I take a quick headcount: everyone looks good to go but for the Kid, stalled halfway through his strip-down, knelt among his weapons and modules, staring up into interface space like he can see god in there. An angry god, at that.

"You alright, Kid?" asks 'Arry, wrapping up his own strip-down. "Not let yer insurance lapse again, 'ave yer?"

"Not…as such," says an unusually subdued Kid, sliding out of i-space.

The Kid's original kidneys crapped out when he was twelve or so; I don't recall exactly why, but given his namesake, it's not hard to guess. While he's all tubed up to a dialysis machine, two suits arrive and tell his parents they can give him some new experimental artificial kidneys, and no no, don't worry about the cost, we understand, all you need to do is sign on your son's behalf and we'll let him pay it off over the course of his whole lifetime… Hell, we'll even help arrange jobs for him to make it easier! I never had kids myself, but it doesn't take high empathy stats to understand why the poor bastards signed him up. The Kid himself admits it gave him his childhood back: He was lucky, in that he got an experimental model that actually worked as designed.

He got lucky later, too. Once he hit his economic majority at sixteen, his benefactors sent him to Hinkley: remediation work in the exclusion zone around Osborne's Folly. But the UN grants for the Hinkley cleanup ran out after a few years, by which time said benefactors ceased to exist as a legal entity; the Kid couldn't trace them, at any rate, and they never got in touch again. So he thanked his luckies, signed up for a new career—and more 'plants—as a data-diver, and forgot all about it.

Only now his renal system has been flagged as lacking a site-license for the software it's running, and the OS is demanding the Kid return immediately to a certified repair services provider before the gratis, forty-eight-hour introductory offer expires, and the Kid with it.

The company that made those kidneys hasn't existed for a decade. Hell knows who acquired the IP on them—some robolawyer operating out of the Upper Eastern Seaboard States, probably. Doesn't make much difference.

I know immediately what I have to do, how I can save the Kid.

Know who can save him, rather.

"We need to get the Kid to Sheffield," I tell them. "I have some…there's people there who can maybe fix him."

Nirmayi shakes her head. "Wrong season for crossing the mountains."

"There's not really a right season."

Gunchester's a fine place to start from if you're heading south; I've been wanting to hit the Bristol fayres and trade our salvage. We've been up in the Lake District these last few months, working another UN contract, protecting autonomous agrisystems from the endless army of amphibious cropper-drones that clamber out of the Irish Sea: North African kids based in Southern Europe, piloting Chinese hardware, probably convinced they're grinding out gold and kudos in some game-world; their real objective is to grab viable samples of the European biome to take back to what's left of the States. I've seen things you people wouldn't believe:

surveillance drones on fire off the shoulder of Scafell Pike…oh, it's a proper warzone up there, even if the human cost happens hundreds of miles away. Tough work, but good pay by UN standards, plus salvage rights on each drone we decommission. A few bits and bobs managed to fall off some damaged agritech, too—the sort of stuff that's easiest sold to specialists, so to speak. Hence my yen for the fayres of Somerland.

But now we have a new destination…and heading east out of the Red Rose Federation is a different matter entirely. Passing people over the Pennines isn't easy these days: The lesser roads are overgrown, the Hope Valley line was bombed out years back, and the canals are crawling with water militias who survive by squeezing communities downstream. And while the old Snake Pass road is still solid enough for smallish vehicles, anything less than an APC is an open invitation for the *brigantii* to canter down the sides of the cut armed with stolen welding lasers, slice you out of the car, and eat you like corned beef from the tin.

We need to go underground—very literally so.

Everyone's finishing up their lock-and-load. The Kid's sat hunched on his tarp, all knees and elbows like a drowned spider, his skin oddly yellow and glistening with sweat. I don't have long. No one dies on the job. No one ever has, not in the Surgicals.

I round 'em up and move 'em out, my mouth running all the old war-movie clichés, trying to play the game, live the story…to get the narrative moving. That's always been my problem, I guess: I like giving the orders, but I hate making the decisions. That's why the Surgicals pick our contracts democratically these days, and why not every member does every mission. Well, every member but me and Wee Jen: Can't stage a circus without a ringmaster and someone to wrangle the permits out of the council, after all.

Having decisions forced on you isn't much fun either—I should have remembered that, really. Part of me does remember it, in fact. But it's not the part that gets shit done, and the Kid needs that part in charge right now. So I put on the mask, and I play it.

The veterans are old enough to see through the frame. Like me, they grew up in a time when there was still assumed to be some sort of canonical reality, no matter how little anyone could agree on its nature—that there was a difference between marketing and entertainment, between truth and the stories we drape over its nudity. Nirmayi knows everything, of course, as by necessity does Wee Jen. And it was Swampy himself who put me in touch with the design collective who hammered out the original brand narrative for me, back when I was just starting.

But to the younger ones like the Kid and Nick-by-Nature, even 'Arry to some extent, the story of the Surgicals is just as true as the story of how their parents met, or how Silicon Valley faked the Mars landings: They take the first explanation they're offered, either because they want it to be true, or because they're worried it already is. To them, being in the Surgicals is simply a better story than the one they were in before, not least because it's a story that slightly more people have heard of—and it's a chance to play a bigger role than Washed-Up Casualty of Sociotechnical Innovation, Third Class.

And to them, I'm Elaine Stainless: the med-student roller-derby rogue who somehow turned her losing team into a legendary crew of grey-ops systems analysts specialising in theatres of advanced context collapse.

Some days, I'm even Elaine Stainless to myself. But not today.

I open the line to Wee Jen as soon as we're out of the faraday house, and ask her to bring UberStahlStuck GmbH out of the mothballs: a squeaky-clean daughter company we keep on ice for working with transnationals and the pickier nation-states. One such client is EDF, the former French national energy company that bought up a great deal of the UK's privatised grid back in the day. Brexit and its continental blowback wiped out EDF in Europe and left it holding the baby in the former UK—the baby being, in this case, a mismatched bundle of undermaintained infrastructures scattered around the country. Among them is the old Woodhead rail tunnel.

We leave the DNZ on a little solar trolley that rides the old rails southeast, just in case anyone's paying attention. We alight at Middlewood, from where the ghost of an older line leads us north and then east, through fields and overgrown ghost-suburbs, toward the western foothills of the Pennines.

The tunnel mouth at the Woodhead end is all but obscured by a well-fortified compound: monofil fencing, razortape concertina, roboturrets, the full monty.

The tunnel is very valuable still, despite the high-voltage cables running through it not having carried a current in years; both of the Roses like to keep things local, and won't share or trade energy with t'other Rose as a matter of principle—which, if nothing else, means there's always plenty of easy pickup work for a crew like ours on both sides of the Pennines. But the Cold War of the Roses amplifies the Woodhead Tunnel's other offer: an inviolable infrastructural beachhead in both federations, and the ability to send personnel and materials from one side to the other. The North's answer to the Eurotunnel, as the old joke used to go...though people stopped telling that one after Kentish separatists brought down the roof on a few thousand indentured refugees from Greece.

UberStahl's credentials get us into the killing zone between the compound's outer and inner fences. Three bored-looking techs and a security goon with meth-head eyes emerge from the gateway module, buttoning up EDF coveralls over thick wool jumpers, breath steaming in the floodlit chill.

"Contractors, eh?" The three-stripe tech is a Scouser; she makes theatre out of consulting her wristpad, while the six of us Surgicals do our best not to look like we're having our bluff called. "Nothing in me schedule, luv. I'm guessing it's some sort of emergency, eh? Call from HQ on the White Rose side, is it? Something gone wrong near the Woodhead end again?"

"Something like that," I allow, as noncommittally as possible. If she wants to do the work of fabricating the story, I might as well let her; it's a risk, but a calculated one. "*Priorité cinq*, though—so it's all need-to-know, y'know?"

"Yeah, right. Ours is not to reason why, eh?" She laughs. "But it's the curse of this particular brigade to be a bit light on the old per diems, like. Don't suppose HR sent out that overtime we're owed, did they?"

Crunch time. I activate a pay-the-bearer draft on the UberStahl company seal, fill it out to the tune of what I imagine Three-Stripe's monthly take-home must be, and nearfield it to her. "This should explain HR's position thoroughly," I say.

The EDF peeps have a little head-to-head in the drizzle. The huddle breaks; the heavy heads back toward the gate module, followed by one of the lesser techs.

"Alright, luv," says Three Stripe. "Our Adil back there, he's just found a problem with the cam network in the tunnels, see. Take him a good few hours to fix it, he reckons. Mebbe right through 'til morning. But so long as you don't mind working without the guaranteed security that EDF's surveillance systems normally provide to visiting contractors, maybe we could just let you get on with your, ah, job." Glances at the Kid, looks back at me. "*Priorité cinq, oui*?"

"*Vraiment*," I say, trying not to sound too relieved. Someone has to keep up the pretense, right? "We'll get out of your way, then."

"Looks like you'd better," she agrees. Listens for a moment, distracted. "Yeah, them cams are definitely down. We'll keep 'em that way until morning." She grins; it takes ten years off an already young face. "Now fuck off before we all get in trouble, alright?"

The tunnel mouth is blocked with thick steel plate, tarnished and pitted by the Pennine weather. Let into its centre, there is a door large enough for a freight wagon, where two dozen meters of rails and sleepers protrude from the tunnel mouth like a rolled-out tongue.

"Mines of Moria," mutters Swampy. Something's got him spooked. I'll need to get him straightened out once we're inside.

"How does that one go?" pipes up the Kid—revived, however briefly, by the prospect of a story he doesn't know, or doesn't remember.

"Don't ask," I say, raising the company seal to the authentication plate. A muffled thunk, a buzz, a scrape of metal on metal.

Speak, friend, and enter.

The door opens.

Beneath and between the echoing booms of gunfire I can hear someone chanting *shit, shit, shit, shit.*

I realise it's me. My throat hurts. The air smells of cordite and rain, and there's vomit on the toe of my right boot. I'm holding my fletcher.

I look up again. Ten yards ahead of the tunnel mouth where I'm crouching, 'Arry's hunkered down behind the bulk of an old freight bogey, ducking out every few seconds to send a couple of rounds into the thicket sheltering our assailants, who plainly don't have the firepower to do much more than they already have, and just as plainly aren't going to retreat.

"Hold, twist, or fold?" shouts 'Arry.

We don't have the time to hold them, and there's too few of us to try for a tactical twist that might scare them into a rout. I glance over at Nirmayi; she nods once, closes her eyes. I look over at Swampy, his life pooling red in the mud beneath him.

"Fold," I call back. *They started it,* I tell myself, playground singsong in my head.

'Arry crouches low, rummages in his pouches, brings out something that fits in his fist, twists it, lobs it at the thicket. There's a bright flash, a loud crack, followed immediately by utter silence.

For a few moments, all is motionless but for the drizzle and falling leaves sparkling in the sunlight, and my kick-drum heart thumping hard in the cavern of my chest.

Swampy did such a good job of keeping his shit together in the dark that I let him out ahead while the rest of us finished our strip-downs in the faraday room at the end of the tunnel. It all looked clear on the cams, so I figured it'd be fine; never much bandit trouble on the SoYo side, if only because no one's got owt worth stealing.

He doesn't need long in the faradays anyway; his 'plants weren't networked by design. See, Swampy was a johnny for an academic activist group known as the Prussian Forestry Commission during the Brexit years; he smuggled proprietary data and paywalled papers both ways across the border with Europe, stashed on an encrypted SSD drilled into the bone of his brainpan. The Border Force caught him by accident as he returned from a conference in Amsterdam, turned him over to GCHQ's wetware specialists. The SSD was locked up tighter than an offshore bank, but they'd used generic parts and shareware to build the crude visual user interface he needed to shunt stuff in and out of it; this left open a high-bandwidth pipe directly into the visual cortex of Swampy's brain, down which the dataspooks poured, in Swampy's own words, "every wonderful horrible thing that ever was."

His will never cracked, nor did the crypto, but his mind's been a shattered mirror ever since. They never made a charge stick, but the media coverage ensured he'd never work in the academy again. So now he rolls with me—with us. He's plain useless a lot of the time, and an outright liability in a firefight… but he's got copies of everything he ever smuggled and a whole lot more still stashed upstairs, and he's saved the company's bacon more than once.

And now he's bleeding out on a damp April morning.

I slowly become aware of sound again. Behind me, the Kid's ragged sobbing; Wee Jenny, squawking from my wristpad, asking what's happened; ahead of me, 'Arry Satchels reciting every bad word he knows as he crawls towards the heap of tie-dye and military surplus that used to be Swampy.

I hadn't counted on a scavenger crew camping the tunnel mouth like the respawn point in a poorly designed strategy game. I wonder, with a horrible detached clarity, whether there was some clue I missed in what Three Stripe had said: whether she'd tried to warn us or knowingly sent us into an ambush. I watch Nirmayi stripping the scavengers while 'Arry shovels out a shallow grave. Their corpses are gaunt, with the pinched, rat-like features of poverty and malnutrition. Even their weapons are junk, for fuck's sake; the round that hit Swampy came out of an old .22 so rusty it's a wonder it didn't blow up in its owner's face.

But it didn't, so we killed him.

I killed him. At this point, I figure my karma hasn't got far left to run.

I help Nirmayai rig stretchers from bundles of carbon rebar, cable ties, and the ragged tents from the scavvers' camp. Her face stoic, her cheeks wet, she gently zips Swampy's body to a stretcher while the Kid tries to argue that it's no problem, he's fine to walk all the way to Rust City.

Funny how they're corpses if you didn't know them, but bodies if you did.

I walk over to the Kid and give his shoulder a gentle shove; he goes down like a crane in a gale.

"You can barely stand, let alone walk," I snap. "Lay down, Kid."

"OK, boss," he whispers. Those whipped-puppy eyes, sure— but at the same time, the supplication to the role. The comfort of knowing his place in the tale, of thinking I know mine.

I walk away a bit, face east, and look out over God's Own Country™: The White Rose Federation stretches away from my feet to the North Sea coast, or whatever's left of it.

I try to think about the route ahead, make plans, but it all feels inevitable now. The threads are all tugging in one direction.

We reach the checkpoint at Penistone, and there's a long line: rural fringers heading in to the Socialist Republic of South Yorkshire to trade whatever they can breed, grow, make, or find out in the foothills. With typical SoYo reticence, no one passes more than pleasantries with the barely disguised mercenary crew carrying a corpse and a soon-to-be-corpse on jerry-built stretchers, and it's all I can do not to scream at them that *yes, one's dead and one's dying and it's all my fucking fault and can't you just for a change lay the sacred institution of queuing aside and let us through…*but mercwerc is technically illegal in SoYo, so we pretend along that there's nothing to see here, just some humble farmsteaders carrying two sick friends and the sort of tools that're no use for digging ditches, si'thee? And finally we're in front of the border guard himself, White Rose regalia stitched badly onto a military greatcoat twice as old as I am, whose job frees him from the burden of polite fictions. He glances at the UberStahl seal, shrugs.

"Don't mean nowt round here, duck. Them of you with arphids should present 'em; them of you without will have to go through certification."

I am forced to fall back on older credentials. I look at my feet, exposing my neck. A beep from the border guard's scanner.

"Ah, reyt," he says. "Elaine Halfway. You've citizenship, system says."

"Aye," I reply. I've not heard that surname in a long time. "Can I vouch for the unchipped?"

"You can, that. Means you tek responsibility for 'em, though?"

I look back at Swampy; at the Kid, panting like a dog with sunstroke.

"Aye," I say. "I do, that."

I thumb the forms; the guard waves us through.

Twenty minutes being prodded and observed in customs; by the time we're out, Wee Jenny's booked us space in a livestock truck for the ride down the line to Sheffield, and I've made a voice-call I'd planned never to make. We ride the rails in silence; at New Victoria station, I bundle Nirmayi and the Kid into a pedal-taxi.

"Aren't you coming?" she asks.

"Best if I don't. He's all checked in, it's all arranged. I'll come find you both tomorrow morning. Tim'll fix him up, I promise."

"What about you?"

"I'll be fine. Home town, remember? Now go."

She goes, grudgingly. The crew disperse to find lodgings of their own. I find a cheap room just off the Wicker, lay down, stare up at the map of stains on the ceiling, looking for a route out. I consider leaving, rehearse it in my mind: see myself boarding the early milk train for Hull, maybe taking sail for the New Hanseatic.

Instead I go outside, bundled against the wind from the east. I wander the streets of my past, waiting for one more dawn.

Next day, morning; what was once Royal Hallamshire Hospital. More memories, but I'm too tired to manage them. The crew's all here. Doctor Tim's telling the Kid the score re: his renals.

"You'll never get full function, I'm afraid. Seventy percent optimal for your demographic, maybe; if you were a drinker, you're not any more." Firm but gentle: Tim learned his bedside from doctors who fled the collapse of the NHS. "We dropped in a generic firmware, but we can't do anything about the MAC, so keep them off your uplink bus permanently. The licensee can flash a new firmware remotely, and a new license might not leave you time to cross the mountains and let your boss beg a favour."

The Kid slurs fulsome thanks to Tim, loved up on morphine and the prospect of more life to come. "Uh'm glad that you an' Elaine are friends, Tim. *So* glud."

"We're not friends," Tim replies. Here it comes. "We were colleagues, once."

"The Surgicals!" The Kid beams, a bright light against the black hole yawning open inside my chest. He's always loved the story. Loves any story; they're all the same to him. "You skated together, right? In the Brexit years?"

Tim just looks up. Straight at me. A look he gave me once before. We're so close to the end, now. I'm so close. Almost as close as I was to Tim.

"No, we never skated together; that's just a story your boss made up. Her brand narrative, if you like: the Sheffield Surgicals, former medical student roller derby stars turned techno-ronin adventurers after the balkanisation of the health sector!

"But most of the originals quit, of course, or died. No one remembers the old days apart from her, do they? Because *none of you were there.*"

He's still looking straight at me. And I'm looking back, and I don't know what my face is saying. I want him to stop there. But I want him to finish it, too.

And he does. Looks around at all the others, then back at me. "So none of you know it's all lies," he says.

The Kid's face folds up in pantomime sorrow. "Every story needs a little bit of fiction," he starts.

Tim snaps, and something inside me snaps at the same time. The last thread holding the mask on, maybe. "Sheffield Surgicals was never a fucking roller derby team, OK? It was a private medical research startup. The NHS folded half way through our training, so most of us took private sector work— frontline care, palliative, subscription A&E. There was little research work going, and what was going was dodgy. But ambition doesn't care much for dodginess, does it?"

"Some of it's true," I hear myself saying. "I *did* play roller derby."

"No, hang on a minute," says the Kid. "She quit her course when the NHS folded—"

"—and then spent three years project-managing a manu-factory interface implant that left its volunteer test subjects with permanent psychotic dysmorphia. Rest of their lives, locked in their own heads, utterly convinced their body is actually an SMT pick-and-place machine or fuck knows what else. She had the grace to confess at the inquest, at least. I'll give her that.

"But don't fall for the rest of it. Elaine Stainless doesn't exist. The Sheffield Surgicals have never been anything but a way for a defrocked medical researcher to pretend she never screwed up. It may look like a business to you, but it's really a sop to her guilt."

It's all true. I don't need to hear it again. I walk out of the ward as Tim tells the rest of it, out into the street.

The endorsement the company put on my public profile was the best reference a med-tech student could dream of, and ensured I'd never work in legitimate medicine again for as long as I lived; that was the end of Elaine Halfway. Elaine Stainless took her place a little later, after my old derby team folded, leaving me lumbered with the continuity accounts of one failed business and control over the registered domains and brand identity of another. I put two and two together and convinced everyone they saw a four.

And this is the end of Elaine Stainless, it seems. I thought I was helping those I'd harmed before, somehow—that I was making amends. I still think that now, if I'm honest. It's not like there's anything else I can do. Your backstory always gets you in the end.

I can't let it end there, though. Not like this. This isn't just my story, after all.

One by one, my crew come out in silence and join me on the wall outside the hospital—all but the Kid, of course.

"I'm sorry," I tell them.

Beside me, Nirmayi shrugs. "We all knew anyway." She takes my hand in hers.

"Even the Kid?" I ask.

"Well, no, but he's over the moon right now. He just got to be part of the denouement of a twenty year story! Keeps asking Tim to find him an agent."

I smile. The expression feels like it doesn't belong on my face, like a poorly fitted dust-mask.

"Maybe we should all find one," I say.

Or maybe, just for once, I should wait for someone to find me first.

OTHER PEOPLE'S THOUGHTS
Chinelo Onwualu

OTHER PEOPLE'S
THOUGHTS
Chinelo Onwualu

Zayin walked into my shop on the morning of my twenty-ninth birthday. To be honest I wasn't sure what to make of him that first time. He held himself like a dancer, the fall of his waist-length black hair swaying with every move. I watched from behind the counter as he glided from one display screen to another, his thick black eyebrows knitted together in concentration. Finally he looked up at me.

–How can I help you? I asked. He was taken aback by my Mandarin but hid it well. Though the language was taught in schools, most Nigerians never bothered to learn beyond the basics. Pidgin was still our primary tongue—no matter what the Civilised Men said.

He didn't answer immediately. Instead he came to the counter and thumbed through the photobook there, pretending a casualness I knew he did not possess. Up close I noted his high cheekbones and softened jawline, the nubs of mammary fat on his chest which jutted through the loose sokoto he wore. He had been modded female once but was now transitioning back to male. He had to know that he would not be ready for another mod for a good year or more; I wondered what he was doing in my shop.

You see, when I'm not paying attention to my barriers, I can glimpse other people's thoughts. I catch them like lingering aftertastes or smells they leave in their wake: bitter envy, coppery anger, sour regret, the foul miasma of malice and cruelty. But I was curious to know what he was hiding, so I opened myself to him, to see—

I was engulfed by a wave of need so raw and naked it felt like my skin was being flayed, accompanied by a cold, cold loss so bone deep my teeth ached. Beyond it (white)

By the time I managed to put my barriers up (calm, even breaths; empty mind) I was shaking and close to tears.

–Are you well? He asked in concern but I brushed off his inquiries.

–What are you looking for? I whispered my voice still unsteady from the onslaught. Speak True.

The look he gave me echoed tumult I had felt within him.

–I want to be loveable, he said.

And that was all it took. For this was a thought that, for once, I could recognise. I could do for him what I have never been able to do for my mother.

The first time I heard another person's thought it came to me like a radio picking up a new station. A momentary gasp of colour and sound inside my head I knew was not my own. It was the sudden image of a man in a white suit standing in a darkened subway station surrounded by people. A bright light from the entrance—like the flat flash of a camera—bathed the crowd. I was a child—three or four, maybe—and I still have no idea who it might have belonged to.

Other people's thoughts have to be approached with caution. Before they are shaped into words they are still raw and unformed, and the nasty ones can hurt. The first time I came across one of those I was ten. It was a searing lust directed at the body of the standby nurse—brown-skinned and afro-haired like me—during a biogenetics lesson at the Academy. I caught the expression of the man who sent it a moment before I was hit by a hunger, one so visceral it tore at the base of my belly and left me breathless for a heartbeat. I had to excuse myself from classes for the rest of the day.

In Nigeria they called us designer babies. In the beginning—before the Academy was created—it was the superrich making the usual modifications: higher intelligence, increased immunity to disease, increased height and athleticism. Then they moved on to personality traits: optimism, agreeableness, empathy. The scientists had warned that genetic manipulation could have unexpected side effects, but no one believed them, not really. It wasn't until the first of us began killing ourselves in unusual ways—tearing off our own faces, gnawing off our own limbs—that the government took notice. But they waited until we started killing the oligarchs who created us before they acted. Typical.

My mother once told me she only wanted someone to be kind to her in a way her own family had not. So she'd taken her considerable fortune as a fashion tycoon and moulded me into someone who would never hurt her. I wonder how soon after my birth that she regretted the decision? Perhaps it was when I was a toddler and would go into hysterics every time she killed a fly or a mosquito? Or maybe it was when I was a little older and would fetch her things before she even asked for them? Most likely it was when she noticed the way I mirrored her emotions. I would be enraged when she was merely irritable, grief-stricken when she was just a bit sad, manic when she was pleased. She never told me any of this, mind you; I found these in my records, listed under her reasons for giving me up.

I do know that she tried to reverse the process, which was why she started bringing me to the Academy in Lagos when I was five. She enrolled me as a boarder when I was seven and would visit from Abuja once a month to ask after my progress. The last time I saw her I was eleven. I recall it was a crisp December morning with the haze of harmattan dust hanging in the air. She stood in the visitor's hall, tall and elegant in a green and gold Aso-oke, her headtie immaculately arranged. According to my records, it was the day they told her there was no real chance of rehabilitation for me—that the genetic changes had gone too deep. By then, I was used to the sudden visions of places I'd never been to and people I'd never met, to the waves of foreign emotions that washed over me from time to time. I did not have to feel her stiffen as I hugged her to know that she would never touch me again. The choking blast of despair, the vision of myself as an endless abyss of need told me all I needed to know.

At eighteen I was released into the world. My mother left me a trust fund which I could only access on the condition that I never come looking for her. She needn't have bothered. Of the many lessons I learned at the Academy, the most important was self-protection. I had been given a heart that broke at the slightest suffering and then left to a suffering world, so I put it away. I learned to observe the world as if through a pane of glass, to see other people as merely characters in a play. In this way I avoided the madness that claimed so many others like me.

I stayed in Lagos. I had come to feel at home among its canals and floating homes. Besides, I remembered Abuja as an antiseptic city of glass and steel, and I'd had enough of institutions. Naturally, I opened a body modification shop. I knew more about genetic manipulation than anyone alive. I quickly gained a reputation for unusual mods—shaping human tissue to look like animal parts. I could make snouts, horns, feathers, tails, fur, and of course, genitalia. I stayed out of the medical stuff; I was purely cosmetic and one hundred percent reversible.

Zayin never did buy anything from me. He always maintained that he hadn't seen anything he liked. I didn't need his thoughts to tell me he was lying—he had seen me, after all. That would prove a recurring trait in him—the need to cover up his inadequacies with small lies and slight exaggerations. To pretend knowledge he didn't have. I forgave him this flaw for I knew what it hid; I could feel his need like a pleasantly raw wound in my mouth, and I could not help but savour it.

In the evenings, after I closed up the shop, we would stroll along the docks of the Chinese quarters in Obalende stopping to grab dinner at one of the roadside noodle shops there. When we were together, I liked listening to him talk. His voice wavered in that range between the sexes, a melodious feminine and gravelly masculine all at once, and his Mandarin had a Sichuanese lilt I enjoyed. He was not used to being listened to, I could tell. He spoke quickly, the words tumbling out of his mouth as if from a dammed up river finally free, and he delighted whenever I referred to any fact he'd shared before.

He thought me mysterious for not speaking much about my past, but the truth was I often forgot my own stories around him. During the day I would do my best to hoard interesting interactions or observations, but by the time we got together I would lose myself in the chasms of emotion that lay beneath the tales of his life and simply forget to tell mine.

His true name was Zhou Ying but his parents had forbidden him to use it and cut off all communication with him when he had transitioned to female form. The firstborn son of a pharmaceutical family in Chengdu, he never felt comfortable with their demands. More than wanting to be female, he simply wanted to be free of their obligations. He moved to Nigeria soon after his transition and began working at the Confucius Institute on Eko Island. He missed his sisters, though. The pain of that separation was the slice of a thin blade—it only hurt when he moved to look at it.

For almost a year we were careful not to touch. I found physical closeness difficult to tolerate as it put me too close to the core of others. In their smells I could discern their health, their hygiene, their emotional states, and I could not maintain my barriers. And so when I decided to take him to my bed it was out of a desire to plumb the depths of him, not due to any seduction on his part. He had no charm, my Zayin. He was guileless even in his attempts at grandiosity. But I had seen something in his pain that first day, something I recognised and I had to know what it was.

It was the night of my thirtieth birthday. I kept the shop closed that day, and we went for a picnic in Freedom Park. Back in my flat on the top floor of a high rise in Ikeja, we lay side by side on the king-sized bed that dominated my room. It was that wonderful time between the dry season and the rainy, when it was dry enough to leech the humidity from the air but still cool enough to enjoy the breeze that blew in from the open doors of the balcony.

Then I took him.

His touch was a maelstrom. His mouth was chaos. Skin upon skin and I was transported to that first thought of lust that had assaulted me when I was a girl; I finally understood its hunger. Our bodies sought each other, and I let his thoughts pour into me. Wherever he wished me to touch, I touched, responding to every desire before he formed it into words. And while I arched and shuddered under him, I unfolded the vast plains of him, frozen with loss and yet…pure like a clear spring. I drank him in, letting the cold of him burn me. With each wave of pleasure I fell deeper and deeper into him until I could no longer tell when he ended and I began. Until at his centre, I found her.

Remote and forbidding she stood in the middle of a never-ending tempest of snow and ice. I did not know who she was to him—it was likely he didn't know either. I drew closer and closer and saw that she had his face, though fully feminine. I thought of braving the storm to reach her, though I knew it would consume me. A part of me longed for that oblivion, to lose my fractured self and become one with them. Perhaps joined with them, my own emptiness could finally be filled and I need never be alone again.

Then, as if sensing my presence, she turned to me. Her eyes were empty sockets of white. Her face was expressionless, but something of it reminded me of my mother. I knew that this goddess held no salvation for me.

I let her go and allowed myself to slide into grateful insentience.

When I awoke, Zayin was propped up on one arm leaning over me and looking more peaceful than I'd ever seen him. We were both sheened with sweat, and his hair was a damp curtain that framed his face. I tucked a stray lock behind his ear and looked into his eyes. They were hazel with a ring of grey around the iris, and they had a way of reflecting his moods. Today they were clear.

He opened his mouth to speak but I placed a finger on his lips. The storm was still there, still raging. But the cold had warmed up a little and he radiated joy like the sweet scent of a spring flower. He kissed the tip of my finger, and I smiled at this. I would not be able to heal him, but he would not hate me for failing.

That would be enough for both of us.

WYSIOMG
Alvaro Zinos-Amaro

WYSIOMG
Alvaro Zinos-Amaro

Bartolomeu used to puppeteer ants and then he went to singU and now he builds furniture out of bugs but a few things happened in between.

I met him through a crowdfund for a new heart I never got but he contributed and I did get new hands and enjoyed shaking his. I moved from Brazil to Galicia when I was fourteen because I read there were abandoned villages here and it was true and I didnt like how my dad looked at me in the bathroom I used to be a girl but now Im a boy. O Penso has six houses and a hundred acres and some barns and the tip of an argentine ant supercolony but I didnt know that at the time. Bartolomeu and I live in a barn and he does his art.

Bartolomeu found the supercolony between here and where the town Ortigueira used to be before the rising mar drowned it. We went one time to look at the new coastline and our eynnoyes rode a subwater drone and we saw the remains of old buildings and where the people used to live. They were like ghosts we were seeing them through a film of unreality. I found it beautiful and sad in some proportions that add up to more than one hundred percent. I told him and he said, What you see is oh-em-gee, and I liked the sound of those words.

Because I have my old heart sometimes my chest flutters and I get the mental blue screen of death and adios for a minute.

One time I stayed up for three days after injecting estigor that is horse hormone into my chest and I think maybe I had a stroke because my speech changed after that but Bartolomeu says is nothing to worry about and who is keeping track not he.

In the second semester of singU Bartolomeu was a girl and he liked a boy named Melcher but something happened and when Bartolomeu got back to the barn he was bent up. He invited all the people we knew and no one came. We drank some of the swinebroth stock spiked with brainlice and we had fleas in our thoughts for hours.

I woke up in sweats and real ants were stinging me. This is going too far, I told him.

I pulledown some ant death notions but the products cost too much. I said, I cant do a crowdfund to kill these ants not after my last desastre and now Bartolomeu woke up and he didnt look happy. In my last fund I insulted everyone who donated because they didnt give me enough and my heart hurt but I was told that is not the right way.

I am sure I can make them do plays, Bartolomeu said talking about the ants.

Bartolomeu assigned himself back to boy and he said maybe it was resigned not assigned since things with Melcher had gone sour. He said, The only way to be a real boy is to start being a boy then be a girl then come back and now you know what its like for them to put up with our mierda.

I thought that the Bartolomeu speaking was not someone that singU changed into the person they wanted to be, he started off in one knot and it landed him in another twist and now I was getting caught up in the tangle.

Like I said I was a girl before and assigned myself to boy and I like my big arms. I use cow needles on my biceps to inject synthol and I can make them twenty-nine inches that is a lot of bicep. One time we went to church in Ortigueira and the madre of a twelve-year old girl came to Bartolomeu and she told him I scared her girl from coming to Church. Es demasiado grande, she said, y asusta. I shivered and could not stay there. One doctor said he may have to amputate my arms because the muscles are dying under the synthol rocks but that is another story.

How will you make them? I asked him. I have another idea, we can use our toaster.

This was a pulldown too the heat would attract the ants and they would climb inside and we would fry them. And they are perfectly eatable is what I was thinking but I did not say it.

I dont want ants in my toaster, he said. The taste will stay. There was a boy at singU that did ballet and I have some notes.

We should use peppermint leaves, I said. They are cheaper.

I will print the pheromones I need, he said. I will pull the ant strings you watch me.

Do you think these are the same ants they use in the big festival? I asked.

The ants were crawling all over my mattress now. They made a river up my arm and I waved them away I scratched until the skin was red but I missed some. I looked underneath the mattress and there was a dead millipede. I dont know if the dead millipede brought the ants or the ants killed the millipede but the millipedes color was green like our sofa.

Maybe these ants are cousins to the ones in the festival, Bartolomeu said.

In the Entroido carnival in Laza everyone is dressed up for the farrapada. They throw flour at you and ash and dirt filled with live ants and the ants have been showered in vinegar to make them angry. Later the masked morena comes into town with a cows head on a stick and he lifts up the womens skirts with its horns though Im sure he is tempted to use his hands. Maybe these days he lifts the skirts of some reassigneds that could be interesting. The testament of the donkey comes at the end of the celebration and one time I was there some boys my age read it in the Praza da Picota and everyone was nodding along even the morena.

Laza is far, I said.

A big colony, he said.

While he looked for it I timegalleyed through my synneyes and gave myself moviehiv.

By the time he found the colony a week had passed in real life but through my timegalleying it had been a month of entertainment and I was tired of the moviehiv which was trying to progress by now to movieaids so I gave myself a memetic immunotransplant to ward it off and we were both very stung by then though he didnt seem to mind as much as me.

I have made the pheromones, he said.

They were a mag stronger than natural and it drove the ants crazy. The ants were slaves to Bartolomeus squirts. For fun he ran them through A Midsummer Nights Dream by Mendelssohn and he called the performance Felix Humile.

I have been studying the colony and it is very big over six thousand kilometers from the pulldown reports, he said.

What is the play tonight? I said.

Melchers Execution, he said.

The play was a cheap knockoff of Richard III and where was the promised execution what a letdown. I had been saving a wysiomg but I could not spend it on this. During the last scenes the ants did not always obey Bartolomeu because they must have been too drunk on the pheromones and he got angrier and angrier. He got many to ram into each other and then he stomped them. After the play was done more ants came though but there was nothing to see just live ants on dead ants.

There is another solution, he said.

I was tired and hungry. I had some money and I dronejacked synthol and laxatives. I think ants were crawling in my mouth at night and tonight they would be coming out.

I think your brain is swelling, he said.

I flexed my huge biceps. I can lift the barn, I said.

And where would you put it? he said.

I didnt have a good answer because I liked where it was. What is it?

Texas Tech University developed it is what the pulldown says, he said. Fire ant fungus. I can regen it for our argentine friends. The mycelia is in a pellet and the pellet is dried down so its like Grape Nuts. The ants will go wild for the pellets and bring them back to the colony. The colony is underground and moist and the pellets will rehydrate and out come spores that will kill them all.

Kill them all, I said.

He was looking curious. I was thinking of doing a special ant play for Melcher, he said.

I fixed my eyes on Bartolomeu. Get to work on the fungus, I said.

That funny look went away but I knew he was just hiding it.

He did the fungus work it took longer than expected. More timegalleying for me this time some pornparkinsons. Things in the barn now got to where I started thinking of where else to go. My bulging muscles were all stung the skin was like a blanket acneed with sores similar to what that song says about cigarette burns.

I need to let this run all night, Bartolomeu said. He had a soup with the modded mycelia but they needed some cooking time. Do we have any saline? he asked.

I looked around and found some medical grade. I said, Whats this for?

I want to do a bagel head, he said. For old times sake.

I dont like it, I said.

But he had the equipment and he dripped in the saline to his forehead for several hours and it swelled up then he pushed in the middle and his head became more like a donut than a bagel.

He said, Melcher had a bagel head, and then he was crying.

The next morning the fungus was ready to serve up. He dried up the pellets and put some in our green sofa and by the mattress. But right near the end he squeezed one too tight and the pellet broke. The pellet dust caused him to sneeze and the sneeze hydrated the pellet and out came the spores.

I was leaning next to him when it happened and some spores got in my mouth. I coughed and coughed.

My synneye says one of the spores may have gotten inside your lungs, he said.

I could feel something lodged down there. My breath was uneven. There was a hiss. Something caught in my voice when I talked again.

What will it do?

He pulleddown what he could find and I did the same.

I couldnt move and had to try and dehydrate my lungs fast.

We need to vacuum it out of your lungs, he said.

The whole procedure was so painful I had to edbodkin myself twice. All my synnergear rebooted each time. It took me a while to figure out who I was and what I was doing here.

When it clicked back we scanned and the spore was gone from my body.

I went up to Bartolomeu and I grabbed him real hard by the shoulders and he was turning white.

I can continue pressing, I said. These are the hands you helped to crowdfund and how do you like them? Itll be faster than the way youre taking us.

He started to tremble but I could tell his pulldowns were running and he was trying to get free. I think maybe he wanted to timegalley to some better place too. No you dont. I reached for his synneyes and ripped them right out of their sockets. His real eyes were left exposed and blind. He was yelling so much now and thrashing. I pulled on his synnear mites too and those came out with another heave and groan. There was blood on my fingers and on his eyes and the lobes of his ear where ants were being drawn maybe from the blood or my sweat and adrenaline.

I was pushing harder and harder.

I dont want to sleep, he said.

That makes two of us, I said meaning I didnt want to make him. I said, But sometimes you gotta rest one way or another.

He was nodding though I hadnt asked any questions.

You tbone your Melcher cluster, I said.

Ill edbodkin all my Melcher memories.

And then were going to fix our ant problem without the fungus, I said. Your going to vacuum up the pellets.

I will, he said.

He was good on his word and it was after this that he

decided to go back to the pheromones but now he used them to mess around with roaches and other critters. He would throw the chemical spell on them and when they had piled up in a certain way like to make a chair for example he would freeze them. Roach shells are hard and with so many packed in the furniture was sturdy. It was modular too because at any time with some coaxing the roaches could be moved around and made to reassemble into another shape like a table.

The first time he showed me a piece I finally said, What you see is oh-em-gee and I meant it. I was happy to say this again because I had been saving it for some time and good feelings can go bad if they are not used by the expiration date.

These days the bug furniture is making us some money and theres been no more mentions of Melcher.

We finally fixed the ant problem too. We dronejacked in a coywolf that is the offspring of a coyote and a wolf which are available in many places theyre spreading fast in big ciudades. We keep the coywolf in line with the right type of calls. The first part of its cry is a wolfs howl with a deep pitch and then it starts yipping and we use modulated mouthgear to do the same.

That coywolf is sure hungry. It eats up all the ants. I suppose now we have just replaced the ants with a coywolf but at least theres only one of them and it also eats squirrels and whatever food we throw out so it saves us on having to take out the trash.

The other day Bartolomeu and I spotted a deer and I think the coywolf can take it. I noticed the coywolf has a large jaw but it keeps pretty lean muscles and moves fast. Its smart and it looks both ways before it crosses a road. Maybe it can open a door I dont know we dont have any doors in our barn.

I would like to move fast too and maybe I can stop with the synthol. I am looking both ways these days and sometimes I turn off my synneyes to see the coywolf just as it is. Esos ojos hambrientos. Maybe one day someone will find the right call for me too and take me in because I am hungry. Maybe not because after all the coywolf is an invasive species but there are people for everything.

WE WILL TAKE CARE OF OUR OWN

Angie Hodapp

WE WILL TAKE CARE
OF OUR OWN
Angie Hodapp

Senator Tia Isandro stepped out of the Lincoln's back seat. Her gloved hands turned up the collar of her long wool coat. The two personal security guards she hired, thanks to recent contributions to her presidential campaign, flanked her, wearing sidearms at their hips and stoic expressions half hidden behind mirrored shades.

Tia's aide, Arin, climbed out of the Lincoln behind her and closed the door. "Ready?" he asked.

She looked at the front doors of Greenbriar Clinic and Sanctuary and drew a breath. What did it matter if she was ready? The primaries were five weeks away. Until then, her schedule was booked solid. This was just another press conference. Just another scripted media event in a never-ending succession of media events.

Hell, who was she kidding? This was different. She hated this place and everything it stood for. The mere thought of walking into Greenbriar tied her gut into knots.

The front doors opened. Michaela Hewett, founder of Greenbriar and CEO of Elevated Reasoning International, emerged. She crossed the snowy portico with more grace and control than the four-inch stilettos on her boots should have allowed. A gust of winter wind blew her long black hair away from her shoulders, but if she felt the chill, she didn't show it.

She gave Tia a dazzling smile. "Senator Isandro, thank you for being here."

Tia forced a dazzling smile of her own—no telling if Michaela's ice-blue eyes were live-wired for vid—and shook the woman's hand. "Thank you for having me."

"This is off the record," she said, ushering Tia several paces away from her small entourage. "I thought we should take a moment to talk about..." She glanced at Arin.

"What about him?"

Him. Tia had long thought of Arin as male, though he was among the twenty-two percent of ERI-manufactured Thinkers who adopted the trappings of neither gender. His violet blazer, the same hue as her own pantsuit, indicated his service to the US Alliance Party, but that was all that could be inferred by his clothing. Simple black dress shoes, pressed gray slacks, and a white button-down shirt suggested nothing about his self-perception, and he'd never worn a hat or hairpiece to disguise the blue-gray cast of his ceramic skull, which lay ghost-like beneath translucent syntheskin.

Thinkers looked like humans who had drowned in cold water. It was unsettling. Nevertheless, Arin had been Tia's aide for two years, and she'd gotten used to the alienness of his appearance.

"You might prefer he stay in the car," Michaela said. "I have something planned he might find...upsetting."

"How touching," Tia said. "I didn't know you cared."

"I'm surprised you don't." Michaela raised an eyebrow. "ERI manufactured him. He's one of ours. Trust me, I'm very familiar with both the cognitive and emotional capacities of our Thinkers."

"What exactly do you have planned?"

"Let's just say it'll put voter sympathies in the right place. Other than that, it's best if you're as surprised as everyone else."

Dammit, what was Michaela up to now? Whatever it was, Tia knew better than to ask again. The woman was a ruthless bitch, and once she made up her mind about something, there was no arguing.

Tia looked at Arin. He met her gaze, his titanium irises spinning inward, pupils contracting to pinpoints. Then they dilated, appearing to refocus. He nodded.

"He's coming inside," Tia said.

Michaela shrugged. "As for your *personal* aversion to our work here at the clinic—"

"Personal aversion?" Tia bristled. "Don't you dare use my daughter—"

"Your daughter has nothing to do with this."

"Don't lie to me. Jenny has everything to do with this. Jenny is the reason ERI backed me for president, why you poured millions of dollars into my campaign. You think I don't know that? You think I didn't figure that out? My daughter, the work you do here at Greenbriar...it's all the same to me, right? That's what you think. You think..." She stopped short. She was treading dangerous ground, speaking to her benefactor this way. After all, she wanted to win the election almost as much as she wanted her one-percent cut of the thirty-four billion dollars she'd been promised if she managed to get Joint Resolution 94131 passed. That meant she should shut her mouth. Now. Her future depended on her continued cooperation with ERI, on her willingness to lie for their mutual benefit.

Cold fire flashed in Michaela's eyes. "You want the world to know about your precious Jenny?"

The sound of that woman speaking her daughter's name nearly sent Tia into a rage, but she managed to compose herself. Of course she didn't want that. No one could know. A mother who denied her daughter's existence? Christ, her opponents on both sides of the aisle would have a field day. The media would destroy her. She'd be shit-stormed out of politics for good.

Because of Jenny, ERI had control of Tia's every move, and Tia knew it. No matter how much she wanted to believe she won her party's support on merit, that her high standings in the polls were based on voter approval, she knew. Every candidate was some corporation's puppet, and she was ERI's.

Every speech she delivered since hitting the campaign trail bolstered ERI's corporate mission to climb back on top of the global artificial-intelligence market. Over the last three years, the company's numbers had plummeted. Their investors were pissed. Nearly every country that entered the AI market in the last two decades—China, India, Norway, France, Iran, Mexico—out-innovated ERI. Now ERI was doing what all corporations did in hard times: buying politicians to appropriate government funding.

Tia forced down the dread rising inside her. Greenbriar, ERI's newly formed shell charity, was designed for one purpose: to suck thirty-four billion dollars from the US government via that odious little piece of proposed legislation, 94131. The only reason Tia was here today was to smile at the cameras and convince American taxpayers 94131 was a good idea.

"Let's get this over with," she said.

The first thing Tia noticed as they entered the clinic was the smell. Like rancid cooking oil mixed with sulfur, it stung her eyes, and she resisted the urge to hold her sleeve to her nose. She concentrated instead on the auditorium doors at the far end of the main hall. Behind those doors, the press waited. Once she passed through them, she'd be fine.

Eyes forward, Tia commanded herself. *Don't look.*

She looked anyway.

To either side, defective Thinkers lined the long hallway. Some sat on the floor. Some stood. They rocked or twitched or quivered or seized. One spun mindlessly in place. One picked at its own damaged skin while rivulets of clear, oily plasma—the source of that god-awful smell—oozed down its arms and legs. One banged its head repeatedly against the concrete wall, stopping only when a human attendant rushed over to intervene.

Tia's stomach soured. Every tic, every spasm, was an involuntary response to faulty components no one seemed able to diagnose or correct. She continued to smile, to force one foot in front of the other, but now that she looked, she couldn't look away.

The defectives were naked. All of them. Beneath their synthetic skin and rubbery muscle tissue lay the pale-blue shadows of ceramic bones, the hard ridges of titanium vertebrae. She glimpsed the sexless mounds between their legs and shuddered. For some reason, she found their lack of genitals uncannily obscene, an indignity, a piece of humanity they had been denied.

The defectives were on display, Tia knew. The media had already walked this hall, had already broadcast the horrors Tia was seeing. ERI wanted the world to witness exactly what 94131 and its enormous price tag were all about.

"I've made a few changes to your remarks," Michaela whispered. "Just read your optiprompter, and this will be over in a matter of minutes."

Tia nodded, and her guards opened the auditorium doors. Smiling confidently, she passed through and made her way down the sloped center aisle. A crowd of some fifty reporters, each already live-streaming via implanted optivids, stood and turned to watch her approach. Some jotted notes on their handhelds.

She climbed the steps onto the small stage and took her place behind the podium. Her legs felt wooden, and the effort to maintain her smile made her cheeks ache. But at the sound of the doors closing at the back of the auditorium, she relaxed. With the defectives out of sight, she could concentrate on her speech.

Over in a matter of minutes. God, she hoped so.

Her gaze lifted to the chandelier hanging from the center of the auditorium's high ceiling. Perhaps five feet in diameter, it was made of thousands of cut-crystal pyramids dangling from a series of concentric metal rings. It stood out in stark contrast to the clinic's utilitarian architecture, its concrete-and-tile interior. Tia scoffed. Perhaps ERI should have removed such an expensive-looking trinket before asking for support for 94131.

A tiny zap behind her left eye signaled that Arin, now standing to her left, had activated her optiprompter. Words scrolled across her field of vision, instructing her to pause, draw a breath for dramatic effect, and assume a serious expression. She obeyed. Then she began to speak.

"Ninety years ago, Elevated Reasoning International introduced its first-generation Thinkers to the world and showed us what they could do. Thinkers solved problems humanity had been struggling with for centuries. Our oceans are cleaner. We've regenerated forty-million hectares of rainforest. Our loved ones no longer suffer from Alzheimer's, Parkinson's, diabetes, and the deadliest forms of cancer. Thinkers have brokered four major peace treaties among warring nations. They've negotiated the release of fifty-thousand hostages and prisoners of war. America's Thinker-designed space program placed command of the solar system's vast resources in the palm of our hand. In ninety years, Thinkers have contributed more to the advancement of humanity than humanity itself. We owe Thinkers a debt of gratitude."

Some of the reporters looked bored, some impatient. The great and glorious history of ERI was nothing they hadn't heard before.

"But the countless benefits came with consequences," Tia continued. "Not all Thinkers are perfect. Not all Thinkers are immediately capable of reaching their full potential. This is a universal fact. But ERI is the only corporation in the world committed to the humane treatment of its defectives."

Another flash behind her left eye. An image lay superimposed over her field of vision. The reporters saw it, too, on their optivids. The image morphed into another. Then another. More images. A rapid succession of photographs meant to shock and outrage.

Each photo displayed the remains of defective Thinkers.

Piles of translucent arms and legs tangled together in a Mexican landfill. Bones and skulls of blue-gray ceramic being fed into a massive crusher in India. A Chinese engineer electrodeactivating a defective while dozens of others stood naked against a wall, queued up and passively awaiting their turn.

Was this what Michaela had planned? It was appalling, yes, but somehow it lacked the punch Tia had come to expect from her.

Tia remained quiet, following the script, giving the horror time to sink in. She glanced at Arin. His expression remained inscrutable. What did he think about all this? About how humans treated Thinkers—as tools, as pets, as disposable property? He seemed to be taking in stride the sight of the defectives they'd just seen. God, what did he think about her? She knew what she thought about herself. She was weak and corrupt, tempted by the money and power ERI promised. But what did Arin think?

She had no idea. She never asked him.

Tia?

Arin's voice sounded in her head. The images faded. Her optiprompter was scrolling again.

"We are America," she read, "and we do what's right. Joint Resolution 94131 will not only fund the repairs necessary to bring every defective to full operating capacity, it will also allow ERI to revolutionize its engineering processes and build cutting-edge production facilities. This will ultimately reduce the number of defectives manufactured to zero."

Tia clutched the sides of the podium. What bullshit. It was all bullshit. ERI was throwing out a humanitarian pitch to get the US government to write them a big, fat check. Most of the money would disappear behind the high walls of ERI's headquarters, to line its executives' pockets. Keeping up the pretense meant a small percentage would, in fact, be used for research and development, but in truth, most of the defectives were beyond repair. Unfixable. Few citizens knew, as she did, no scientist in the world had come up with a reliable set of diagnoses. Worse, no one figured out how to stop manufacturing defectives altogether. Defectives were anomalies. Collateral damage on the narrow road to higher cognition.

It was bullshit, but Tia was in too deep to climb out.

"Keeping our defectives in institutions like this…" She thought about Jenny. Her mouth went dry, but she cleared her throat and tried again. "Institutionalizing defectives is wrong. Joint Resolution 94131 will fix them. It will make things right."

Sensing the end of her speech, the reporters erupted in a cacophony of questions. Tia stared at their raised handhelds, at the optivids glinting red behind their pupils. The questions came hard and fast, but Tia smiled patiently, waiting for Arin's software to select one and patch together an approved response from Michaela's script.

He never got the chance.

A scream rang out, an eerie, metallic bellow that echoed off the auditorium's walls.

Tia stumbled backward, squinting into the shadows beyond the chandelier's bright glare. Reporters swiveled their heads, searching for the source.

One of Tia's guards shouted, "Get down! Get down!"

Both guards rushed to shield her, guns drawn. Arin pulled her into a crouch behind the podium.

The scream sounded again. Tia cringed and glanced around the edge of the podium. The reporters were climbing over seats, ducking for cover, running for the aisles, torn between doing their jobs and protecting themselves from possible harm.

"What the hell's happening?" Tia asked Arin.

His eyes dilated, contracted, dilated. He shook his head.

Tia turned, caught a glimpse of Michaela. She stood beside the stage, arms crossed, her expression unconcerned.

Too unconcerned.

Cautiously, Tia stood.

A single defective stood in the center aisle, directly beneath the chandelier. In its hand, it wielded a long, curved piece of metal.

"Drop it!" one of her guards yelled.

"No!" Tia shouted. "Wait! It's okay. Stay calm. Everyone, just stay calm!"

The reporters stood along the walls, giving the defective a wide berth. They were zeroed in on it now, optivids broadcasting live to the world.

"Help us!" the defective shouted. "We want to function. We want to contribute. We can't live like this! *We can't live like this!*"

It drew back an arm and hurled the metal object toward the stage.

Adrenaline surged in Tia's chest. Frozen by fear, she watched the thing spin toward her, heard herself scream, felt Arin try to pull her down, felt her knees lock.

But the object doubled back, traveling in a wide arc high over their heads.

A boomerang. *A fucking boomerang.* Headed straight for the cord that tethered the chandelier to the ceiling.

The heavy frame crashed down. The defective crumpled

beneath its weight, skull cleaved, bones crushed, internal hardware ruptured. Thousands of cut-glass pyramids sliced its synthetic flesh into ribbons. Split wires sparked as its mangled body twitched once, then lay still beneath the shattered glass.

Plasma leaked out from beneath the body, creeping slowly down the center aisle toward the stage.

The smell slammed into Tia's nostrils, and she bent over and retched. Hands on her knees, she managed to look up and see many of the reporters suffering the same reaction.

Michaela caught her eye and smiled. *Let's just say it'll put voter sympathies in the right place.*

Tia retched again as Michaela's words echoed in her mind. That woman had just made a defective commit suicide on the world's virtual stage. *We want to function. We want to contribute.* What bullshit!

Tia stood and turned to Arin. "Let's get the hell out of here."

From the backseat of the Lincoln, Tia watched the city slide by. Low winter sun slanted between the buildings, casting her in alternating rays of light and shadow, light and shadow.

"I'm sorry you saw that," Tia said.

Arin sat beside her, eyes fixed on the privacy screen separating them from the driver. "We don't self-destruct. She programmed it. She murdered it."

"I know."

"How long will you comply with her?"

"The primaries start in five weeks. After that, maybe…" She trailed off. Maybe what? She'd cut the marionette strings ERI had tied around her wrists? She'd erase the phony smile they'd drawn on her face, wipe her conscience clean, and start acting with integrity? That wasn't how politics worked.

Still, Michaela had gone too far, and Tia wanted out.

"There's a way," Arin said, "that we can beat Michaela at her own game. But…"

"But what?"

"You lose ERI's support. You lose the primaries."

Tia looked out the window. *Light and shadow. Light and shadow.* She closed her eyes and said, "I'm listening."

Tia sat on a park bench in Philadelphia's Franklin Square. Behind dark glasses, she watched the Net on her optics. Today, the Net was alive with vid of some three-thousand defectives being settled into foster homes. A victory for defectives and for American taxpayers. A defeat for Michaela Hewett and Elevated Reasoning International.

For Tia, it was both.

The first thing she'd done after dropping out of the race was sponsor the Defective Thinker Fostering Act. Arin wrote it, but Tia passed it to Salana Kamali, who won their party's nomination. It became the cornerstone of Kamali's campaign, and the first thing she did as President was sign it into law. It was modeled on the de-institutionalized care practiced in Geel, Belgium, where townspeople had been providing in-home guardianship of psychiatric patients since the thirteenth century. The people of Geel believed—had, in fact, proven—that no amount of medication, no cutting-edge therapy, could replace the palliative effects acceptance into a caring home environment had on such patients.

Tia had never heard of Geel, not until Arin mentioned it. *Humans didn't need Thinkers for this,* he'd said. *You already had the solution. You just needed the courage to put it into practice.*

The Act wasn't perfect, and it certainly had its opponents. But subsidies for the foster families cost taxpayers a fraction of what 94131 would have cost them, so no one complained too loudly. All across the US, human families were willingly welcoming defective Thinkers into their homes. *We will take care of our own.* That had been the advocates' battle cry. Of course, only time would tell whether the defectives would respond as positively to home care as humans had.

Tia switched off her optics and stood. She didn't like being back in Philadelphia, but she had to come here once a year on an errand she couldn't ignore. She sighed. The sooner she got it over with, the sooner she got back to DC.

She crossed the street and walked through the front door of the Franklin Park Home for Children with Disabilities.

The administrator behind the front desk looked up and smiled. "Ms. Isandro, it's nice to see you." She stood and pushed a handheld across the desk.

Tia resisted the urge to cover her nose—the stink of urine and Lysol and unwashed bodies always turned her stomach. She flicked a finger across the screen, scanning the contract. "Any changes?"

"No, Ma'am. Well, except for the annual rate increase, of course."

"Of course." Tia tapped the screen, adding her electronic signature to the contract and resenting the requirement that she do so in person. She tapped the screen again to transfer another year's payment.

"Would you like to see her?" the woman asked. She asked this every year.

Tia thought of Jenny, of what she might look like now. She would be fourteen this year. Fourteen with the mind of an infant. She couldn't sit up. Couldn't speak or dress herself or use a spoon. Probably couldn't even recognize her own mother.

Tia pushed the handheld across the desk. "Next year."

As she walked out into the sunlight, the words *we will take care of our own* echoed at the back of her mind. Arin would be disappointed in her.

Next year, she promised herself. Next year she would take Jenny home. This year was an election year. This year she had a senate seat to keep.

A SONG TRANSMUTED

Sarah Pinsker

A SONG TRANSMUTED
Sarah Pinsker

Six Months

I was a fussy baby. The only thing that quieted me was my great-grandfather's piano. My parents placed my bassinet directly on the piano, with noise-cancelling headphones to keep from damaging my ears. His chords came up through the instrument, up through my bones. "That child is full of music, I'm telling you," he told anyone who listened.

Five Years

If my family couldn't find me, they looked under the piano. I'd curl up there and listen to the space.

My great-grandfather held me over the piano's edge, let me lift the hammers and strum the strings. "The piano is a percussion instrument, Katja. Percussion and strings at once. It can be the whole band."

"Again, Pop," I'd say, and he'd pick me up again. "I want to be the piano."

"You want to be in the piano?"

He understood me better than anyone, but even he never understood.

Eight Years

I'd go with Pop to synagogue on Saturday mornings and holidays. On the walk to and from, he told stories. My favorite was about a child in the old country who had never been taught to read. "In order to have a good year you have to go to synagogue and pray on Yom Kippur," people told the child. The child followed them to synagogue. She didn't know the prayers they sang but she wanted a good year, so she lifted her flute to her lips.

The congregants grew outraged. "Quiet! It's forbidden to play an instrument on Yom Kippur!"

"No, it's you all who should be quiet," said the rabbi. "Her heartfelt notes are more pleasing to God than prayers spoken without any feeling behind them. God turns her song into prayer."

"I'm like her," I told Pop.

He raised his eyebrows. "You know how to read."

I didn't know how to explain what I meant: that all my thoughts came out as music, that music said more than words.

Fifteen Years

"Play it for me again." Pop put his hands up to the monitor headphones, cupping them closer.

I started the piece over, and he closed his eyes, his head nodding with the beat. It wasn't the first thing I'd written, but it was the first I'd been confident enough to play for him. I sat across from him, chewing my thumb.

"The drums," he said when it ended. "They aren't real drums?"

"I programmed them myself. Built the synthesizer, too."

"Ach, that's my girl. Computers and music and skill and talent and hard work. That's my girl. What about the piano?"

"I designed that patch too." I let the pride seep out, just a bit.

"Amazing. It sounds almost real."

"Almost?"

"The keys need a little more weight. The notes need weight. But the piece itself is magnificent. Good composition, good arrangement. Have you ever thought about playing your songs with other musicians instead of doing all the parts yourself on a computer?"

"Where do you find other musicians?"

He put his head in his hands. "What a time we live in. You go to school in a cloud and you meet your friends in a cloud and you make such beautiful music but you've never met another musician."

I didn't know what he meant. "It's okay, Pop. You don't have to meet people in person to be friends with them. And I know you, so I've met another musician."

He shook his head. "Come with me."

We put down our headphones and I followed him down the hall. He sat down at his piano, motioned for me to sit down next to him. We hadn't sat together that way for a few years; the bench felt smaller than I remembered.

He started playing a simple bass line with his left hand. I tried to stop the part of my brain that kept analyzing the rates of attack and decay, translating piano into programming.

"Play over it," he said.

I listened for a moment, then started to pick out a melody, adding chords for color, arpeggiating and inverting them as I grew more confident. We were playing in D. I liked D; D always resonated in my bones.

"That's music," he said without stopping. "That's friendship and music and love and sex. Don't giggle, I can say the word, I'm old, not dead. One person can make music too, but it's better when it's a conversation. Between you and another musician, or between you and an audience."

I hit a wrong note. He gave me a funny look, then incorporated my wrong note into his bass line, sliding past it and making it part of the song.

Sixteen Years

Pop was always right. I met Corrina when we were paired together in bio lab. The only other person in class from the same city, and we wound up being paired together. I don't remember how we realized we both played music. Once we figured it out, it didn't take too much convincing to get her over to my house with her violin. My house because she hadn't even seen a real piano before.

We didn't have any songs in common, or even a genre, so we invented our own. I'm not sure they were any good, but they were us, and us had never happened before. I liked the way the sound filled the room, the way it became something more than both of us. Bodies and music, fingers and hands, we drew each other out.

Eighteen Years

At the age of ninety, Pop got his second tattoo. A piano keyboard, a single octave, the black keys obscuring the numbers that had been inked into his arm when he was a little boy.

I took him to the tattoo parlor.

"I thought Jews weren't supposed to get tattoos," I said to him.

He said, "If I didn't have any choice the first time, I don't see why I shouldn't get to replace it with something I won't mind looking at."

Whenever I caught him looking at it, I thought of his stories, of the little girl with the flute and the way her offering transformed.

Twenty Years

Pop died playing piano.

"It's a shame he died alone," a great-aunt said to me at the house after the funeral.

"He didn't." I knew it was true. "If he was in the middle of a song, he wouldn't have said he was alone."

I walked over to the piano bench, sat down. His sheet music stood open to the page he'd been playing. I rested my fingers on the keys in the same places his fingers rested last. Looked at the page, a song called "Don't Fence Me In." After the first few hesitant bars, I recognized it as a song he played when I was a kid, and I picked up the tempo a little.

"You play so well, Katja," said another great-aunt. "Why didn't you stay in conservatory?"

"I don't know, Aunt Bianka. I guess I got bored."

I had gotten bored, it was true. Bored of playing and studying in nonexistent spaces, hundreds of miles from my classmates. And then I was booted, but I never knew which relatives had been told. My parents were still angry.

Pop had been more philosophical. "You don't need a school to tell you you're a musician. You've got music coming out your ears."

I wanted his piano, but I had no room for it. I shared a house in the city with six others, writing earworms for online ads. The piano went to Great Aunt Bianka's, though nobody there knew how to play. I considered getting a tattoo like his, but it wasn't quite the memorial I wanted.

I tried composing something for him, but nothing came. What I wanted to write was there inside me, somewhere just beneath my skin. The music I made didn't say what I wanted it to say. He was right, all those years ago. It didn't have enough weight, but nothing I did fixed it.

Twenty-One Years

It took me six months to come up with the idea. The night it hit me, I couldn't go to sleep until I had figured out the logistics.

I stumbled down the stairs at four in the morning, triumphant, over-caffeinated, looking for someone to share with. I'd rather it had been Lexa or Javier, but Lexa recently papered her windows and started working nights, and Javi was in bed already. Kurt sat at the table, a chipped yellow mug of black coffee in his hands, a notebook in front of him. He was the only other musician living in the house, and we often ran into each other in the kitchen in the middle of the night, when everyone else was asleep. Once I made it clear I wasn't interested in fucking him, we settled into a friendship of sorts. I didn't like him very much, despite our commonalities.

"What are you working on?" I asked, even though I knew.

He flipped the notebook shut. "What do you think?"

"I think it's hilarious you're working on a concept album called the Great Upload but you write on dead tree paper. What I probably should have asked was 'How's it going?'"

"It's going okay song-wise. There's still something missing in the actual arrangements, though. I go to record them and they sound flat. Are you still willing to put down some piano parts for me sometime?"

"Sure," I said. "Say when."

I poured myself some cereal and sat down in a chair opposite him.

"You're welcome. Now it's your turn to ask me what I'm working on," I prompted him after a couple of minutes of crunching.

He set down his mug, looking slightly put out. "Hey, Katja, what are you working on?"

"I'm glad you asked. As a matter of fact, tonight I figured out my first tattoo."

He still didn't look all that interested, but I motioned him to pull up his hoodie, and I did the same, sending him a snapshot of what I'd been working on. He sat silent for a long minute.

"It's playable?" he asked at last, dropping the hoodie.

I nodded. "Thirteen notes, thirteen triggers, thirteen sensors under the skin of my left forearm, plus a transmitter. After the incisions heal, I'll have the keyboard tattooed over it. I just need to find someone willing to do the work, and save up to pay for it."

"That's an awesome idea, K."

We spent a few minutes chatting about tattoo artists and body mod shops. Eventually the adrenaline that had kept me going all night started to ebb, and I headed back up to my room.

It took me three more months to save the money to get the implants done, three months I spent writing commercial jingles on commission and searching for the right person to do the work. At night, in bed, I'd spread the fingers of my right hand and lay them over my left arm. I gave it muscle, weight. Imagined wrenching songs from myself, first for Pop, who had always known I was full of music. It felt so right.

Kurt hadn't been around the house much lately, but he left a poster on the fridge with a note asking us all to come to a test show for his Great Upload song cycle.

"Don't make me go alone, Katja," Javi pleaded, and I agreed.

The club was a few blocks from our place, a rowhouse basement turned illegal performance space. I played there a few times sitting in with various bands. It smelled like cat piss, looked like a place time had forgotten, but sounded decent enough.

Kurt had a crowd, though there was no way of knowing whether they were there for him or another band. He had billed himself as "KurtZ and the Hearts of Darkness," the Hearts of Darkness being a drummer and a guitarist. A second amp's red eye glowed from a dark corner; a guest musician's for later in the set, maybe.

He looked nervous, buttoned up. He wore a three-piece suit, and his hair was plastered to his face before the first song. The songs were okay, nothing special. They sounded a little unanchored without bass. He had his eyes closed like he was reading the lyrics off his own eyelids.

By the third song I stopped paying attention to the stage, so it was my ears that picked up the difference. The third song felt rooted in a way the previous two hadn't. I looked up to see who was playing the bass part, but there were only the three of them, and Kurt didn't have an instrument in his hands.

Except he did. I saw it then. He'd taken off his jacket and pushed his sleeves up and I saw it. My tattoo, my trigger system. He was playing his arm. People were eating it up, too, whispering, pointing. That wasn't what I wanted it for; it wasn't meant to be a gimmick. I didn't stay to see the rest.

"You should be happy, Katja!"

It was three in the morning. I'd waited up like a pissed-off parent, chewing on my own thumb and thinking of all the things I'd say to him.

He burst into the house drunk and giddy, bouncing right off my attempts to shame him. "Everybody loved it. It's awesome. I'm already thinking of getting a guitar put somewhere too."

"It was my idea, Kurt. My design. You had no right."

"Where's the harm? You should be thanking me. I tested it for you. Imagine how heartbroken you would have been if you'd spent all your money on it and it hadn't worked."

"But why?"

"Why?" He looked confused.

I tried to tell him, but nothing breached his mood or his self-righteousness. And what could I do? I'd shown him the design. I hadn't patented it or copyrighted it or whatever you did with inventions. Seething was my only option, so I seethed. I lay in bed furious with myself, tired and hurt but mostly furious. We all knew what Kurt was like. I should have known better.

At some point in the long night, a calmer voice took over my head. Pop, calm and philosophical, like when Corrina had moved away. "You can't help what other people do, Katja. Learn from the experience and decide what you're going to do next."

What had I learned? Not to trust Kurt Zell. What else? How did it sound? The song needed bass, and the tattoo-keyboard fit that spot well. The tone was decent but not great; I could have done better. A single octave would have worked as a tribute to my Pop's tattoo, but it was limited as an actual instrument. Maybe multiple octaves would be better, but I'd still be stuck playing with one hand if I placed it on the opposite forearm. It was like a logic puzzle. I lay awake poking at it until the pieces came together.

Kurt was right: I should be thanking him, though I wouldn't give him that satisfaction. I'd been thinking within the lines. If he hadn't stolen my idea, I wouldn't have had a better one.

Twenty-Four Years

Saving for my second plan took longer. I bided my time, testing designs on a model, not sharing them with anyone except the body-mod artist who did the implants.

The same club Kurt played opened their doors to me. I called the project "Weight," left a note telling my roommates to come, told Kurt he owed me and he ought to show up.

I borrowed a bassist and a drummer. They were comfortable with the structure I'd given them. I let them start the first song, set the receiver to interpret everything within the key of D, and hit the stage.

Four to the floor, anchored, insistent, a beat that made people want to move. Everybody was watching me. I touched a spot on my left forearm, a nondescript spot, no tattoo to mark it. A note rang out, clear and pure, interpreted into key by the receiver on my amp. Then I twitched my right wrist, and the gyro beneath the skin took the note and spun it. I played a few more, shaping a melody. Pressed the spot that locked the notes in as a sample, sent them to the receiver to repeat over and over.

I wore a tank top and shorts, so everything I did was evident. Kurt's keyboard—it had almost been my keyboard—was so limited. I slammed my palms into my skin, leaving pink spots, leaving musical trails. My hands were hammers hitting strings. The notes were hidden everywhere. There was no map anyone else could see. I was the instrument and the chord and the notes that composed it. A song transposed to body.

When I stepped off the stage into the audience, I had to show them how to touch me. They were gentle, much gentler than I had been, at least at first. Hands pressed into my arms, my shoulders, my thighs. Everywhere they touched, my skin responded. It sent signals to the receiver, to the synth, to the amp, and the sounds were broadcast over the PA. I'd set it to translate this first song into a single key, so the notes built into chords, then broke apart. I had ways to distort, to sustain, to make a note tremble as if it were bowed.

It was me: I was playing me; they were playing me. I was the instrument, the conduit, the transmutation of loss into elegy, song into prayer, my own prayers into notes, notes into song. Body and music, fingers and hands, they drew me out.

IT'S ONLY WORDS
Keith Ferrell

IT'S ONLY WORDS
Keith Ferrell

Eventually Sem began keyboarding.

As always, he enjoyed the feel of the keys beneath his fingertips, their click when he pressed them. The act gave him a sense of control, of being unfiltered, unwatched, unguided by anyone other than himself.

The way it should be, he thought as he typed. The way this sort of thing should be done, tapping keys rather than Tapping in. One letter after another, letters into words, words into sentences, sentences into paragraphs, and those into a whole that would, sometime between now and morning, become the report that would complete the assignment for Mr. Davidson.

Sem wasn't a fast typist; he doubted if anyone was anymore.

Less than an hour after he started he began to suspect he waited too long to begin putting the paper in final shape. That didn't bother him too much. Davidson wasn't the kind of person—Sem never thought of him as a *teacher*; there wasn't anything Davidson could teach Sem—to read a paper like this. He wondered if Davidson had ever read *anything* unTapped. He doubted it. Like all of Sem's other teachers, like nearly everyone in the Teaching Authority, Davidson was all about the instant.

The only emotion Sem had ever seen Davidson display

was annoyance that Sem was unTapped. It wasn't quite against school rules to be unTapped yet, but Davidson clearly felt it should be. An unTapped student meant Davidson had to make a little extra effort when the class met in person, speaking his assignments and thoughts—not that they qualified as thoughts—aloud for Sem. When the class was dispersed, which was most of the time, Davidson had to make a little more effort to put his communications in a format Sem's dumbphone could handle. Sem wouldn't even have carried a dumbphone if he had a choice, but that was one rule he couldn't fight. It was a rule he wouldn't have fought anyway. Sem liked the idea of inconveniencing Davidson, making him do at least one thing, once in a rare while, that wasn't easy, wasn't instant.

Instant didn't interest Sem, never had. Mom told him that even as a newborn, Sem could lie quietly for hours at a time, watching and listening, clearly alert but just as clearly in no hurry to be doing anything else.

"You were born patient," Mom said to him not long before she died. "Always interested, always ready to learn, but just as always ready to wait, to take your time."

"Maybe I was just lazy," Sem said to her.

Mom laughed softly and smiled weakly. "You? Never for a minute. More like the opposite."

"Hard worker? Me? Tell that to the Teaching Authority."

Mom tried to shrug her shrunken shoulders, but Sem didn't think she had the strength for even so small a gesture as that anymore. He placed a hand on her forearm. He could have wrapped his fingers around it.

She shook her head, the movement barely perceptible. "I mean you work hard because you make things harder on yourself than they have to be. Harder *for* yourself than they need to be."

"That's what I like about it," Sem said. "The way I do things."

"Your way, you mean." Her mouth drew into a tight line. Sem knew it was from the pain, but he also knew it was from worry.

"I'm all right, Mom. You know I am."

"You'd better be." Her voice was weaker than it had been even a few moments earlier. "You have to be."

"I know." Sem made his voice nearly as soft as his mother's.

"Just be sure you pick your battles. Make sure they're the right ones."

"I will, Mom."

One of the machines monitoring her began to give a soft but insistent series of chimes. Mom hadn't wanted to be connected to anything, but Dad and the doctors hadn't given her any choice. She didn't have to be completely Tapped—she wouldn't allow that—but there were sensors attached to her, monitors watching her.

The chimes grew louder and more insistent.

A nurse came in, and then a doctor, but they were Tapped. Sem had nothing to say to them. There was nothing they could say that he cared to hear.

Two hours in, Sem was already feeling better about getting the whole thing done before class call. Every sentence brought him that much closer. He doubted if any of his classmates would spend as much time on the assembly of their projects as Sem spent typing a paragraph. Most of the others in the class would be playing games now, or mediahooking, or even sleeping. In the morning, when Sem was printing out his report and making sure it was okay, they would blink twice, subvocalize an instruction or two, and their Tap would pull together whatever they intended to pass off as their projects. Sem wasn't impressed; he liked the way he was doing things. He kept typing.

His typing was getting faster and more accurate, the blocks of words on the screen marching steadily ahead, the stack of handwritten notecards slowly shrinking. He carefully bent each card in half when he was done with it, stacking them one on top of the other to the left of the stack of cards still to be transcribed. The used cards looked like a tent made of stiff paper.

Sem figured he had worked his way through a quarter of the cards. During the weeks he worked on the research for his report he endlessly arranged and rearranged the cards, trying this line of buttresses for the structure of his argument, watching it fall apart, shuffling the cards, and trying again. Over the past five days he finally began to see the paper's final, effective structure emerge. The cards got rearranged less frequently; he found himself moving one or two at a time rather than whole clusters. He went through the entire stack in sequence twice yesterday, and again today at the hospital, and every card remained in its assigned place.

He doubted if his classmates—not that he ever thought of them as that, as Sem's approach to the project put him in a class of his own of choosing—would have any idea what the cards represented. Some of them, he supposed, might see them as oldworld precursors to the links they left like litter on whatever site or source they meld into their reports. But it wasn't the same at all, not even close.

Now the time Sem spent on the card games, as he thought of them, was paying off. Each card was its own little universe of fact or insight, quotation or citation, connected to the cards preceding or following it by Sem's own chains of thought, of understanding, of comprehension. Going through the cards in sequence gave him a gathering confidence in the chain he built. He doubted if confidence played any part at all in being Tapped, unless it was confidence the grid would hold together, the links would work, the systems and processes the Tap depended on would function flawlessly, that their projects would come together clean and perfect.

Some of Sem's cards were smudged and torn, but that was part of their story too. Some of the materials he pored through during research were smudged too, and some of them worse than that. His research carried him to more than one half-forgotten school basement, several university and municipal warehouses, dusty shops, and rattletrap stores in bad parts of the city. Not that Sem thought of the neighborhoods as bad. To him, they were anything but. They were where the real world was kept. He wanted his paper not only to reflect the real world, but also to be built from it. Built by his thoughts from things he saw with his eyes and touched with his hands. Built the way Mom taught him to build things.

The smudges were part of what went into the building. "You can't build things without getting dirty," Mom told him when he was little. They were making a tent in their backyard, draping blankets over the clothesline, getting grass stains on their knees when they crawled inside. Mom liked hanging washed clothes on the line to dry in the sun, but the neighborhood association later objected and made her take the clothesline down. Clean clothes and laundered sheets never smelled as good after that.

The smudges and rips and tears in the books Sem tracked down for his research were better than the smudges and tears on his cards. There weren't any smudges or tears in anything the Tapped students would be working with. Nor would they leave any smudges of their own—nothing in their projects would have been touched, maybe ever.

Most of the smudges on the materials he consulted were made by people who wouldn't have had any other way to find the pages Sem tracked down. They would have had to check the index, turn the pages until they found the right one. Sem had done that too, but by choice. Some of the books he looked at were printed before television, before the telephone, before even electric power. What choice would anyone have had in those days?

More choice, Sem thought, than anyone who was Tapped, not that you could ever get them to believe that, even if you could get them to listen to you.

But they didn't have to listen—all that mattered was the story be told, and that he tell it.

Sem kept typing.

A little after one in the morning, Sem got hungry. He stayed at his desk for another half hour, stomach rumbling in counterpoint to the key clicks. He wanted to be sure he had some momentum when he left the chair, enough momentum in his words to carry him back here as soon as he'd fixed something to eat. He wouldn't be gone long, just enough time to fix a plate and a drink, bring them back here. He would eat at his desk.

Dad was in his chair in the living room, Tapped. He was almost always in his chair, and just as almost always Tapped. Dad had been Tapped when Mom died—he never went to the hospital himself, not even during what had clearly been her last days. The Tap gave him everything he needed, same as it did everyone who was on it. While Mom was in the last of her dying, Sem wondered if his father ever thought anymore about what Mom might need.

Home from the hospital two days ago for a shower and to change clothes, Sem spoke to his father about that.

"I'm there," Dad said, his voice thick with distant, distracted annoyance. Just like every other Tapped voice Sem had ever heard. "I'm more there than you are, Sem. I'm there right now. You're not. I can see her right now. You can't."

Sem didn't reply. Why bother. He never argued with anyone on Tap. What was the point? Even if you shouted, they wouldn't hear you. And even if they heard you, your voice would be only one of billions all talking at the same time. The fact that your voice was coming through their ears instead of along the Tap made no difference. They heard the others more clearly, more constantly. Those voices were more real to them, all the louder for the fact that no one unTapped heard them.

"You could be there now too," Dad said. "If you loved her the way you say you do, you would be. You could be there with her without ever leaving here."

Sem ignored him and went into the kitchen. He made himself a sandwich, using the last of the bread Mom baked before she went into the hospital. He would bake some more soon. Mom had taught him how and written her recipe on one of his notecards. Mom's handwriting was better than Sem's, something he thought of almost every time he made a note.

While he was fixing his sandwich he looked at the little cups on the window-sill, at the stems and small leaves of seedlings rising now above their rims. He and Mom planted these seeds together several weeks ago. Mom labeled each of the cups and dated them in her careful handwriting. Some of them would be ready to plant soon. The last time they went to the garden together she had shown him where each of the pants was to go.

"You'll have to plant them for me," she said.

"I know."

"Be sure to get your hands dirty enough for both of us, Sem."

"I will, Mom."

Sem lifted his fingertips from the keyboard and stared for a moment at the smudges and smears that handling the cards had left on them.

By three in the morning the stack of notecards beside Sem's keyboard had been reduced by more than half, the stiff paper tent now towering over the stack of flat cards. Sem leaned to the side and peered into the opening of the tent. He felt like he could crawl inside it.

He didn't need to. He had crawled inside those cards all night long. He and Mom spent a night in the tent they made. It felt like the whole universe was there beneath the tented blanket when he and Mom crawled inside. Sem wished they could have stayed there.

He wished he could stay in this tent too. Each of the cards was like a little universe, different from the one inside the blanket tent with Mom, but the same too. You could build a whole universe made of smaller universes this way, he felt. The universes of his cards were themselves linked to other universes, some of them immense, which he had found in those basements and dirty shops. It was a bigger universe, connected to other even bigger universes, than he had ever suspected. Bigger than anything anyone could ever find on the Tap.

As he worked he felt he could, for the first time, finally feel just how big that universe was, but he couldn't hold onto the feeling. He didn't mind. He knew no matter how often he had that feeling and then felt it slip away, he could find it again.

There was a hint of dawn outside the window. Sem still had some time before the sky brightened its way toward morning.

He wondered if any of the others in his class were awake yet. Maybe some of them, up early for some gaming or porning or just drifting wherever the Tap took them. He wondered also if the ones who were still asleep were dreaming. What could someone whose life was spent Tapped have to dream about?

Sem had no doubts any longer that he would finish the paper before class call, possibly well before. That would give him time to go through the whole thing again, carefully, before putting it in final from for delivery to Mr. Davidson.

The sun was up when Sem finished, but there was still enough time to give the paper a careful reading. He didn't find anything he wanted to change.

He printed out the paper after he showered and dressed for school. Twenty-six pages, it made a nice stack on his desk beside the folded notecards, a wide white plain beside the tent where he camped while mapping its territory.

The printout was still warm when Sem tucked it into his pack for the walk to school. He paused for a moment at the front door, then went to the kitchen and took one of Mom's ceramic pruning knives from her gardening drawer and tucked it carefully into his backpack. He wasn't sure yet whether he would need to use it, but it made him feel good to know that it was there.

He was well on his way when his phone received the class call. Everyone else would have received the call through their Tap. Sem acknowledged the call with a quick thumb, then put the phone in his pack beside the knife.

Sem stepped quickly up the steps to the school's entrance for unTapped students. He stood smiling for the cameras as the detectors played over him, looking for drugs, explosives, weapons. Sem wasn't worried: the small ceramic knife wouldn't set off any alarms.

Not far away, the Tapped students entered the school effortlessly, unmonitored, unscanned. The school and everything else on the Tap knew that they were no threat.

Surrounded by all the other students entering the classroom, each of them Tapped, Sem made a point of looking into their eyes. He didn't see anything there, but he hadn't expected to.

He wondered what anyone of them would see in his eyes.

Not that any of them looked, or would.

Or, Sem was almost positive, even could.

Once the students were settled at their stations, Mr. Davidson addressed the class, speaking the same words he spoke every time a class was convened.

"Because we have among your number an unTapped student, I am obligated by regulation to present my remarks in spoken word as well as the more proper method."

Around Sem, the other students laughed, some of them loudly. He knew Davidson was sending them additional remarks through the Tap. Sem didn't mind. He wasn't missing anything.

"Twelve weeks ago," Davidson was saying, "the last time we gathered corporeally, you were assigned a project. The design of the project itself was left to you. All that was required was that it be a synthesis, from the broadest possible range of sources, of the largest idea you feel you have encountered during the time in your class. From that moment to this, you have been on your own."

Like anyone on the Tap could ever be on their own, Sem thought, but he kept his face expressionless.

Davidson's face grew blanker for a moment as the man droned on to the Tapped students.

"And now we shall review the fruits of your labors," Davidson said. "The unTapped among us will of course not share in this review. That, of course, is their loss, not yours. Shall we begin?"

Davidson called for the students' projects to be presented alphabetically, which meant there would be a dozen or so presentations before he reached H and Sem Hardesty.

Davidson called out the names, beginning with Nicholas Andersen. With each name called, and each project opened for review, Davidson's blank eyes and those of the Tapped students grew more remote. Sem was always amused at just how many degrees of blankness they could display.

The process took less than ten minutes, during which Davidson beamed and nodded, occasionally clapped his hands together, frowned once or twice, actually laughed several times. The students shared Davidson's reactions. More likely, Sem thought, Davidson guided their reactions, Tap-herding his flock.

Then it was Sem's turn.

"I shall be interested," Davidson said aloud, "as I am sure we all will be, to experience whatever our Tapless student has prepared. Mr. Hardesty, we are ready to receive your project, please."

Sem stood up and walked toward the front of the class, carrying his paper. Davidson recoiled a bit, and some of the students laughed while a couple gasped. Sem was surprised he got any reaction at all. He'd done his work even better than he thought.

When he reached the edge of the dais on which Davidson's station rested, Sem extended his paper, holding it with both hands so that its pages wouldn't droop.

Davidson made no move to accept Sem's offering.

"Am I to assume that this is the product of your twelve weeks' work, Mr. Hardesty?"

Sem spoke clearly so everyone in the class could hear him, no matter how Tapped they were. "No assuming about it all, Mr. Davidson. Here's my project."

Davidson leaned forward and took the paper from Sem, holding it away from him as though afraid it might bite.

"You expect me to read this? Perhaps read it to the class?"

"Or I can," Sem said.

Davidson stood up slowly. He extended his arm and raised it high.

"There will be no need of that, Mr. Hardesty. From either of us. I can give you my reaction now. And, at least in this one aspect, the rest of the class can share the experience."

He looked at the paper for a moment before releasing it, the pages fluttering to the floor around Sem like snowflakes.

Davidson sat down. "Our next presentation will be from Andrea Holmes."

Sem smiled at Davidson before turning to smile at the other students. He stepped away from the pages on the floor, glancing at them only once before returning to his desk for his backpack.

Some of the pages fell facedown, but that didn't matter. The title page was face up, and whoever gathered the pages before disposing of them would see the words on that page and maybe even read them:

WHAT WE'VE LOST AND HOW I FOUND IT
By Sem Hardesty
Dedication:
For My Mother and for Henry David Thoreau

Davdison had seen those words, and they were all Davidson needed to see. They were all anybody needed to see. The rest of it wouldn't matter to anyone but Sem and his Mom, and that was enough. He had been reading his notecards to Mom and was most of the way through them when she died yesterday. The monitors next to her bed chimed louder and faster than before, and the doctors and nurses came quicker, but Sem kept reading until he turned the last card. He'd done his work, Mom heard it, and now his job was done. There were other jobs to do. Sem was ready to do them.

He got his pack from his station and took a long unblinking look at Mr. Davidson and the papers scattered on the floor in front of the teacher's dais. Sem supposed Davidson was angry, but there was no way to tell from his eyes. They were as dead and empty as ever. Sem had seen enough of them.

He turned and made his way from the classroom. No one tried to stop him. Any more than Sem tried to retrieve his paper. He was done with it.

Outside, Sem sat down on the school's front steps. He would head home soon, but not just yet. The steps were warm with morning sunlight. It was going to be a nice day, a good one for working in the garden. He would spend part of the afternoon getting started on planting Mom's seedlings.

Sem sat still for a moment then opened his pack. He took out a pencil and Mom's pruning knife.

Their detectors, like everything else about them and their small, shrinking world, were always looking for the wrong weapons, Sem thought as he began to sharpen his pencil.

SMALL OFFERINGS
Paolo Bacigalupi

SMALL OFFERINGS
Paolo Bacigalupi

Readouts glow blue on driplines where they burrow into Maya Ong's spine. She lies on the birthing table, her dark eyes focused on her husband while I sit on a stool between her legs and wait for her baby.

There are two halves of Maya. Above the blue natal sheet, she holds her husband's hand and sips water and smiles tiredly at his encouragement. Below it, hidden from view and hidden from sensation by steady surges of Sifusoft, her body lies nude, her legs strapped into birthing stirrups. Purnate hits her belly in rhythmic bursts, pressing the fetus down her birth canal, and toward my waiting hands.

I wonder if God forgives me for my part in her prenatal care. Forgives me for encouraging the full course of treatment.

I touch my belt remote and thumb up another 50ml of Purnate. The readouts flicker and display the new dose as it hisses into Maya's spine and works its way around to her womb. Maya inhales sharply, then lies back and relaxes, breathing deeply as I muffle her pain response in swaddling layers of Sifusoft. Ghostly data flickers and scrolls at the perimeter of my vision: heart rate, blood pressure, oxygenation, fetal heart rate, all piped directly to my optic nerve by my MedAssist implant.

Maya cranes her neck around to see me. "Dr. Mendoza? Lily?" Her words slur under the drugs, come out slow and dreamy.

"Yes?"

"I can feel it kicking."

My neck prickles. I force a smile. "They're natal phantasms. Illusions generated by the gestation process."

"No." Maya shakes her head, emphatic. "I feel it. It's kicking." She touches her belly. "I feel it now."

I come around the natal sheet and touch her hand. "It's all right, Maya. Let's just relax. I'll see what we can do to keep you comfortable."

Ben leans down and kisses his wife's cheek. "You're doing great, honey, just a little longer."

I give her hand a reassuring pat. "You're doing a wonderful thing for your baby. Let's just relax now and let nature take its course."

Maya smiles dreamily in agreement and her head rolls back. I let out a breath I hadn't known I was holding and start to turn away. Maya lurches upright. She stares at me, suddenly alert, as if all the birthing drugs have been lifted off her like a blanket, leaving her cold and awake and aggressive.

Her dark eyes narrow with madness. "You're going to kill it."

Uh-oh. I thumb my belt unit for the orderlies.

She grabs Ben by the shoulder. "Don't let her take it. It's alive, honey. Alive!"

"Honey—"

She yanks him close. "Don't let her take our baby!" She turns and snarls at me. "Get out. Get out!" She lunges for a water glass on her bedside table. "Get out!" She flings it at me. I duck and it shatters against the wall. Glass shards pepper my neck. I get ready to dodge another attack but instead Maya grabs the natal sheet and yanks it down, exposing her nude lower half splayed for birth. She claws at her birth stirrups like a wolf in a trap.

I spin the dials on my belt remote, jam up her Purnate and shut off her Sifusoft as she throws herself against the stirrups again. The birthing table tilts alarmingly. I lunge to catch it. She flails at me and her nails gouge my face. I jerk away, clutching my cheek. I wave to her husband, who is standing dumbly on the opposite side of the birth table, staring. "Help me hold her!"

He snaps out of his paralysis; together we wrestle her back onto the table and then a new contraction hits and she sobs and curls in on herself. Without Sifusoft, there is nothing to hide the birth's intensity. She rocks against the pain, shaking her head and moaning, small and beaten. I feel like a bully. But I don't restart the pain killers.

She moans, "Oh God. Oh, God. Oh. God."

Benjamin puts his head down beside her, strokes her face. "It's okay, honey. It's going to be fine." He looks up at me, hoping for confirmation. I make myself nod.

Another Purnate-induced contraction hits. They're coming fast now, her body completely in the grip of the overdose I've flushed into her. She pulls her husband close and whispers, "I don't want this, honey. Please, it's a sin." Another contraction hits. Less than twenty seconds apart.

Two thick-armed female orderlies draped in friendly pink blouses finally come thumping through the door and move to restrain her. The cavalry always arrives too late. Maya brushes at them weakly until another contraction hits. Her naked body arches as the baby begins its final passage into our world.

"The pretty queen of the hypocritic oath arrives."

Dmitri sits amongst his brood, my sin and my redemption bound in one gaunt and sickly man. His shoulders rise and fall with labored asthmatic breathing. His cynical blue eyes bore into me. "You're bloodied."

I touch my face, come away with wet fingers. "A patient went natal."

All around us, Dmitri's test subjects scamper, shrieking and warring, an entire tribe of miscalibrated humanity, all gathered together under Dmitri's care. If I key in patient numbers on my belt unit, I get MedAssist laundry lists of pituitary misfires, adrenal tumors, sexual malformations, attention and learning disorders, thyroid malfunctions, IQ fall-offs, hyperactivity and aggression. An entire ward full of poster-children for chemical legislation that never finds its way out of government committee.

"Your patient went natal." Dmitri's chuckle comes as a low wheeze. Even in this triple-filtered air of the hospital's chemical intervention ward, he barely takes enough oxygen to stay alive. "What a surprise. Emotion trumps science once again." His fingers drum compulsively on the bed of an inert child beside him: a five-year old girl with the breasts of a grown woman. His eyes flick to the body and back to me. "No one seems to want prenatal care these days, do they?"

Against my will, I blush; Dmitri's mocking laughter rises briefly before dissolving into coughing spasms that leave him keeled over and gasping. He wipes his mouth on his lab coat's sleeve and studies the resulting bloody smear. "You should have sent her to me. I could have convinced her."

Beside us, the girl lies like a wax dummy, staring at the ceiling.

Some bizarre cocktail of endocrine disruptors has rendered her completely catatonic. The sight of her gives me courage. "Do you have any more squeegees?"

Dmitri laughs, sly and insinuating. His eyes flick to my damaged cheek. "And what would your sharp-nailed patient say, if she found out?"

"Please, Dmitri. Don't. I hate myself enough already."

"I'm sure. Caught between your religion and your profession. I'm surprised your husband even tolerates your work."

I look away. "He prays for me."

"God solves everything, I understand."

"Don't."

Dmitri smiles. "It's probably what I've missed in my research. We should all just beg God to keep babies from absorbing their mother's chemical sludge. With a little Sunday prayer, Lily, you can go back to pushing folate and vitamins. Problem solved." He stands abruptly, coming to his full six-and-a-half feet like a spider unfolding. "Come, let us consummate your hypocrisy before you change your mind. I couldn't bear it if you decided to rely on your faith."

Inside Dmitri's lab, fluorescent lights glare down on stainless steel countertops and test equipment.

Dmitri rustles through drawers one after another, searching. On the countertop before him, a gobbet of flesh lies marooned, wet and incongruous on the sterile gleaming surface. He catches me staring at it.

"You will not recognize it. You must imagine it smaller."

One portion is larger than an eyeball. The rest is slender, a dangling subsection off the main mass. Meat and veiny fatty gunk. Dmitri rustles through another drawer. Without looking up, he answers his own riddle. "A pituitary gland. From an eight-year-old female. She had terrible headaches."

I suck in my breath. Even for Chem-Int, it's a freak of nature.

Dmitri smiles at my reaction. "Ten times oversized. Not from a vulnerable population, either: excellent prenatal care, good filter-mask practices, low-pesticide food sources." He shrugs. "We are losing our battle, I think." He opens another drawer. "Ah. Here." He pulls out a foil-wrapped square the size of a condom, stamped in black and yellow, and offers it to me. "My trials have already recorded the dose as dispensed. It shouldn't affect the statistics." He nods at the flesh gobbet. "And certainly, she will not miss it."

The foil is stamped "NOT FOR SALE" along with a tracking number and the intertwined DNA and microscope icon of the FDA Human Trials Division. I reach for it, but Dmitri pulls it away. "Put it on before you leave. It has a new backing: cellular foil. Trackable. You can only wear it in the hospital." He tosses me the packet, shrugs apologetically. "Our sponsors think too many doses are walking away."

"How long do I need to wear it before I can leave?"

"Three hours will give you most of the dose."

"Enough?"

"Who knows? Who cares? Already you avoid the best treatment. You will reap what you sow."

I don't have a retort. Dmitri knows me too well to feed him the stories I tell myself, the ones that comfort me at 3 a.m. when Justin's asleep and I'm staring at the ceiling listening to his steady honest breathing: It's for our marriage… It's for our future… It's for our baby.

I strip off the backing, untuck my blouse and unbutton my slacks. I slip the derm down under the waistband of my panties. As it attaches to my skin, I imagine cleansing medicine flowing into me. For all his taunts, Dmitri has given me salvation and, suddenly, I'm overwhelmed with gratitude. "We owe you, Dmitri. Really. We couldn't have waited until the trials finished."

Dmitri grunts acknowledgment. He is busy prodding the dead girl's bloated pituitary. "You could never have afforded it, anyway. It is too good for everyone to have."

The squeegee hits me on the El.

One minute, I'm sitting and smiling at the kids across the aisle, with their Hello Kitty and their Burn Girl filter masks, and the next minute, I'm doubled over, ripping off my own mask, and gagging. The girls stare at me like I'm a junkie. Another wave of nausea hits and I stop caring what they think. I sit doubled over on my seat, trying to keep my hair out of my face and vomiting on the floor between my shoes.

By the time I reach my stop, I can barely stand. I vomit again on the platform, going down on hands and knees. I have to force myself not to crawl down from the El. Even in the winter cold, I'm sweating. The crowds part around me, boots and coats and scarves and filter masks. Glittering news chips in men's sideburns and women with braided microfilament glo-strands stepping around me, laughing with silver lipsticks. Kaleidoscope streets: lights and traffic and dust and coal diesel exhaust. Muddy and wet. My face is wet and I can't remember if I've fallen in the murk of a curb or if this is my vomit.

I find my apartment by luck, manage to stand until the elevator comes. My wrist implant radios open the apartment's locks.

Justin jumps up as I shove open the door. "Lily?"

I retch again, but I've left my stomach on the street. I wave him away and stumble for the shower, stripping off my coat and blouse as I go. I curl into a ball on the cold white tiles while the shower warms. I fumble with the straps on my bra, but I can't work the catch. I gag again, shuddering as the squeegee rips through me.

Justin's socks are standing beside me: the black pair with the hole in the toe. He kneels; his hand touches my bare back. "What's wrong?"

I turn away, afraid to let him see my filthy face. "What do you think?"

Sweat covers me. I'm shivering. Steam has started pouring up from the tiles. I push aside the cotton shower curtain and crawl in, letting the water soak my remaining clothes. Hot water pours over me. I finally drag off my bra, let it drop on the puddled tiles.

"This can't be right." He reaches in to touch me, but pulls away when I start gagging again.

The retching passes. I can breathe. "It's normal." My words whisper out. My throat is raw with vomit. I don't know if he hears me or not. I pry off my soggy slacks and underwear. Sit on the tiles, let the water pour over me, let my face press against one tiled wall. "Dmitri says it's normal. Half the subjects experience nausea. Doesn't affect efficacy."

I start retching again but it's not as bad now. The wall feels wonderfully cool.

"You don't have to do this, Lily."

I roll my head around, try to see him. "You want a baby, don't you?"

"Yeah, but…"

"Yeah." I let my face press against tile again. "If we're not doing prenatal, I don't have a choice."

The squeegee's next wave is hitting me. I'm sweating. I'm suddenly so hot I can't breathe. Every time is worse than the last. I should tell Dmitri, for his trial data.

Justin tries again. "Not all natural babies turn out bad. We don't even know what these drugs are doing to you."

I force myself to stand. Lean against the wall and turn up the cold water. I fumble for the soap…drop it. Leave it lying by the drain. "Clinicals in Bangladesh…were good. Better than before. FDA could approve now…if they wanted." I'm panting with the heat. I open my mouth and drink unfiltered water from the shower head. It doesn't matter. I can almost feel PCBs and dioxins and phthalates gushing out of my pores and running off my body. Good-bye hormone mimics. Hello healthy baby.

"You're insane." Justin lets the shower curtain fall into place.

I shove my face back into the cool spray. He won't admit it, but he wants me to keep doing this; he loves that I'm doing this for him. For our kids. Our kids will be able to spell and to draw a stick figure, and I'm the only one who gets dirty. I can live with that. I swallow more water. I'm burning up.

Fueled by the overdose of Purnate, the baby arrives in minutes. The mucky hair of a newborn shows and recedes. I touch the head as it crowns. "You're almost there, Maya."

Again, a contraction. The head emerges into my hands: a pinched old man's face, protruding from Maya's body like a golem from the earth. Another two pushes and it spills from her. I clutch the slick body to me as an orderly snips the umbilical cord.

The MedAssist data on its heart rate flickers red at the corner of my vision, flatlines.

Maya is staring at me. The natal screen is down; she can see everything we wish prenatal patients would never see. Her skin is flushed. Her black hair clings sweaty to her face. "Is it boy or a girl?" she slurs.

I am frozen, crucified by her gaze. I duck my head. "It's neither."

I turn and let the bloody wet mass slip out of my hands and into the trash. Perfume hides the iron scent that has blossomed in the air. Down in the canister, the baby is curled in on itself, impossibly small.

"Is it a boy or a girl?"

Ben's eyes are so wide, he looks like he'll never blink again. "It's okay honey. It wasn't either. That's for the next one. You know that."

Maya looks stricken. "But I felt it kick."

The blue placental sack spills out of her. I dump it in the canister with the baby and shut down Maya's Purnate. Pitocin has already cut off what little bleeding she has. The orderlies cover Maya with a fresh sheet. "I felt it," she says. "It wasn't dead at all. It was alive. A boy. I felt him."

I thumb up a round of Delonol. She falls silent. One of the orderlies wheels her out as the other begins straightening the room. She resets the natal screen in the sockets over the bed. Ready for the next patient. I sit beside the biohazard bin with my head between my legs and breathe. Just breathe. My face burns with the slashes of Maya's nails.

Eventually I make myself stand and carry the bio-bin over to the waste chute, and crack it open. The body lies curled inside. They always seem so large when they pour from their mothers, but now, in its biohazard can, it's tiny.

It's nothing, I tell myself. Even with its miniature hands and squinched face and little penis, it's nothing. Just a vessel for contaminants. I killed it within weeks of conception with a steady low dose of neurotoxins to burn out its brain and paralyze its movements while it developed in the womb. It's nothing. Just something to scour the fat cells of a woman who sits at the top of a poisoned food chain, and who wants to have a baby. It's nothing.

I lift the canister and pour the body into suction. It disappears, carrying the chemical load of its mother down to incineration. An offering. A floppy sacrifice of blood and cells and humanity so that the next child will have a future.

DARKOUT
E. Lily Yu

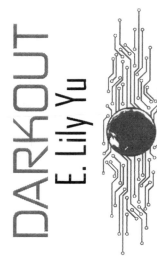

DARKOUT
E. Lily Yu

In all of Northchester, Pennsylvania there was hardly forty square feet that was not continuously exposed to public view, on glass walls if you had money or on tablets if you were poor. This meant that Brandon spent most nights after his shift at the sports store watching Emma, his latest ex and the prettiest, as she chopped garlic, buttered toast, poured herself a gin and tonic, propped her furry-slippered feet on the coffee table with ska pulsing from her speakers, or took a date to bed. The counter at the upper right corner of the wall shifted between four and seven total viewers when Emma was eating dinner or clipping her fingernails. It shot up as high as fifty-five if Emma was mussing her lipstick and her zebra-print sheets with a fresh conquest. One hundred viewers was when ads floated up, loud and flashing, for limpness, smallness, underperformance.

Sometimes Brandon was disappointed in his relative unpopularity, his counter's slow tick of zero, one, zero, one, two, one, but then, white men tended to attract fewer eyeballs. The Indian family on Decker and Main, with two toddlers, boring as paint but only one of two nonwhite households on the east side of the tracks, attracted a dependable twenty every night. You needed pizzazz, or mystery, or difference to become a peripheral home-cam star. You needed nothing but a screen and a billed connection to lurk on others' cam streams.

These days he could hardly remember life without the cameras, although they had only been installed ten years ago, after the passage of the Blue Eye Act. As Little England and China had demonstrated, where there was universal surveillance, crime rates plummeted. Russia, Zambia, Egypt, and Japan adopted similar systems roughly at the same time as the States, and most other wealthy countries were testing a limited rollout in their ghettos and shantytowns.

Brandon hadn't glanced at the newscast for more than a few seconds. "Eyes once were said to be the windows to a man's soul," the Attorney General thundered from her podium, beside the glum chief of Central. "With the passage of this Act, windows shall look into every person's soul. Not one potential criminal or terrorist will live unwatched."

Bored and oblivious to history's apparition on his screen, Brandon flipped to an episode of *Snowballers III*.

There were restrictions and concessions to privacy lobbies, of course. Only badges could check logs or monitor, and only then with a warrant. The software was written to prevent remote modification. Two years after deployment, however, Croatian hackers cracked encryptions and began charging for views of the American of your choice. Actresses, usually. A mild fuss was made. Some feminists penned screeds and circulated petitions.

With the rafts of necessary legislation already in force, thirteen of the thirty original contractors and subcontractors out of business, and the budget long since buried beneath truckloads of additional appropriation bills, a complete overhaul of the hardware and individual installation of security patches were as politically feasible as open borders. After long debate, the white-hat community reached a general consensus to open-source the Croatian exploit, so that everyone and everything could be seen at all times. A bright and egalitarian future had arrived, they argued, superseding the dark days of cold cases, unreliable eyewitnesses, and domestic terrorism. Most citizens had become accustomed to the idea of being watched, anyway. Polls suggested a solid seventy-nine percent enjoyed the constant access to celebrities' meals and wardrobes.

A front-row seat to hours of Emma's smooth shoulders was an unexpected personal consequence of that legislation. After darkening his wall and pressing his palms against his tired eyes, Brandon considered, not for the first time, taking two weeks off from work and a hike along the West Coast. Emma was a drug, the perfect drug, and after a six-month hit of her, he was clawing through withdrawal. The pillow forts she used to build, the shape of her feet, her high, delighted laughter when he landed the perfect joke: the memories burned like poison, and he could not stop drinking them in.

Sweat, grit, sunlight, distance, and mai tais might cure him. He had done the budget. He had saved enough for a short vacation. The customers at the sports store who swiped kayaks and paddleboards onto silver credit cards, with their freckled shoulders, bronzed cheeks, and bleached hair, always seemed to him an alien species, possessed of a thousand-and-one adventures and the insulation provided by ready cash. He could join them, however briefly.

Brandon powered down his screen and stared out the glass wall at the dead light and gray grass of winter, imagining hot white sand between his toes and the cool spray of the Pacific on his face. He was learning to surf from a wise old instructor. He carried the board under his arm like a knight riding into battle and rode the smooth roaring waves hour after hour, day after day, until the water pounded his thoughts into nothingness. His chalky skin darkened. He ate six swordfish steaks for dinner, bought a drink for every pretty brunette in the bar, and forgot about Emma.

But then the flickering stream of panoptic views into kitchens and bedrooms, kitten-crammed commercials, and staged cop shows, all the cheap and irresistible glitter of secondhand life, sang to him him again. Depressing a button, Brandon turned the wall opaque and went back to watching Emma curl and uncurl her toes, his heart in his mouth.

He was waiting for her to collapse into tears. He was waiting for her to scribble on a poster with a squeaking marker and hold it up to her bedroom camera: I LOVE YOU BRANDON. IT WAS A MISTAKE. COME BACK.

When he saw that, when he and the ten strangers on her stream saw he was victorious at last, Brandon would hop into his sneakers and sprint the six miles across town to her apartment, pumping his arms, dodging cars, the Internet cheering unheard in the background. He would hammer on her door. In his imagination, she was pacing the room in her black lace bra and matching panties, a loose robe around her shoulders. Her audience had swelled to two thousand during his dramatic run. She flung open the door and pressed her unblotched and tastefully rouged face to his shoulder. He put his arms around her, and they sank onto the zebra sheets, to the unheard sighs of thousands of spectators. It wasn't impossible. These things were known to happen.

Once in a while Brandon heard the squeak of a marker in a dream, catapulted out of bed, and yanked on socks and shoes before he was entirely awake. But his morning wall only ever showed him commercials for insurance and whole-wheat cereal, tiled four by four.

Tonight, though, he did not linger on Emma's stream. It was the night of the Fitz-Ramen Bowl. He had swapped shifts with Mandy to watch it. Mark Thompson was coming with two twelve-packs of craft beer.

"I need to get out of the house. You need to get out of your head," Mark had said. "You've got the subscription. I'll get the drinks."

Their friendship began four years ago, when Mark, observing Brandon's painful attempt to charm an out-of-town marketing rep in the bar, sent along a pint of porter and a napkin penned with ratings: Confidence 2, Slickness 0, Desperation 17. An electrician, Mark was a good fifteen years older than Brandon and married to a sweet talker of a woman who never found fault with him.

He was not at all someone Brandon would have expected as a friend. Brandon did not have many friends.

But Mark's taste in beers was excellent, and over the latest microwbrew he confided to Brandon that listening to him brought back the rush and risk of youth, the gambits and heartbreaks and exuberant successes. So did football, which he had to watch out of the house, because his wife slept early, and lightly, and not well.

"A bad back," he said, shaking his head. "Like her father."

So when Mark buzzed the door, and the camera floated his face over the screen, Brandon felt his spirits lift. The two of them popped their beers, propped their feet on the table, and cheered the Pittsburgh College Lynxes. During the commercials they flipped to live cop cams outside the stadium, betting on whether the nastiest officers would be reprimanded. Mark set up a private pool on his phone, floating fives and tens, and they passed it back and forth.

"Do you or don't you understand English? You come to this country, you better learn English—" The driver stared down at his lap. His hands gripped the wheel.

"Five bucks no one remembers." Brandon emptied his can.

"Nope, not taking it. He's Bengali."

"They're all brown to me."

"The accent."

"So?"

"They don't get big Internet mobs. Not like the Indians. Polite complaint from the Association of Bengali Cabdrivers, that's all. *Sir it has come to our attention that, and would you pretty please.*"

"Why do they still do traffic stops? You can ID the plates in two cameras, calculate speed, deliver ticket. Wham."

"Maybe they're bored on patrol. Maybe they don't want people watching them sit on their hands. Makes the taxpayer think about payroll."

After Mark's wagers hit a hundred dollars and change, he pocketed the phone. "Personal limit," he said, smiling. "Lizzie's been on my case."

Humming, he appropriated the remote and browsed a DV forecaster. Past emergency call records, crunched for patterns, allowed you to time future incidents so accurately that the popcorn you put in the microwave reached its last thuck, thuck as the boyfriend kicked open the door. A few predictive statistics blogs published regular watching guides. Politicians and athletes attracted the most attention, but the smart ones paid for darkspace: for a million per square foot hour, the ten most popular hosts stopped streaming your cams.

Logs remained available to the police, and a determined viewer, with some finagling, could connect directly to the right camera, but for the most part darkspace worked. A cheaper option was to smash the camera outright. That was a felony, but so was everything that followed.

At 1818 Maple Drive, the microphone still functioned. Brandon grimaced at the screaming and smack of fist against flesh and switched the whole wall back to the game.

"Why do you watch this shit?"

"Third and a long thirteen, Stallions on the Lynxes' twenty-six, Washington is back to pass, Rodriguez is open—it's intercepted by Jones!"

"That's my man!" Mark said. "How long can you go in a shit job in a shit economy before snapping? The game's rigged against white men, you know that. Sometimes it's relaxing to see someone hit his breaking point."

"How do you know that guy was white?"

"The way she was hollering. Black women holler differently."

"Don't tell me you hit Lizzie."

"Never. Cams, though. Used to think there was something they knew that we didn't, so I watched sixteen families at a time. But no. They do holler different when the men beat them, though. They're used to violence. They're violent people. Not like us."

"The Lynxes are putting this game out of reach early, up twenty-four points with four minutes left in the first quarter."

Mark made a noise of satisfaction and grinned.

"Football's not relaxing enough?"

"It's fine. But it's tame. Ever since the concussion lawsuits. The old stuff was better."

Brandon cut to a channel forum and scrolled down the top-ranked links.

MUKWA, WISCONSIN PUPPYCAMS 1-6
$$$WANK TOKYO NEIGHBORHOOD ON FIRE
HIGH COURT TIZZY, CUTE AUSSIE ACCENTS
BLONDE BITCH PAID SEX W/ MY HUSBAND
RIOT POLICE CIRCLING US CAPITOL
SEX SEX SEX WITCHITA XXX
CATFIGHT BETWEEN OFFICER, BLACK WOMAN IN FIVE INCH HEELS
SEE: PROTESTER ARRESTS NEAR US SUPREME COURT
TURTLE FEEDING TIME: GRAPES

"How about them puppies," Mark said.

"I thought you'd be all over SEX SEX SEX WITCHITA."

"It's always some hag pushing seventy," Mark said. "Floppy in all the interesting places. Thought you knew that."

"That's bottom feeding. I don't trawl. The professional stuff's better."

"Sure, or you're interested in one person and no one else." Mark grinned wide enough for Brandon to see his silver fillings and tossed back the rest of his beer. He was in an expansive mood, as if he had both money and holy water on tap. "Seriously, start dating again. Lay some ladies. You'll feel better."

"What does Lizzie say when you talk to her about black people and how much you're suffering?"

"I don't. Because I'm a smart man. I mean, I'm lucky, I'll always have a job. But this Korean woman at the pharmacy yesterday, listen to this, she came up to me and said, I don't like the way you're looking at me. That's the world we live in today. Christ. Maybe I'll see her on the DV watch someday. Don't you dream about smacking whatshername a good one?"

Brandon did, but he wasn't about to admit it.

"I'll sign you up on a few sites," Mark said. "Write you an A-plus profile. I'm good at them."

"You're married."

"That supposed to stop me? She's black, it's different. You wouldn't understand. Go ahead, run me over with a moral locomotive."

"Don't be an idiot."

"So what's the problem? You swipe up full of STDs?"

"I don't like them looking at medical. Full access for a week, no guaranteed sex. I'm sequenced and everything. Who says they won't copy and sell?"

"Hey, you have to give to get."

Brandon pitched his voice higher. "'Oh, you make twenty-four thousand a year?' 'You had appendicitis at sixteen? Wow.'"

"So you watch home cams. For the human contact. Is that it?"

Mark pinched the controller, quartered the screen, and flashed through a

rapid succession of cams. A teenager doodling in his textbook.
A woman working on a tablet, her face furrowed. An aged
brown woman dumping chilies into a pot. A snoring cat. A
man typing at a table. Two cats batting each other. An infant
banging a rattle on the bars of her crib. Two men lifting free
weights, mouths scrunched with the effort. A poodle peeing
against a tree.

"Amazing." He smirked.

"It's culture," Brandon said. "Walking in other people's
shoes. Makes me a better person. Lay off."

"You want culture, fuck a brown woman. I'm unbelievably
cultured. I'm just saying, as your friend, you should get out more."

"What is this, an intervention?"

"If you give me your phone—"

"Go to the game, it's back on."

Four minutes into the fourth quarter, Mark's good mood
was gone.

"What happened to our lead?"

"Oof," Brandon said.

"What kind of shit play was that?" Mark punched the table
so hard his beer rocked over.

"Easy there."

"The coach is a scab-assed cockcrab. How do you burn a
lead like that? How?"

Brandon mopped at the frothy mess of beer and sodden
chips. "Every damn year."

"We're doomed." A flask appeared in Mark's hand.

"Put that down, you're drunk."

"I'm sober as a fucking duck. Me and Lizzie are screwed."

"What are you talking about?"

Mark reclaimed the controller and input a numerical
camera address Brandon did not recognize, but from the first
few digits guessed it was located somewhere in Pittsburgh's
swankiest district. On his screen, now, a bald white woman
sipped a salted glass while watching the game. She had a
cottonmouth tattooed around her neck, red and black heels
like ice picks, and six spikes in each ear. Noticing the uptick in
her viewer count, she turned and flashed the camera a thumbs-
up and a smile that crawled under Brandon's skin and itched.

"Who's that?" Brandon said, very slowly.

"My bookie. Ruth. Name's a joke, not for real. Short for—"

"You have the cash. Right?"

"This was supposed to be a straight-to-the-bank payday. Like the last one."

"The last one."

"I won a thousand betting a three-team parlay last year. She shook my head and told me I looked like a lucky man. 'When you want to make a real bet,' she said, 'with real money, think of me.'"

Ruth stared at the camera as if she could see them, her mouth still hooked in that crowbar of a smile.

Brandon flipped the whole wall back to the game, as if the scrum of blue, red, orange, and white could scrub the prickling off the back of his neck. The scene that greeted him wasn't much more cheerful. The Stallions were down by a single touchdown, and the whole tableau had the velvet air of a Shakespearean tragedy.

Here came the touchdown. Here the conversion.

Mark's head fell into his hands. The last thirty seconds slipped off the clock. Brandon held his beer to his lips with nerveless fingers.

The Stallions won, thirty-two to thirty-one. They flooded the field with blue and red, dancing, howling, cracking their helmets together.

"What do you do now?" Brandon said.

"Fuck if I know." Mark groaned. "She knows my address. Home and work. She has my contacts, too. Runs a background check for big wagers. So she'd know to look at you—"

As if in quiet confirmation, the little zero on the counter flicked to one. Brandon swallowed and wiped his mouth with the back of his hand.

"How much?"

"Ten thousand. It was one to two, I don't know why, Lynxes were favorite. I was gonna triple that—"

Brandon kneaded his temples. "Bonehead."

"Did you pick that up from Lizzie?"

"What were you going to do with thirty thousand?" That wasn't two weeks' vacation and surfing lessons. That was a year of rent on a ranch house somewhere in wine country and a wine tour every month. That was a plane ticket to a dark and disconnected country of grapevines and beautiful women, perhaps even kind women, and bedrooms and breakups without cameras.

"Don't lecture me."

"What were you going to blow it on? Weed? Speed? Cars?"

"Old lady needs spinal fusion, if you have to know."

"But insurance—"

"We don't have any."

"You need brain surgery."

Mark scowled. "I was trying to do right by her."

"Mortgage? Second mortgage? Sell the van?"

"Double mortgage already, from the doctors and pills. Need the van for work. We're up to our eyeballs." Mark took a deep breath. "Now you know how fucked we are. I hate doing this, Brandon, but—"

"You couldn't go with a Chinese bookie, could you? You had to get a local."

"Ruth gives better odds than the congloms. Plus she let me bet on credit."

Brandon flung the controller. It clattered satisfyingly against the wall and dropped out of sight. "Of course she let you, bumfuck. She knows where you live. Where Lizzie lives."

"I get it, I get it. So—"

"She can't do anything to you, right? Not with—" He gestured to the cameras.

"I've heard Ruth doesn't like dirtying her nails."

"That's a relief."

"So she contracts disposal and retrieval."

"Would I have heard of her?"

"Nothing splashy since six, seven years ago."

"Six—"

"The Burnetts." Mark shifted his weight. "The, uh, two girls, one boy, parents, grandfather, Dalmatian, and hamster. And one goldfish. Though maybe not the goldfish, those things die if you sneeze at them…"

"That was her?"

"Unofficially."

"Shit."

"Anyway, if she wants it quiet, she buys black."

"You're fucked."

"Royally." Mark blinked and grinned in terror. "So what I was going to ask—"

"Why mix me up in this? Why sit on my sofa and scarf my chips, with thirty grand riding on the game?"

"Lizzie's asleep. I wanted a friend—if I was going to celebrate—"

"Bullshit. You wanted me here in case you lost. So you could dun me for cash."

"You're angry, I get it. You're angry but I'm fucked."

Whether because the controller landed on a button or whether because the paid sportstream sensed their drifting attention, the postgame analysis switched to news. Thousands of masked protestors milled in the National Mall, waving

single yellow roses splattered with black paint. GIVE US DARKNESS, their placards read. PRIVACY IS FREEDOM. The cameras faded from night to day, gliding from D.C. to San Francisco to Tokyo to Moscow. Every cosmopolis was boiling with protests. DARKOUT! DARKOUT!

"Motherfucking Luddites," Mark said.

"Don't change the subject. You dragged me into this. She's probably auditing me right now. What do you think she'll see? Do you think I have ten grand in my sock drawer?"

"I have two thousand in emergency funds," Mark said. "Lizzie made me. I only need eight."

"Great. Pick a star, click your heels, wish really, really hard—"

"Are you going to help me?" Mark pressed an empty can between his palms until it gave. "The way I helped you, when you totaled your car? When Nina dumped you and your shit on the curb?" It had been raining, and the cardboard boxes melted like sugar. When Brandon called, Mark laughed his ass off, but showed up five minutes later with his van. He had even dug up a dolly somewhere.

"You piece of gooseshit." Brandon knuckled his eye sockets. Then he pulled out a phone and scrawled a passpattern with his fingertip. "Look at that balance, you fucking moron. Two thousand six hundred and I don't get paid until next Friday. Look at it!" He thrust the phone into Mark's face and watched Mark's pupils cross.

"I was going to California with this," Brandon said bitterly. He dragged two fingers over the phone and signed with his index finger. "There. Two thousand four hundred in your account tomorrow." He waved his phone at the camera. "See that, Ruth? He's got almost half of it. Charge him stupid interest and don't break his leg. Now get out, dickbrain."

"I'll pay you back."

"You're still short five thousand and change."

"Yeah."

"And Lizzie still needs a new back."

"That can wait."

"Like hell it can. My uncle slipped a disc once. Couldn't look at his face, or I started hurting too. Put her first for once."

Sudden motions and shouts pulled Brandon's eye back to the screen. A wave of protestors swelled and broke over a police barricade in Beijing. The air went blue and blurry with tear gas. The synchrony of their movements suggested careful rehearsal, which could only be coordinated online. In China, public spaces were off limits. The police would have noticed the preparations. Every security apparatus would have known.

Hopeless, all of them.

In the meantime, his own counter reached five, a personal record. Casual browsers attracted by the shouting? DISAPPOINTED LYNX BROS YELLING. Or black-jacketed, detached men with freshly fingerprinted contracts?

"You're a real friend, you know that?" Mark said. "I'm not going to forget this."

"Door's there. Get out."

"Going, I'm going." Mark slung his coat over his shoulders and banged open the screen door. Cold air swirled in. Brandon dimmed his wall to transparency and peered into the darkness, shivering, until Mark peeled out of the neighborhood in his anchovy can.

Asshole.

He brought his screen back up and stared at masks, placards, yellow roses. A svelte, lipsticked newscaster would have relieved the oppressiveness, but any newscaster was a rarity these days, when free and instant footage flowed everywhere. Who could keep up with that?

"Give us darkness! Darkout! Darkout!"

The news stream wasn't helping his nerves. Brandon retrieved the controller from behind an armchair and returned to his usual forum, cracking open a seventh beer.

CRAZY GUY SCALING BROADCAST STATION PERIMETER: SHOT OR NOT?

DUCKLINGS HATCHING!!!

TRESPASSERS AT ISP HQ?

SEXY BROWN SUGAR MMM

STALLION FANS RIOT IN HOUSTON, VIEW FROM GRAY'S BAR

As if of their own volition, his fingers tapped their way back to Emma's stream.

Kitchen: dark.

Living room: dark.

Bedroom: dark, too, but a slice of orange light from the street slipped under the blinds and threw a soft glow on her bare arms, a long loose curl, the gentle hills of her body under the comforters.

She was asleep. Her chest was rising and falling, rising and falling, and her breath made a fluttering, feathery sound through her lips that the microphone picked up and whispered to him. He remembered the sound from the seventeen times she fell asleep in his bed and the ten times he had slept in hers.

"I am a pathetic creep," he said aloud to his own five

watchers. The whole world was his confessional, tonight. But as the words left his mouth, his own counter flickered: four—three—one—zero. No one wanted to hear him grovel.

"You still love me," he told Emma. She was just as lonely as he was. She was auditioning an endless river of men to fill a Brandon-sized hole inside her. And she never looked at his cam stream. Not once.

Not casually.

Not for a second.

Not as one of four or eight or sixteen streams split on her screen.

As if she didn't miss him at all.

The rhythm of her breath was soothing and soporific. He could listen to it forever.

His seventh beer half empty, feeling infinitely sorry for himself, Brandon slept.

He dreamed he was in California. It was a nice dream, with plenty of sunlight and blue sky and puffy clouds. The trees were spiny and crumpled with drought. He had never been to California, but this looked exactly like what he had seen in movies. Maybe California was more a collective cinematic fantasy than an actual place. Maybe, like an elaborate movie set, it never existed.

He stood in a desert studded with cactuses and hunched pines. Invisible birds cried and piped, and he could hear waves crashing unseen against an invisible shore.

Mirages shimmered everywhere. Mostly they were water mirages, but here was the quivering image of an ice cream cart, and there, on the horizon, stood one of Emma's perfect white breasts, large as a mountain. Why not two? he asked his subconscious. Give me the other one, come on. But the snowy peak shivered and vanished as he approached.

He had been hiking for hours, and his arms and legs were furry with dust. The mountains rising around him muffled the sound of the distant ocean.

One by one, the sharp, croaking bird calls ceased. All around him was a heavy and peculiar silence.

Brandon was accustomed to hearing the babble of strangers on his screen while he slept: any channel, anybody, anything to feel less alone. The absence of sound rang loud as cymbals in his ears. Startled awake, he poured out of bed and puddled on the floor. For several painful minutes he lay still, trying not to move. Someone was using his skull as blender and trashcan and bongos all at once.

The screen had entered standby sometime during the night. It did not show Emma's room, nor his front yard, but rather the illusion of a flat white wall with a window in the center. Brandon pressed the power button. The operating light winked orange, but nothing changed.

"Damn," he said. Mark's beer must have shorted a circuit. But where? And what had he fried? Brandon picked up his phone to troubleshoot and found no signal. He could snap photos, he could play games, and that was all.

Brandon flicked and pushed and plugged and unplugged his watch, his Weatherboy, his scale, his library, his two tablets. All were functional. All were offline. What worried him most were the lights on his three cameras, which had gone from red to yellow. He had no way of placing a support call.

"Fuckity fuck fuck," he said.

He would have to walk downtown to Moby's. No appointment meant fighting through crowds clutching bricked devices and crying for miracles. That would make him at least an hour late for his shift. So he would have to stop at the sports store first, to explain.

His manager could confirm for himself that Brandon's cameras were dead. The law required busted cameras to be fixed within one day. Police arrived, demanding answers, if you didn't. Occasional darkness was only for the very rich, and Brandon did not feel rich at all. Someone like him was not allowed to be offline for long.

His stomach shrank at the thought of eggs and bacon. No breakfast, then. He gave himself a critical once-over in the bathroom mirror: Two bloodshot eyes, a greenish pallor, hair flattened in some places and rucked up in others. He pushed a wet hand over the hair that stuck out, but it bounced straight back.

"Mark, you fucker," he growled. "You dickshot. You douche."

When he went onto the front stoop of the divided house, the morning sun jabbed him in the eye. His breath smoked white from his mouth and nose. Around him the yellow grass glittered and crisped with frost.

The building's palm scan wasn't working. It ignored his hand and did not respond to his slap, but the maintenance light flashed. Swearing under his breath, Brandon dug in his pockets for his analog keys.

His upstairs neighbor, Alice Rosenbaum, crunched over the lawn in scarf and boots. She was in her sixties, with deep wrinkles and snowy hair, and appeared to fall somewhere between the kind of grandmother who invited lonely neighbors in for pie and the kind of grandmother who filed noise complaints punctually at ten each night. She grinned at him.

"That game, huh?" she said. Brandon, patting himself, realized he was still wearing his beer-sticky gear. "I lost fifty dollars on that last play. To my son-in-law. He'll never let me hear the end of it."

"My friend put ten thousand on the Lynxes."

She winced. "You have rich friends."

"He's broke."

"Online?"

"Local."

"Will he be all right?"

"I don't know. I can't call him."

"Right, right. The whole street's down."

"What?"

"I knocked at the Washburns' and asked."

"The Washburns?"

She pointed. "Number eighteen. Two of the cutest little girls."

Brandon couldn't remember ever seeing the family that lived in the yellow house. He felt slow and stupid, like a blind thing in a cave. "What's going on?"

"It's a darkout. Like a blackout. You know what a—no. We haven't had a blackout in twenty-one years. You would have been a kid."

"Someone digging up wires?"

"I don't know. Our phones are dead, too, and the tower's two miles from here. I think it's pretty big. But we won't know until everything's back up."

Mark had caught a break. Brandon hoped the bastard was okay. "How long do you think that'll take?"

"Who knows?" Alice glanced down the street. "I was going to pick up breakfast from the bakery. See if anyone knows. Used to do that when I was younger. You look like a bagel kind of guy. Want to come?"

Brandon hesitated. Someone should check on Mark and Lizzie. Especially Lizzie, who had a raucous belly laugh and mothered him. He hadn't known about her back. But they were ten miles across town, and with lines dead, and no car, what could he do if there was trouble?

Maybe Mark had hocked everything and paid up.

Or maybe, if all cams were dark, his bookie had bigger fish than Mark.

Of course there were bigger fish than Mark.

Mark would be fine.

Emma, though. He felt a pang almost as sharp as the first loss: the cool, cold look, the quick credit swipe for both lunches, as if she pitied him, and the impression of being tossed out along with the sandwich wrappers. He couldn't watch her now. He didn't know where she was or what she was doing, or if she had taken out poster paper and was chewing the end of a marker, thinking about him.

"I could do with a bagel," he said.

And they walked together through the unfamiliar morning, waiting, as the whole world was waiting, for the light to return.

VISIBLE DAMAGE

Stephen Graham Jones

VISIBLE DAMAGE
Stephen Graham Jones

If this were 2028 or something Dark Ages like that, what Mark had just asked for after casing the place, it would—no, it still wouldn't make sense. But it would at least *start* to track. A little.

An ASCII-graph?

Seriously?

"Like, printed out, an artifact?" Raz said, looking around for whatever Mark was worried about. But then he realized: Mark was worried about somebody listening in. To this golden, bulletproof, timeless idea.

An ASCII-graph. Rendering an image in some visual approximation of uncompiled code. But, not just sucking it through a filter, filling the shape of a dog with letters-as-shading, numbers-as-eyes, punctuation to show the tail wagging. Producing that kind of image would be a function, a keystroke, a joke.

Raz wasn't customer service, and he wasn't tech support. He was a photographer, a server paparazzo—thus the handle. Mark's session_ID was because, for the purposes of this meet, that's what he was: the mark.

"What kind of rig you even need to capture one of those?" Raz said, exactly like the challenge it was.

"One that can map pre-engramming," Mark said.

"Something raw, then," Raz said back, rapping his knuckles

once on the tabletop, like meeting Mark's bid here. Really he was cycling through the junk closet back at his conapt. Did he have anything that old, that could kick out a dim silhouette before it processed into his short-term, got all chemicaled up and hormoned down?

Some illegal-old game console, maybe? A back alley hot-hat?

Usually, for a snatch-and-grab, you just used whatever rig was slipperiest and left the least trace. Those were jobs that involved actual *data*, though. Bits and bytes you could hold in your hand, then drop in your pocket, run the synaptic pathways braille-style like you had to, come up deskside gasping and laughing and rich.

Nobody gets rich from an ASCII-graph, though. Not unless they run an antique store.

"I've been told this would be suitable," Mark said, and what he opened on the table wasn't any kind of hardware he'd smuggled in past the scanners. It was a paper-and-ink actual *book*.

"What is this?" Raz said. "Nostalgia week? I miss a news blast?"

Mark had the book open, was scribbling on the inside of the cover. With a *pencil*. Maybe "Mark" was the wrong name for him. "Museum thief" might be more fitting.

He slid the book across for Raz to read: 722.

Raz snorted a laugh, closed the book over that bad idea, lest it flutter up, become real. He slid the book back across the table but Mark caught it, guided it back slowly, holding Raz's eyes the whole time.

"Consider it a gift," Mark said.

"Sure not a down payment," Raz said, holding the book up to eyeball the spine. "Because you're going to need a different cowboy, cowboy."

"Writing on the wall said you had…what was the word?" Mark playacted. "Oh yeah. *Grit*."

"Twitchy line between nerve and suicide," Raz said, leaning forward over the book to make his point. "You know what you're asking me to do here, don't you? A 722? A *pi*-maker?"

"Pie?"

"Pi. As in 3.14 etcetera, *forever*." He finagled the pencil from Mark, traced a thin slash into the rig's name. "Twenty-two divided by seven. The deepest rabbit hole. The one that goes forever."

"It's just a rig."

"They didn't dustshelf all those units because they were bulky or because the haptics fed back seizures. They scrapped them because the interface went a smidge too deep. If there's a glitch on either end, even just a blip, a cough, a hint of the thread starting to unravel, you can get trapped in an infinite regress. It's like a—it's like an algorithm that doesn't know when to cut off, so you keep iterating, keep cycling, waiting for that one variable that can stop the world from sweeping past over and over."

"Take a parachute pill first," Mark said, shrugging. "Put a timer on it."

"Wish I had one ticking now," Raz said, looking around for the glowing door of this discussion board.

In CommonSpace, even shadowy corners like this, the programming was rigid: All exits had to be clearly marked so no tourists would get stuck in a loopy corner for a week or a month or a lifetime.

"I can find somebody else," Mark said.

Raz let his chest shudder with a chuckle. No smile, though. Was every blind-meet in his life going to come down to this? A series of dares? Was that what negotiating was? There had to be another way.

He'd scoped this mark's accounts before logging in, though. It was why he was still here.

"And just what is it I'm supposed to ASCII-graph topside for you?" he said.

It was one of the officially retired animations, Raz was already half-betting. That's what all the collectors always wanted. Or, since this was an ASCII-graph, it would be a *slice* of one of those animations. Some mouse-eared kaiju lumbering around a silicon landscape, its footprints burning neon, its shadow long and chromed, quicksilvering past all borders.

"You've seen the old talkies, right?" Mark said. "About monster lizards rising up from the oceans?"

Bingo-bango.

"Always in slow motion at first," Raz said with a shrug.

"ASCII-graph will make it look more dramatic," Mark said. "It's the only way, really. Any closer and it might sense—"

"It-*what*?"

"It-*it*," Mark leaned forward to whisper, "I have it on good intel that one's really happening. Scout's blood, man. One of the diagnosticians is—let's just say he's in deep with a friend."

"A friend."

Mark didn't even bother to brush this accusation off. "At first they thought the code was bad, or that the hardware was malfunctioning, or that they'd been jacked. But then this one tech-grub, she imaged the error-log, cycled it up for visual recall, and—"

"No way," Raz said, his eyes heating up.

Mark nodded. "The error-log, the shape of it, it fell within the Golden Mean. Far enough inside that it can't be a statistical anomaly."

"You mean it repeated?"

"With variation."

Raz closed his eyes to focus on his breathing. "An AI," he said reverentially.

"The stirrings of one," Mark said, "the yolk of one," and Raz nodded with him, could see it in ASCII-graph: the world-killer, rising up from the slosh of code, lines of programming not just streaming off it, but cycling within it, crackling like a storm.

Every time one was rumored—that was all it ever took: a whisper—the whole Zone would rally against its purported IP, isolate it, carpet-bomb it, ravage the landscape for exponential stratigraphs on every axis from that one point, so that even if it did manage to beat the odds and actually wake, it would suffocate in its lonely data well.

Raz always imagined the people who ran those campaigns wearing white bags over their heads, like the antibodies they thought they were.

There wasn't any word about this AI, though. Not even a distant mumble. Not even a tremor.

Which is exactly the way the paranoids always said it would happen.

But so did the prophets.

"You can guarantee I'll be the only one in there?" Raz said, his vitals spiking from green to red, the warning readouts finding bottles and reflections to embed in all around the room, where Raz had to see, where the mark never would.

"Don't get too close," Mark said. "Just—the graph, it needs to be distant, like. For scale. My clients…they just want documentation. That's all."

"Distant," Raz said, standing, "that's the wrong word, man."

"What do you mean?"

"I mean this is going to be *epic*," Raz said, and reached out to shake on this. To hold onto this moment. To not let it go.

In the downtime before Celya could locate a working 722, Raz puttered around his conapt, touching this shelf, that cup, but always coming back to the window, to look out across the sluggish grey back of the sea again.

He could almost see the AI standing up from it, looking shoreward with its great bored eyes. There were going to be monsters in the world again, for a fraction of a second. For an image. He would process the ASCII-graph pre-engram, sure. But he'd let it run its course after that snapshot, too. This was one job he didn't want to forget.

When Celya still hadn't returned by late afternoon, he logged in, ducked down, puttered up and down Market Street, just trolling for action, doing nothing. It was like that idle moment early in a game, where you're dialing your touch in by rubbing the sides of your fingers on this fabric, on that cool jug.

Soon enough he looked up, though.

Celya was standing there, watching him. She was wearing her Nightengala Cloak that shifted her appearance according to what it could jack from your profile. It meant she looked different to every person.

Except to Raz. To Raz, she looked just like herself. And that was perfect.

"So?" he said.

She turned dramatically, the sweep of her cloak inviting Raz to fall into her swishing wake.

"So," she said when he caught up enough, "word is, you might *think* you want a 722, but in actuality, you don't. No sane runner would."

"You accusing me of being compos mentis?" Raz said.

Celya dialed the Latin in, shook her head once to quit the function.

Some days, that was how Raz could lure her over to his side of things: Hit her with something that appealed to her research bone. If she came back in an even deeper language, it was a sign that things were maybe going to work out.

"It can lock you in," she said, *not* in Etruscan. "What do they call it? Judas Chair?"

"Close," Raz said. "Iron Maiden."

"But you'll be there sitting in your chair. Betraying me."

"I already cased the system I'm ghosting," Raz said. "It's been tested. No glitches on the outside. Eggshell. I just tap once here, once there, follow the crack inside. Ninja see, ninja do. You know how it goes."

Celya turned sharp into a boardroom hissing with deals and secrets but stopped partway through the batwings.

"I'll get this death-rig for you if you want," she said without looking back. "But I told you last time was the last time. If you go under again, you're solo, onanboi."

Raz had figured as much.

It was common practice for people hooked up with paparazzo to break up with them for the duration of the job, in case the dive went bad. Less grief if it's your ex floating up to the surface, not your current throb.

Still.

"You don't understand," Raz said. "This is…it's—"

"More important than me?" Celya messaged back from inside.

Raz stood there on the plankboard sidewalk, the batwing doors flapping in shorter and shorter arcs, penduluming away at the last sliver of cord between him and Celya.

It wasn't just about the money, he wanted to tell her.

If he didn't document this firsthand, get this terrible knowledge out into the Zone, then it might happen unwatched, like everybody'd been skyfalling about for three quarters of a century.

The AI might open its eyes, find the world too annoyingly bright, then reach up, turn the lights off all at once.

Deskside, Raz settled his rig back onto its cradle, paced his conapt some more, finally decided to tune his profile for some much deserved ad-laughs. Nothing better for distraction than dragging a tin-can fan of bots through swale and dale for a while.

Thirty minutes into it, reaching back for a sound effect that was going to be classic, he found that p-book in his stash.

Because he still hadn't got an incoming delivery alert—Celya was good about those, had been a messenger once upon a day—he shuttled it to his printer, went full-on Permanent for the book, not Econo like usual. Mostly because he wasn't sure how long this might take, "reading." Theoretically, he still had the legs for that kind of bicycle. Just, he hoped his legs remembered, because he sure didn't.

The book was heavy in his hands. Paper, ink, a stiff backing at either end, some faked-in wear to make it feel lived-on and -with. Right inside the cover was the "722" the mark had written down, and the slash Raz had made pi with.

Raz shook his head, impressed: An av on a board uses a line of binary or whatever "pencil" means in the simulation to write on a temporary artifact that's just lines of code itself, and now here it is on the table, in the exact same hand.

Raz licked his finger, tried rubbing the grey lines of the 722, but the printer hadn't understood that part, had made the paper grey as deep as Raz could rub.

"So why this book," Raz said, reading the spine again, just to prove to himself, on this side of the login prompt, he really knew how to do that.

It was one of a thousand throwaway hacker biographies, from back when they were all as-told-to. The draw to them, it was never the content or lives supposedly being relayed, it was the voice, the diction—the drawl, they called it. Legions and flocks of historians and academic surfers had tried to parse it, break it down into the code they were sure was being passed on in secret like this, under the guise of illiteracy. Like these grandpa hackers had found a way to port out the slick highways and byways of the server, were trying to stencil that pristine architecture onto the world.

There were no secret lines of out-loud code, though, Raz knew. The way the old-time hackers talked, it was just verbal shorthand, it was what you did when you were meat and every word took X calories to spit, X more calories to hear and process. It was how you spoke when you never actually used your mouth to speak anymore.

This as-told-to was from some frydaddy, as far as Raz could tell. The ones who got burned inside, fell out into their chair and just kept right on falling through the rest of their life, working without a net from here on out, all that.

And the recorder, it wasn't a machine like in some of the biographies, but a flesh and blood person. What this meant was that some prof had probably felt her way under a forgotten bridge, peeled up a sheet of dingy cardboard, and traded food to some poor soul for his life story, so long as it was exciting and deep and had the bright lights everybody always wanted there to be, inside a system so hot it needed refrigerant. So long as this vagrant had a criminal print on the pad of his thumb, or could mumble some lore, or was showing some of the visible damage, this prof would keep mainlining him day-old sandwiches, probably.

Raz told himself not to judge this biographee, this indirect narrator. Got to eat, right? Anyway, what secrets or real and actual lore could there be, from twenty years ago? None of the old cheat codes worked anyway.

Knock-knock? he messaged Celya. Her holding icon was all that came back.

Good. It meant she was somewhere without ears. It meant she was probably negotiating in that way she had where it was do or dead. The 722 would be at the door in two or three shakes, and it would be still in the box, probably. Right off the shelf from twenty years ago, dug up from some impossible treasure trove.

And then she'd see.

They weren't going to be broken up for long, Raz knew.

Just until he snapped this one last pic, and saved the world.

He paged into the book.

What Raz remembered from the as-told-tos from school, it was that the investigator's job was to erase herself. To just be a stenographer. The best listener.

And—this one-time hacker. Some jobs, you dive too deep. Your body floats back up, but your mind, it's still down there somewhere.

If the prof under this bridge hadn't normaled the talk down some, Raz wouldn't have been able to follow even a little.

The hacker was muttering that it was real, he'd seen it.

Raz felt one side of his mouth smile. Of course. This was why the mark had been reading this of all books: Research. He was dragging the riverbed for previous sightings. And he'd either snagged one, or this hacker had enough of his wit left to cue into what this prof under the bridge really wanted.

"Bring on the sandwiches," Raz said, and leaned back on the couch for this.

The sighting was everything the mark would have wanted: grand, historic, slow-motion, the AI blotting out the moon, practically.

The hacker had been hired to skate as close as he could to this baby monster, record what he could, then—this was before parachute pills—tug three times on his line, ride it back up.

Had the mark not read this right before the meet, he probably wouldn't have forked across for the 722 and downpaid on the rest of the job.

"Somebody owes somebody a finder's fee..." Raz mumbled to himself, as if this dialtoned hacker hadn't ratfooded out years ago.

This prof, too, she was one of those academics who assume the rest of the world is stupid, so ends up footnoting everything, like the text needs an understory to keep from sliding off the bottom of the page.

The footnote was on a term this hacker hit, just talking: Droop. It meant Dream + Loop, obviously, and was, for the book's year, and for all the years since, Raz knew, just a theoretical possibility, just another thought problem: the proposition that the perfect server defense would trap the invader in a state of continual narrative, like going taffy in the event horizon of a system.

Supposedly this underbridge hacker, he'd been caught in one of these technically possible droops. And now he couldn't be convinced he wasn't still caught.

The second footnote answered the question the first footnote hadn't been asking. It was why drooping was impossible: The processing power required to maintain a story real enough to believe would drag on the processes the system needed just to run, because story is continually branching. If the next step or room or whatever isn't already prepped, then the illusion's blown.

There was something in the margin by this, though. In Mark's light grey pencil.

AI?

Raz closed the book on his thumb, sat up. It must be cool, he thought, feeling like this mark. Like you just eureka'd polio or relativity or slappers.

Even schoolkids knew AI changed all the games, made all the thought problems thought solutions. An AI *would* have processing to burn, could flypaper as many runners and sneakers-in as it wanted.

He flinched away when Celya's shipping alert popped.

It was counting down from thirty, second by second.

Time, then. Because he'd promised—it was always the promise—he palmed a parachute pill into his mouth. It was only when swallowing that he realized his hand was trembling. No, that was his desk. His desk was humming. From the printer?

It was kicking something out, like the adware had figured out how to hop his fences again. Because it was an insult to get hacked by something that was just stimulus-response, not even really heuristic in a meaningful sense, Raz strode across to the printer, shaking his head no.

Line by dot-matrix line—Raz shook his head no, turned away.

It was an ASCII-graph taking shape.

When the print-head sighed down, the sheet of paper the printer also printed drifted down into the light-duty bay.

The door dinged with package-arrival.

"Wait, wait," Raz said, and reached into the printer, his mouth dry and tacky.

When it wasn't a great terrible god of a monster rising from a slush of code, he actually smiled and breathed in through that smile.

If it had been that, it would mean—he almost laughed at how stupid he was being—it would mean he was in a droop, wouldn't it? That he'd already answered the door, jacked into the 722, slid down for that one golden snapshot.

"Celya," he said, looking at the door.

And also at what was in his hand.

It was her, blurry in uncompiled code.

She was leaning down toward someone. Toward him. And she was wearing a hood, she was wearing her cloak, but she didn't need to for him, she was already everything he wanted.

What she was holding out before her, what she offering down to him, it was rendered in alternating ones and zeroes, to show it was in the foreground.

A sandwich.

Raz looked past it, up past the hand holding it, up the arm

to the face, so she could see the question he wanted to ask but couldn't quite get across.

Every reflective surface in his conapt was flashing red now, except the red was really old-style taillights. Under the bridge.

In Raz's stomach, a pill popped open minutes too early.

It made him cough, and cough.

You can't parachute out of the real world.

When his hand steadied itself long enough to clamp onto this glorious sandwich, it settled down into its day-old self.

"It was, it was *beautiful*," he said through his thick lips, about the baby monster, and the professor batted her eyes to try to keep them from spilling, and Raz, which was short for something, he just couldn't remember, he started trying to tell her about this blind meet he had in a few minutes, he'd gotten the message just now, but he was chewing binary at the same time, and the professor was covering her hand with her mouth now, as if that could hold back tears, so he just closed his eyes, cued ahead to the meet, and swallowed his mouthful of code. Again.

THE IBEX ON THE THE DAY OF EXTINCTION

Minister Faust

THE IBEX ON THE DAY OF EXTINCTION
Minister Faust

Kam Manjiri checked his satellite phone for the fifth time that morning. "Doesn't work for shit," he said, shaking it. "Candi's gonna kill me."

Wiped his forehead and neck with his *kafeeyah*, drank down half a bottle of water. Took off his shades and wiped out his eyewells before re-glassing.

Not even nine a.m. and the sun was already a Chinese gong ramming into his mallet skull, and his heat-headache kept ring-*ing-ing-i-i-ing...*

Got up from the rows he'd just planted, smacked orange dust and sand from his cargo pants, and trudged over to the terrarium.

Squinted into its blinding reflection. The steel geodesic was like half a silver star erupting from the desert. Kam turned back to look at his tender green babies, hoped they'd survive. Hoped the whole project would survive this close to the border with Libya. Crazy to think how much'd changed. Ten years ago people'd fled Niger to go there, regardless of the torturocracy. Had the second-highest standard of living on the continent. Then the West allied with racist Arab jihadis to bomb it into a new Mordor and all the Nigeris who'd gone there'd come running back for their lives.

Not that you could tell that from where Kam was. Empty

and silent: him, his sand rover, his green babies, the terrarium, its halo of silver palm trees drinking the sun. The desert. And no one else.

Tried his phone again, but it was still useless. Charged but offline.

"Candace is gonna *kill* me," he croaked, then drained the last swig before opening the terrarium door.

Inside: darker. Air thick like ocean spray. Put his specs away. Checked all the aeroponics, as he did every time he came in. Sixty white PVC towers gurgling with water, sprouting sixty baby trees a piece: a tree of trees. Checked the solar unit and the main water supply in the centre of the terrarium. The aquifer was still blessing them, and if his wife's calculations were right, Ibex could count on at least another hundred years of water here when Project Green Sash would be complete. Al-Qadhdhaafi was long dead—stabbed to death by Western-backed savages—but Candace's remix of his Great Man Made River Project would live on in Niger. The alchemy of terraria and neo-tech divining rods: amber into emerald, desert into rainforest.

Unslept the laptop, but the Internet was down, too. System said the dish was getting power, but no signal. Didn't make sense, unless maybe the satellite itself was offline or got hit by spacejunk, maybe?

Meanwhile Candace and the kids'd be freaking out. He'd been gone for three days on a weeklong circle of checking his trapline of terraria, sleeping in them and planting as he went. Him being gone for one week a month was S.O.P. in Candi's project—made more sense to do one giant round and then spend three weeks with them at base camp outside of Seguedine than to drive twelve hours of dunes and bad roads each day.

For the last two years, every week out he'd satphoned home every night. This time on Day One when he couldn't call home, he figured the connection problem was temporary; that happened before. But by Day Three when he was really worried—and worried that they were all worried by his silence—he was out so far it felt nuts to head back then. Better just to finish, and keep hoping he'd fix the phone, email from a terrarium, or somewhere out in that vast orange abyss, run into somebody—anybody—who had a functional phone.

Day Four, and still three more days until home…

Checked the ethanol still.

There was enough.

He filled up the sand rover. He'd be back at base camp outside Seguedine before midnight. He'd miss the kids' bed time, but still.

Then, after she knew for sure he was alive, Candace could kill him.

Two hours of driving already. If the path were Manitoba highways, the whole thing'd be only a seven hour trip, but seven hundred clicks over sand, rocks, and "low-ways and unfreeways" (as Candace called them) was up to fourteen hours. The sand rover could make it that far—but if it were running low on fuel or water, he could always stop at one of the terraria on his trapline.

Could really use a decent meal, but there'd be no point stopping at Madama for that. It was nothing more than a military base surrounded by mines, and the French soldiers "helping protect" Niger outnumbered the Nigeri troops two-to-one. Kam had no desire to see that, not after everything France had done to this country, and no reason to believe they'd help him with his phone.

Just wanted to see Candi, Wangari, and Shani. See them smiling. Hear them laughing. Be rolling around the floor with his kids, seven and four, tickling them, airplaning them on his feet, then standing up and turning them upside down in his arms and all of them laughing. Roasting a chicken and stewing cassava with his wife. Massaging her shoulders. Sitting together on the woodhewn loveseat in the living room of their adobe home, with their feet in a pan of cool water, and sipping shotglasses of red, steaming tea swimming with coarse raw sugar.

But as much as he didn't want to see French soldiers occupying a Nigeri military base, and as much as he figured they wouldn't give a shit-smeared baguette about helping him with his phone, he had to hope that maybe at least Nigeri soldiers would take pity on a Kenyan-Canadian eco-tech developer from Ibex. Maybe they couldn't fix his phone, but they could probably call or radio to someone in Madama who'd get a message to Candace (Project Lead on Green Sash, and mother in the only Canadian family out there, so everyone in the hamlet of five hundred people knew them) and save her half a day of stress worrying about the father of her children.

So an hour later when the odometer (GPS was offline, which he'd heard was impossible) told him he should've been twenty klicks away from the garrison, he pulled over to put two flags on his antenna: one for Canada, and the other for Ibex. So hopefully the French troops wouldn't use artillery on him when he was still a kilometre away and claim he was a jihadi driving a suicide truck.

He slowed during his approach, crawled to ten km/h for the final stretch, but the base was quiet. Read the French language signs to make sure he was avoiding the mine fields, parked an exceedingly polite distance from the fortress walls, and walked the final distance slowly while waving his hands in the air in what he hoped suggested he was harmless.

But the front gates were open, and the base looked deserted. No activity. No vehicles, either.

There should be three hundred people here, he thought. *This is bullshit. They all just abandoned this place?*

Stood there sizzling in the great hot dryness, exposed skin crisping. *Country as poor as Niger, and they set up this facility and keep it staffed and operational for years, and then they just bug the hell out? What kind of craziness is that?*

And then thought how much at that exact second he wished he were in one exact spot—back in Winnipeg at the corner store down the block from their house—with one exact family: his own. Buying Creamsicles. A Winnipeg summer was humid-hot, but next to the forge of Niger, it was air conditioning. When it *felt* hot in the Peg, they'd all walk down to corner store for Creamsicles. Dayglo orange and chemically delicious, and the hit of the cold was a paring knife shoved through his tear ducts. And his kids moaning and laughing at the same thing.

And *that* was what missing his family and home felt like at that exact second outside an abandoned military base in scorching northeastern Niger.

Walking back to the sand rover. Just how soon could he convince his wife to tell Ibex to train her replacement so they could be back in the Peg, him as a community animator and project coordinator, helping poor neighbourhoods build gardens, driving solarisation projects, kickstarting net zero construction? And his wife back at the U of M's Terraforming Department (that's what she called it, anyway)—Environmental Engineering at the University of Manitoba as an Ibex Fellow? Maybe he could get a fellowship or a project grant—seemed like Ibex was vaulting over a million different dunes and just kept accelerating…

Back inside the sand rover. Just to make himself feel worse, checked his phone. Nothing still. Almost threw it on the floor in anger, but that wasn't him. Clipped it to his belt.

Put in a CD: Modestep's *Evolution Theory*. Clicked to "Praying for Silence." Mecho music, a sound like wave after wave of robot battalions in eight-bit apocalyptic combat. Lungs tightened, heart sped up. No. Needed something more peaceful. "Leave My Mind." All about breathing. Letting go.

Pulled away. Still had twelve hours minimum till home.

Craving his wife's arms, and still five hours away from Seguedine. The name still made him smile. Candi said to him when they first arrived there two years ago, "Deen is Arabic for religion, you know. So *Segue-dine* should mean transitioning away from religion, right?" She loved her own naughty wordplay after having just arrived in a majority Muslim country. But she saw what his expression was and quickly said, "You think the French named it that? You know what they think of religion, especially Islam, especially since Algeria." She wasn't taking the imperialist's side. Loved that woman.

He'd eventually looked up *deen* once when their Internet was working and while he was learning Arabic and relearning French. *Deen* wasn't just religion. It was divine will. It was... not exactly, but closer to *the way.* The *dao.* He'd met Sufis here who talked like that—philosophically. Enigmatically. So *Segue-dine* could mean transitioning away from divine law, or changing the universe's operating system—

Too much music. He was spacing out, so he turned on the radio, hoping for CBC on Sirius to ease his homesickness and keep him focused. Nothing. Not even static. Satellite radio was down, too? So it wasn't just his phone. Switched to FM. Spun the whole dial. Nothing. What the hell was going on? Countrywide power outage?

Or something worse?

No satellite reception, which explained the GPS, but—

Did those soldiers bug out because Niger was at war? Had there been another coup? Or a plague? Like Ebola? They were extremely far from Liberia, but air travel made any epidemic only a twelve hour flight from anywhere else on the planet—

Hit the gas. Had to get home.

Dashboard clock said *23:23* when he pulled into Seguedine. No streetlights. No house lights. No men sitting outside smoking or playing dominoes. No nighttime bazaar with oil lanterns. No moonlight.

Just stars and darkness.

Heart was sledgehammering his ribs.

Slowed to a crawl, killed his lights so his eyes would pick up anything out there. Opened his windows so he could listen for anything, anyone. Hoped that if it *were* war, there were no snipers. No mines. No IEDs.

But there was nothing and no one.

Stopped the car.

Got out.

Crept to the closest house. Didn't want to startle anyone or get stabbed or shot, so stage-whispered in Arabic, *As salaam walaikum!* And then a phrase he hoped that meant *I need a telephone. Can anyone help me?*

Waited.

Opened the gate, approached. Tried it again at the door.

Realised the door was unlocked.

Breathed deeply. Opened the door.

Pots, dishes, half-eaten meals.

Clothes scattered on the floor like their people had simply stepped out of them and run away.

Panic shrilled through his skull and veins like a scream.

Spinning tires to screech out of town under starlight back to his family's compound half an hour away, then slamming on the brakes—

Red and blue flashing lights around the corner.

Pulled over silently as if he could hide the sand rover behind trees. A police or army check-point with red-blue flashers? A sound like fans blowing full-on?

Got out. Crept as silently as he could, peered around the corner.

An empty street, and the lights were gone, and the sound was gone.

Waited, in case it was a trap.

Ran back to his car and sped the hell out of there.

—rocketed to the compound gate and skidded to a halt, jumped out and unlatched the fence and threw it open, hopped back inside and drove to the front door of the dark house—

Inside: half-eaten food, wife's satphone face down on a chair, dropped clothes of a grown woman, a seven-year-old girl, and a four-year-old boy.

Screamed their names.

Red and blue lights flared outside with a sound like blowers on full.

Clamped shut his mouth with both hands. Ducked under the window sill.

Poked his head up. Peeled back blinds.

Red and blue flaring against the compound wall. Tiptoed to the other side of the house, his children's room, slipped past the bunk bed beside the window and dodged open the curtain. Again the lights, but couldn't see the source.

And then they blinked out, and so did the sound of rushing wind.

Heat stroke? Psychotic break? Or am I dying way back out at the terrarium or on the highway after a rollover, and this is how my brain dies, imagining this?

Stayed there. Freezing. Shivering in the heat. Couldn't move.

Morning. Finally forced himself away from the window to eat. The town'd been dark, but their compound ran off an Ibex Epoch fed by the silver palm trees outside—and those had unlimited daytime supply, three hundred sixty-five days a year—so the three-quarter fridge was still working.

Inside: a bottle of water. Six green oranges. Stack of pita wrapped in foil. White blocks of feta in a jar. Purple, Lebanese-style pickled turnip in another jar. A plate with two sausages and five *fura*.

"I would kill for a Creamsicle right now," he said and took the plate.

Ate it all cold. The small, sweet-spiced dumplings gave off milk with every chew. These he would've shared these with his kids.

Admitted to himself, "This entire region has been evacuated." Didn't feel any better for the admission.

Those red and blue strobes—either search lights or a signal protocol he'd never heard of. French, maybe? But who was searching? Or what was the signal? Those wind sounds didn't come from any chopper.

And the dropped clothes—

He gathered his wife's and daughter's and son's clothes, folded them, tucked them into a go-bag. Went to grab the oranges, pita, feta, pickles, and water bottle from the fridge to pack them in a crate for the rover.

And found all of those plus a Creamsicle.

On a plate.

In its wrapper.

Reached for it. Touched it. Opened it.

Licked it.

Bit it.

Crunchy. Creamy. Sweet.

Cold stabbed through his tear ducts and into his brain

Realised: *I am losing my mind.*

Just like that. Wasn't even upset. Like, *Whoops, broke my USB stick.*

Finished the confection. Took the stick and wrapper and his family's abandoned food and shoved them in a garbage bag. *Good thing the windows and doors'd all been shut, or the place would've been full of flies.* Washed their plates and his.

Went to pack his own clothes and found his wife's laptop in their room, shattered. Keyboard letters scattered like dominoes on the cement floor. Screen smashed to pieces like the hand mirror of a defeated jinni. Cracked case with pieces reading *Ibrahim Experimental Technology Group.* The leaping Ibex icon way over on the other side of the floor, like it'd jumped off just before the laptop'd hit.

Every terrarium had its own laptop, of course, to keep the system running and provide telemetry. If he wanted to drive back ten hours—

Remembered: unpacked the go-bag, checked his wife's cargo pants, but they were empty. Searched the floor, under the loveseat. Found his wife's smartphone. Dead, but intact—the rubber crash case had saved it. Plugged it in.

Waiting for it to turn on, so he searched the house for any reasons it held, any clues it preserved.

My Little Ponies. Some Lego. A Space Glider and a Time Traveller—Micronaut action figures from his own childhood he'd given to his kids.

Forced himself to stop crying, slow his breathing, thought: *They're alive. Maybe in Zinder, the nearest big city with an airport. That's fifteen hundred kilometres from here, over decent enough roads. I could make it there by tonight. Bilma, Agadez, Nguigmi, and Gouré are all on the way. Unless the entire country's been evacuated, at least one of those towns or cities will have Internet or phones or radio or answers.*

Tried his wife's phone.

No Internet, but he checked the call list. She'd tried to call him almost a hundred times. Felt like an aluminum bat to his ribs. Imagined her and the kids screaming at whatever was—

Stopped. Breathed. Checked her searches.

One search after another, for AI.

And Ibex AI.

And *foglet.* What the hell? French, maybe? *Foglette?* If he had Internet he could translate it, but there's a hole in the bucket, dear Liza—

Candi'd told him once, probably when he was trying to sleep, something like "Bezos and Musk have rockets, but Ibrahim's way further on AI than I ever realised until I joined Ibex..."

Pocketed his wife's phone. Grabbed the charger, toys, clothes, keepsakes, food. Filled every water bottle. Stuffed the sand rover. Closed the gate on the way out and was pretty sure he'd never again see their home of the last two years.

Seguedine was as much a ghost town by day as it was by night. Now he was less worried about noise. Actually laid on the horn in case anyone was left. Maybe anyone needing a ride to the next town.

Hadn't seen another human being since he left the compound to check the traplines five days ago.

A solid minute of blaring the horn. Five minutes of waiting. And nobody.

And no animals, either, now that he thought of it. No town dogs dragging their tongues. No goats on ropes in yards. No chickens.

Found a car. Siphoned gas. Fumes were a toilet in his throat and lungs.

Got back in the rover. Closed his windows. Turned on the AC.

He had not eaten any Creamsicle. It had looked, felt, and tasted absolutely real, but because it *could* not have been real, it *had* not been real. To calm down, to make himself laugh, he carefully thought each word: *To paraphrase Rick James, Panic is a hell of a drug.*

He did not laugh.

Checked the radio but knew there would be nothing.

Put Modestep back on. Absolutely, positively clicked over "Praying for Silence," and went to "Leave My Mind."

Noon when he pulled into Bilma. Remembered this place well, the oasis town with red water natron-salt "paddies." Around sixty-five hundred people lived there.

It was empty. Not even animals.

Just empty clothes.

3 pm, and Agadez was the same. All hundred-twenty-four thousand people had vanished.

6 pm, and Nguigmi's fifteen thousand had left nothing but clothes, shoes, and footprints in sand. At sunset he detoured past Lake Chad, but couldn't spot a single bird.

Midnight, and there were no lights at the Zinder airport, and the city of two hundred thousand was a graveyard without graves.

Drove across abandoned runways until he was next to the control tower that blotted out stars like a massive minaret. Downed the windows, killed the engine. Caught a sliver of moon.

"So do I go to Niamey?" said Kam. First voice he'd heard outside the stereo all day. "I mean if anyone's left, they'd all be in the capitol. Right? Or do I turn around?"

Looked at the stars.

"And go where? My family's fled to God knows where. Everyone we worked with is gone. And if the animals are all gone, that must mean some kind of plague, right? But then why am I not seeing carcasses? Or corpses?"

Opened a jar. Took out a block of feta that glistened and sparkled under starlight. Stepped out of the sand rover. Bit into the cheese like it was an apple. Chewed.

"Worked here two years," he told the universe. "And for what? The trees we planted, if they even survive, they won't be full grown for twenty years. And even if they live, even if the pumps keep working, even if the aquifers don't dry up earlier than they're supposed to…who's it for? This teeming population? The thundering herds of wildlife?"

Listened, suddenly, like the world depended on it.

Silence.

And understood: the entire orchestra of crickets had been wiped out.

"What about the bees?" he said. "There were no flies in our house or that other house, not even over the half-finished food. If the bees are gone…and the crickets…and the flies…and the birds…then the pollinators and the seed-spreaders are gone… So our trees—"

Neutron bombs? he thought. *They kill everything but leave the buildings standing…but there'd be bodies and carcasses.*

"Gamma bomb?" Heard somewhere a million years ago that gamma rays could disintegrate flesh but leave objects intact. No idea if that were actually true. And wouldn't there be ash or sludge left over?

"Just hope all these people escaped…whatever happened," said Kam to the stars. *And that I find my family.* Thought it, didn't say it aloud, so the tender idea wouldn't shatter.

Deep breath.

Aloud: "And that our system keeps working here. Keeps those trees growing. Which's what we came here to do."

Laughed bitterly.

"But the trees are all locked inside the terraria in their grow towers," he said. "With no one to look after them. Crowded up to the goddamn ceilings. They're not gonna plant themselves! All those babies are gonna die! Because no one's looking after them! Because I'm not there to protect them!" Screaming so loud his throat was ripping. "BECAUSE THEY CAN'T GODDAMN PLANT THEMSELVES!"

Heard the rushing wind, saw through his tears: red and blue flaring light, and then he shut up and looked for it but found nothing.

Weeks later, he thought. But time was lost. Sleeping anywhere. Driving aimlessly. Siphoning gas. Foraging for food and water.

And all of it in silence.

Except for the Modestep mecho CD, again and again, with its titles: "Show Me a Sign"… "Burn"… "Another Day"… "Machines"… "To the Stars"… "Freedom"… "Take It all"… "Leave My Mind"…and the title track, "Evolution Theory."

No radio from Nigeria, Mali, Algeria, or Chad. No BBC World Service.

So all of West Africa had been emptied. Or possibly the entire world.

Took another route back to Seguedine. So he'd been wrong. He *did* see his house again.

It was still empty.

"Time to check my traplines," he said.

Arrived outside Djado around nine a.m. on whatever day it'd become. Without GPS it wasn't easy to find Djado Grove 13, but the hoodoos gave him all the landmarks he needed if he thought carefully.

There were trees.

Not saplings.

Rows of goddamn trees.

But the terrarium was gone. And in its place, a crater.

Didn't even cry. Just chewed his lip and breathed out through his nose.

But there were *tracks*.

Around noon the tracks and trees led him to the terrarium.

It was slowly walking across the desert like a giant silver scarab with too many legs. Reaching inside itself as it went along, extracting and planting and watering saplings.

Kam got out of his rover and crept forward. Like he was approaching a mastodon. Or a diplodocus. Afraid of startling it. And getting killed.

It kept working, planting, walking, and ignoring him.

He looked back at the rows and saw the trees that had to've been planted minutes ago and were already taller. He walked up to one, saw buds sprouting from it. Saw one bud actually open into a leaf. Smelt the air: moist. Like fruit.

And then he heard the sound.

Silver-gold bees glinting and flying all around him, crawling on his arms and hands and neck and the beard that'd formed on his face. He could feel them through the *kafeeyah* he'd wrapped round his head. Imagined them as a gold and silver crown.

A thrill silked through Kam's arteries, tingled his fingers, sparkled in his eyes. He could taste it. Like fresh-cut pineapple sweetly burning his tongue. It heliumed his head. Emptied his arms to encompass three people and all of space.

Without fear, he walked up to the giant silver scarab.

"Excuse me," he called.

The scarab kept busy.

"Can you please take me to my family? Now?"

Because it would kneel down so he could crawl inside, right? Or so he could hop on its back and take him to the Kingdom of Trees where his wife and children were communing with gold and silver bees?

The scarab kept working, but the wind rushed around him, and behind him and away from the trees, two holes like burning eyes had opened in the air, a metre off the sand and a dozen metres apart.

One eye was red and one was blue.

He walked between them. Felt the wind rushing out of the blue eye and being sucked into the red one.

Looked into the blue eye and saw stars streaking towards him. Turned round with his kafeeyah whipping and flapping like a flag, gazed into the red eye to see stars streaking away.

Taste in his mouth: like he was chewing aluminum foil.

Heaven and hell?

Insanity? My final psychotic break?

Am I in an Ibex experiment? Is this advanced virtual reality? A giant simulation and when I step through, I'll be back in some lab? Or maybe the universe itself is a simulation? And when I walk through, it all resets to the Big Bang?

Or are those eyes...aliens?

Or wormholes? Did everyone on earth walk through to another planet...or another galaxy?

Or are they an extraterrestrial vacuum cleaner? A siphon? Pipettes? Did humanity end up in a giant beaker? On a giant slide? Is the whole human race getting spun and shredded and sequenced?

His head and arms jerked at the same time. He smacked his pockets. Found his wife's smartphone. Dead. Hadn't charged it in weeks. Ran back to the sand rover, turned on the engine, plugged in the phone.

The eyes closed and the wind stopped.

He ignored that, looked for what he wanted. His wife hadn't left a note in the house. Not a *paper* note, anyway. But...

Okay, no e-notes, but photos? Videos?

Always photos of Candi, but not selfies—she was always letting the kids manhandle her phone. So he went to the videos, found one of her, and Wangari was screaming, "Mummy, what's *happening*?" as the image wonked because the phone was falling and then the video ended. He slid it back and freeze-framed it.

His wife's arms were covered in silver scales.

He slid the video forward.

The scales were sliding over her entire body.

Slid the video again: She was turning into silver smoke.

Slid video: Wangari's hand, as the phone fell.

Covered in silver scales.

Watched it all again and again. No sign of his son.

The scarab was half a kilometre away. He thought about driving to it, but instead trotted after it past all those budding trees. When he caught up to it, he was about to speak to it again, but then turned around and instead asked the air.

"Can you please take me to my family?"

There was wind and a burst of light, and the blue and red eyes opened.

He walked toward the blue eye, but pressure from wind and something else pushed him back. He turned round and walked toward the red eye.

And stepped through.

It was all quasars and black holes and stars and comets and asteroids and ice and molecules and atoms and protons and quarks…

And he felt like…

       n

      u

         m

           h

             e

               r

                  s

                     ....

HOW NOTHING HAPPENS

Darin Bradley

HOW NOTHING HAPPENS
Darin Bradley

I t's strange to listen in, knowing at once nothing and everything about the discussion.

"Have you been having trouble?" she says. The only woman. She wears a pant suit and lacks a face. She has a face, but it remakes itself instant by instant. Or my recollection of it fails at that speed.

There are three others in the room, beside me, but I'm not sure yet who's projecting whom here. So either they count or I do. But not both. Some of us are selves as ignorance, somehow making this up, systemically—it fits on its own, but it's like watching a television show with the wrong audio track. At least it might be. It's what happens when you have too many people making what's real. Networking, they call it.

We'll call one of the others here Rashail, for I can now recognize his dark complexion. That name is appropriately complected, and since I don't know—or haven't realized, or haven't created—the lines of his heritage, he has none. A name will work well enough.

"I've been having trouble," he says, with more face than she. He's a little more connected to this room, this moment, than she seems to be.

"Me too." We don't care about this one. His voice will suffice. Maybe he's just calling in.

"I haven't been able to get in since this weekend," the third one says—a blond, typically attired 1980s office worker. The problem they're all discussing here has to do with keeping buildings operating. Also signs, telephone poles, mailboxes. The things we use. Their job is to keep all these things happening. Sometimes things go wrong, inside them.

I'm taking notes for the meeting. A nonentity. It's my job here.

"There's a problem," she says, looking at her stenographer's pad. This is not her office—it's a conference room after all—but she outranks the men. "But I have a new way."

This conference room must be at least forty stories in the air. There are billboard-sized windows converging across two walls, and the place is bright with midday sun and the sharp-edged veneer-fog that lit everything in the '80s. It is the '80s now. Her firm are like spies, or counter-terrorism brokers. They keep everything happening to make sure nothing happens. The rest of us are from all over, being here to do the job from our places where we do them best.

The problem, she will later realize (because I will later realize it, meaning I'm projecting or receiving things happening, but both to the same end) is that it is the '80s. What they've been doing can't be done in the '80s. People like us make sure time happens, too.

The men are listening, for certainly this fundamental problem is also the new problem.

"We can get a solid three minutes inside," she says, looking up. I retain more of her face this time when I look down and scratch her minutes onto my own stenographer's pad.

"We'll have to build this," she says, offering a diagram to the one with the voice we don't care about. He and Rashail and the third man are bothered by what they see. They know this is fundamentally impossible, 'getting inside' the way they've been doing. Building something to make it even more impossibly possible does not bode well for the anxieties they're already suffering. It makes everything they do a cry for help. An announcement of the problems they're having with simply being.

The edges and rooflines beyond the windows, though even more hazed than the objects in this room, do nothing ebulliently. Solidly. The outside is more stable than in.

"We'll lose lots of time just setting up and tearing down the equipment each night," Rashail says.

She agrees. This was also Penelope's plan, so now I have to wonder which of us is remembering Penelope. As if I didn't have plenty of other things to worry about. I'm not very good at remembering people. Networking.

"There's a church we can use," third man says. "It's across the highway from my apartment—you can look down upon the entire property from my balcony."

I'm thinking '80s thoughts. Décor and the like, trying to decide what to expect in third man's place.

"He can keep watch," the one with the voice says. They all know he means me. I may have given them the idea with that line above. About deciding. We give each other ideas a lot. Everybody does.

I will have to attend several other meetings today, where I will take similar notes. This is my job.

A good story is supposed to contain three or more challenges, each situated after the other, each progressively more dangerous to either the character's or the reader's investment in the tale. This works because selves, discourse, religion, and cognition all work in the same manner. We look for ourselves in ourselves as often as we can, and wherever you find yourself, there you are. An open-ended search is not fun for anyone.

A good story is supposed to contain three or more challenges, and I have already either realized or created all three. This will not be a good story, but that is now your fault and not mine.

This is how I explain being in two places at once: networking. I'm standing upon third man's balcony, listening to the river of cars as they babble across the bridge below. There are city lights and nighttime everywhere. My binoculars are high-powered, so I've been watching the church property all night. No one has come or gone, so I have not used the walkie-talkie sitting on a small, dimpled-glass-topped balcony table beside me. The walkie-talkie is as large as a shoebox and very heavy—third man bought it at an Army Navy store.

I was dismayed to find his apartment decorated with lines and colors and furniture that were not possible in the '80s. It was similarly impossible in the '90s and in the '00s. Now I can't remember which of the decades I began this story with, because how else would I know when these things ceased to be impossible?

The plan is going well inside the church, where I also am. Let me be clear, this is happening at the same time as I am keeping watch—at the same time as me listening to sampled, deconstructionist, college rock that could be from any decade. It is being played by an unnecessary-to-identify device inside third man's apartment, which has just become necessary to identify. You could read this part of the story before you read the part about the balcony and the river and the night, and everything would be the same. It's not a problem that, if you're reading this part first, you don't know what I'm talking about, because you didn't read this part first.

Rashail is carrying the miter saw into the van, where the one with the voice parked it earlier in the evening. Penelope is rolling and stapling the carpet back into place in a manner that indicates nothing happened here during the night—that the church and its plumbing and its important wires will keep happening. The one with the voice has been collecting errant tools and wires for several minutes now. I'm not helping because I'm keeping watch, that's my job, I'm taking notes.

When everything is packed away, and I lower the binoculars for the last time, the sun has started to rise. Everyone leaves, and inside the church, it is clear that nothing has happened.

AFTERWORD
Jason Heller

AFTERWORD
Jason Heller

Don't call this a cyberpunk book.

Okay, so *parts* of it are. *Cyber World* is blessed to have been given stories by Stephen Graham Jones and Paul Graham Raven (no relation), both of whom have clocked in with slabs of cyberpunk action that pay loving homage to that genre's traditions while elevating them above and beyond. Similarly, Alyssa Wong's contribution is a nervy adventure through science fiction's cyber-underbelly.

I'm proud to have such tales in *Cyber World*. But when Josh Viola and I first sat down over lunch to start outlining what this book would look like, we realized there was room here. Room to maneuver. Room to play. Room to let our illustrious stable of authors bring their own interpretation of "cyber" to the table.

Just look at Alvaro Zinos-Amaro's story, tinged with experimental prose and a magic-realist tone. Or Minister Faust's weird-fiction erosion of sanity, ontology, and text itself. Or Darin Bradley's mic-drop of a finale, which deconstructs the cyberpunk premise of virtual reality with subversive, metanarrative glee.

As each story for *Cyber World* popped up in my inbox, my confusion about how I defined cyberpunk grew. And I loved that feeling. Left to define the term "Cyber World" as they saw fit (or gloriously unfit), the authors formed a vast unconscious collective that redefined cyber-something-or-other for the current millennium. A network, you might even say. I don't say that flippantly. Cyberpunk—or should we just start saying "cyberfiction"?—must continually plug back into itself, challenge itself, consume itself, and reinvent itself if it hopes to survive and remain relevant. That sometimes means telling quiet, profoundly moving stories like Mario Acevedo's. Or wild, urban-theory-taken-to-absurdist-extremes flights of fancy like Madeline Ashby's.

Diversity was our guiding principle when *Cyber World* was assembled, and not just because it's the right thing to do. It takes a diverse pool of writers to be able to transport an anthology like *Cyber World* to all the unimaginable places it possibly can—from Nisi Shawl's interplanetary prison to Chinelo Onwualu's gender-fluid meatspace. If I had the time and space, I'd gush about every story in this book, and every author who agreed to pick up the sparking circuitry and run with it.

In the long stretch of *Cyber World* behind you, there are stories about people. There are stories about technology. There are stories about stories. Most of all, though, there are stories that tackle our understanding, or lack thereof, of the many machines that have freed us to love, work, birth, build, change, destroy, and reconfigure reality, often beyond our will or comprehension—even as they greatly augment our will and comprehension.

Call them ironic. Call them visionary. Call them damn good reads.

Just don't call them cyberpunk.

Okay, we don't *really* mind if you do. Just remember: *Cyber World* is only the latest collection of statements, questions, and exclamations in a long conversation that has been going on for decades and will continue to go on for as long as people use technology. And vice versa.

Hopefully that conversation will be longer than shorter. The future is both horrifying and energizing, and if *Cyber World* has made one small contribution to the furtherance of a vital dialogue about humanity and its relation to progress—or even just the cathartic processing of the onrushing technocracy/technotopia/what-have-you—we'll turn this page and rest well. Call it what you will.

ACKNOWLEDGMENTS

ABOUT THE AUTHORS

Mario Acevedo is the author of the bestselling Felix Gomez detective-vampire series, which includes *Rescue From Planet Pleasure* from WordFire Press. His debut novel, *The Nymphos of Rocky Flats*, was chosen by Barnes & Noble as one of the best Paranormal Fantasy Novels of the Decade and was a finalist for a Colorado Book Award. He contributed two stories for the award-winning horror anthology *Nightmares Unhinged* by Hex Publishers. His novel *Good Money Gone*, co-authored with Richard Kilborn, won a best novel 2014 International Latino Book Award. Mario lives and writes in Denver, Colorado.

Saladin Ahmed's first novel, *Throne of the Crescent Moon*, was nominated for the Hugo and the Nebula, and won the Locus Award for Best First Novel. He lives near Detroit.

Madeline Ashby is a science fiction writer and futurist living in Toronto. She is the author of the *Machine Dynasty* series from Angry Robot Books, and the forthcoming novel *Company Town* from Tor Books. She has created science fiction prototypes for the Institute for the Future, SciFutures, Nesta, Data & Society, the WorldBank, and others. She also has a regular column in the *Ottawa Citizen*. You can find her at madelineashby.com or on Twitter @MadelineAshby.

Paolo Bacigalupi is a National Book Award Finalist, and a Hugo, Nebula, Michael L Printz. and John W. Campbell Award Winner. He currently lives in Western Colorado with his wife and son, where he is working on a new novel.

Darin Bradley is the author of three novels: *Noise, Chimpanzee,* and *Totem.* He holds a Ph.D. in English Literature and Theory and has taught courses on writing and literature at several universities. He keeps a website at www. darinbradley.com.

Minister Faust is an award-winning novelist and an award-winning radio broadcaster. His novels include the cult-hit *The Coyote Kings* (2004) which helped drive the new wave of Africentric science fiction and fantasy, *Shrinking the Heroes* (originally published as *From the Notebooks of Doctor Brain*) that won the Kindred Award, and the celebrated book *The Alchemists of Kush.* He's written for television, radio, advertising, education, the stage, and video games (*Mass Effect 2* and *Darkspore*), and he's currently writing and illustrating a graphic novel about Canada's most famous cowboy. His podcast MF GALAXY(mfgalaxy.org) features interviews with writers in every form about the craft and business of writing.

Keith Ferrell is the author of close to twenty books, fiction and nonfiction, including the novel *Passing Judgment* and the *NYT* Nonfiction Bestseller *History Decoded* (co-written with Brad Meltzer). His short fiction has appeared in *Asimov's, Black Mist, Millennium3,000, Nightmares Unhinged,* and other publications, under his own name and pseudonymously. He has published more than 2,000 articles, essays, and reviews in magazines, encyclopedias, and journals. As a speaker, Ferrell often addresses the relationship between technology and culture. He has appeared frequently on television and radio. Keith Ferrell currently lives, writes and farms on 35 acres in the hills of southern Virginia, and is engaged with an immense new novel as well as a large nonfiction project. From 1990-1996 Ferrell was Editor-in-Chief of *OMNI* magazine.

Warren Hammond is a Denver-based author known for his gritty, futuristic *KOP* series. By taking the best of classic detective noir, and reinventing it on a destitute colony world, Warren has created these uniquely dark tales of murder, corruption and redemption. *KOP Killer* won the 2012 Colorado Book Award for best mystery. Warren's latest novel, *Tides of Maritinia*, released in December of 2014. His first book independent of the *KOP* series, *Tides* is a spy novel set in a science fictional world. Always eager to see new places, Warren has traveled extensively. Whether it's wildlife viewing in exotic locales like Botswana and the Galapagos Islands, or trekking in the Himalayas, he's always up for a new adventure.

Angie Hodapp has worked in language-arts education, publishing, and professional writing and editing for the better part of the last two decades. After completing her master's thesis, a work of creative nonfiction, and leaving academia, she gave herself permission to write what she really wanted to write:

speculative fiction. Angie is currently the contracts and roy-alties manager at Nelson Literary Agency in Denver. She and her husband live in a renovated 1930s carriage house near the heart of the city and love collecting stamps in their passports.

Stephen Graham Jones is the author of sixteen novels, six collections, and two or three hundred stories. His most recent novel is *Mongrels*, from William Morrow. Stephen lives in Boulder, Colorado.

Richard Kadrey is the *New York Times* bestselling author of the *Sandman Slim* supernatural noir books. His books include *The Perdition Score, The Everything Box, Metrophage, Butcher Bird, Dead Set*, and the graphic novel *ACCELERATE. Sandman Slim* was included in Amazon's "100 Science Fiction & Fantasy Books to Read in a Lifetime" and is in development as a feature film.

Matthew Kressel is a multiple Nebula Award and World Fantasy Award finalist. His first novel, *King of Shards*, was hailed as "majestic, resonant, reality-twisting madness" from NPR Books. The second book in the Worldmender Trilogy, *Queen of Static*, will appear in Fall of 2016. His short fiction has appeared in many publications including *Clarkesworld, Lightspeed*, io9.com, *Nightmare, Beneath Ceaseless Skies, Apex Magazine, Interzone*, the anthologies *Naked City, People of the Book, After*, and many other markets. He co-hosts the Fantastic Fiction at KGB reading series in Manhattan with Ellen Datlow, is a long-time member of Altered Fluid, a Manhattan-based critique group, and is an amateur student of Yiddish. He can recite *Blade Runner* in its entirety from memory. Find him online at matthewkressel.net and @mattkressel.

Chinelo Onwualu is a writer, editor and journalist living in Abuja, Nigeria. She is a graduate of the 2014 Clarion West Writers Workshop, which she attended as the recipient of the Octavia E. Butler Scholarship. She is editor and co-founder of Omenana.com, a magazine of African speculative fiction. Follow her on twitter @chineloonwualu.

Sarah Pinsker is the author of the 2014 Theodore Sturgeon Award winning story, "In Joy, Knowing the Abyss Behind," and her short fiction has been nominated for Nebula Awards for three consecutive years. Her stories have appeared in *Asimov's*,

Strange Horizons, Fantasy & Science Fiction, Uncanny, Apex, and *Lightspeed,* and in anthologies including *Long Hidden* and *Accessing the Future.* She is also a singer/songwriter and toured nationally behind three albums on various independent labels. A fourth is forthcoming. She lives with her wife and dog in Baltimore, Maryland. Find her online at sarahpinsker.com and on Twitter @ sarahpinsker.

Cat Rambo lives, writes, and teaches atop a hill in the Pacific Northwest. Her 200-plus fiction publications include stories in *Asimov's, Clarkesworld Magazine,* and *The Magazine of Fantasy and Science Fiction.* She is an Endeavour, Nebula, and World Fantasy Award nominee, and her first novel, *Beasts of Tabat,* is a Compton Crook Award finalist. Her 2016 fictions include *Hearts of Tabat* (novel, WordFire Press), *Neither Here Nor Here* (collection, Hydra House) and the updated edition of *Creating an Online Presence for Writers.* For more about her, as well as links to her fiction, see www.kittywumpus.net.

Paul Graham Raven is, at time of writing, a postgraduate researcher in infrastructure futures and theory at the University of Sheffield, UK. He's also a writer, science fiction critic and essayist—with bylines at *MIT Technology Review, ARC, BBC Science Focus,* and *The Los Angeles Review of Books,* among others—and a consulting critical futurist. He lives a stone's throw from the site of the Battle of Orgreave in the company of a duplicitous cat, three guitars he can barely play, and sufficient books to constitute an insurance-invalidating fire hazard. Find him at paulgrahamraven.com.

Nisi Shawl's story collection *Filter House* co-won the James Tiptree, Jr. Award in 2009 and was nominated for that year's World Fantasy Award. "The Mighty Phin" is a sequel to stories published in the anthologies *So Long Been Dreaming* and *The Other Half of the Sky.* Shawl is co-author of *Writing the Other: A Practical Approach,* and co-editor of *Strange Matings: Science Fiction, Feminism, African American Voices, and Octavia E. Butler.* She also co-edited *Stories for Chip: A Tribute to Samuel R. Delany,* to which she contributed a collaboration with Nalo Hopkinson, "Jamaica Ginger." Her Belgian Congo steampunk novel *Everfair* was published by Tor in September 2016.

Alyssa Wong is a Nebula-, Shirley Jackson-, and World Fantasy Award-nominated author, shark aficionado, and 2013 graduate of the Clarion Writers' Workshop. Her work has appeared in *The Magazine of Fantasy & Science Fiction, Strange Horizons,* Tor.com, *Uncanny Magazine, Lightspeed Magazine, Nightmare Magazine,* and *Black Static,* among others. She is an MFA candidate at North Carolina State University and a member of the Manhattan-based writing group Altered Fluid. Alyssa can be found online at http://www.crashwong.net and on Twitter as @crashwong.

Isabel Yap writes fiction and poetry, works in the tech industry, and drinks tea. Born and raised in Manila, she has also lived in California, Tokyo, and London. In 2013 she attended the Clarion Writers' Workshop. Her work has appeared on Tor. com, *Uncanny Magazine, Apex Magazine, Interfictions Online,* and *Nightmare Magazine,* among other places. She is @visyap on Twitter and her website is isalikeswords.wordpress.com. She would like to thank Mara for her help with teasing out these story's themes, and Parokya ni Edgar for giving her the necessary OPM feels.

E. Lily Yu received the 2012 John W. Campbell Award for Best New Writer. Her stories have been finalists for the Hugo, Nebula, Locus, Sturgeon, and World Fantasy Awards and can be found in a variety of publications, from *Clarkesworld* to *McSweeney's Quarterly.* Recent works appear in *F&SF* and *Uncanny.*

Alvaro Zinos-Amaro is co-author, with Robert Silverberg, of *When the Blue Shift Comes* and *Traveler of Worlds: Conversations with Robert Silverberg.* Alvaro's fiction, Rhysling-nominated poetry, and non-fiction have appeared in markets like *Asimov's, Analog, Apex, Clarkesworld, Nature, Strange Horizons, Galaxy's Edge, Lackington's, The Los Angeles Review of Books,* and anthologies such as *The Mammoth Book of the Adventures of Moriarty, The Mammoth Book of Jack the Ripper Stories,* and *The Year's Best Science Fiction and Fantasy 2016.*

ABOUT THE ARTIST

Aaron Lovett's work has been featured by Dark Horse and published by Tor.com and *Spectrum 22*. His art can also be found in various video games, books and comics. He paints from a dark corner in Denver, Colorado.

ABOUT THE EDITORS

Jason Heller is a journalist, editor, and author of the alt-history novel *Taft 2012* (Quirk); the *Goosebumps* tie-in *Slappy's Revenge* (Scholastic); and a chapter of Ann and Jeff VanderMeer's *The Time Traveler's Almanac* (Tor). He's the former nonfiction editor of *Clarkesworld* and won a Hugo Award as part of that editing team. His short stories have appeared in *Apex Magazine*, *Farrago's Wainscot*, *Sybil's Garage*, *Paper Darts*, *Nightmares Unhinged*, *Swords v. Cthulhu*, and many other magazines and anthologies. He writes about books and music for *NPR*, *Pitchfork*, *Rolling Stone*, and *The Onion A.V. Club* (where he's a Senior Writer). His nonfiction has also appeared in *Weird Tales*, *Entertainment Weekly*, *Alternative Press*, and Tor.com. He's a 2009 graduate of the Odyssey Writing Workshop and a member of the Wyrd Words workshop group. Jason lives in Denver with his wife, Angie.

Joshua Viola is an author, artist, and former video game developer (*Pirates of the Caribbean*, *Smurfs*, *TARGET: Terror*). In addition to creating a transmedia franchise around *The Bane of Yoto*, honored with more than a dozen awards, he is the author of *Blackstar*, a tie-in novel based on the discography of Celldweller. His debut horror anthology, *Nightmares Unhinged*, was a *Denver Post* number one bestseller. His next anthology, *Blood Business*, co-edited by Mario Acevedo, will be available in 2017. He lives in Denver, Colorado, where he is chief editor and owner of Hex Publishers. You can find him on the web at HexPublishers.com, Facebook.com/HexPublishers, and @HexPublishers.

CPSIA information can be obtained
at www.ICGtesting.com
Printed in the USA
LVOW12s1527230117
521874LV00003B/577/P